THE INVENTION OF EXILE

THE
INVENTION
OF
EXILE

VANESSA MANKO

THE PENGUIN PRESS

New York

2014

THE PENGUIN PRESS
Published by the Penguin Group
Penguin Group (USA) LLC
375 Hudson Street
New York, New York 10014

USA · Canada · UK · Ireland · Australia
New Zealand · India · South Africa · China

penguin.com
A Penguin Random House Company

First published by The Penguin Press, a member of
Penguin Group (USA) LLC, 2014

LIBRARY OF CONGRESS CATALOGING-IN-PUBLICATION DATA
Manko, Vanessa.
The invention of exile : a novel / Vanessa Manko.
pages cm
ISBN 978-1-59420-588-0
1. Russian Americans—History—Fiction.   2. Immigrants—United
States—History—Fiction.   3. Exile (Punishment)—Russia—
History—Fiction.   4. Russian immigrants—Fiction.
5. Deportees—Fiction.   6. Domestic fiction.   I. Title.
PS3613.A54565I69 2014
813'.6—dc23
2013039958

Printed in the United States of America
1   3   5   7   9   10   8   6   4   2

Designed by *Marysarah Quinn*

The struggle of man against power is the struggle of memory against forgetting.

Milan Kundera,

The Book of Laughter and Forgetting

I fear I am not in my perfect mind.

William Shakespeare,

King Lear, 4.7.63

When we love, we have, at most, this:
To let each other go; for holding on
Comes easily, we don't have to learn it.

Rainer Maria Rilke,

"Requiem for a Friend"

THE INVENTION OF EXILE

CONNECTICUT

1913–1920

HE ARRIVED IN THE United States in 1913 on a boat named *Trieste*. His face open, the brow smooth, eyes with the at once earnest, at once insecure gaze of hopeful, wanting youth. He began work fast. First at the Remington Arms Company, making ammunition for the Russian Imperial Army, rising up the ranks to become an inspector of the Mosin-Nagant rifle, and later working for the Hitchcock Gas Engine Company. In Bridgeport, Connecticut. His early mornings spent among the others. The hordes of men shuttling to and from factories in lines and masses of gray or black through the dim light of winter mornings and in the spring when the morning sun was like a secret, coy and sparkling, the water flashing on the sound.

They found each other, though. Through all of that, they, the Russians, found each other. They learned to spot each other through mannerisms, glances. This was later. In 1919. Then, the restrictions came at work and in the boardinghouse.

"English! You must speak English! That, or go back home," the foreman always said.

The warehouses loomed up around the men like capes. Their win-dowpanes caked with dirt, small rectangles of frosted, beveled glass. Sometimes, the broken panes were replaced by colored lozenges—sea green, slate blue, dark ruby red. Austin liked to connect them, making up constellations, innumerable designs and geometries.

"English!" The foreman's voice would resound off the tin walls, echo-ing off the glass, the workers all seated in rows solemn and silent, some standing. Once he made the mistake of speaking Russian to a worker.

"Bolshevik! Go back to Russia and bring your revolution with you!" the foreman yelled.

In those early years he sometimes spoke Russian in his sleep and woke in a sweat, the others around him, snoring or stirring as he peeled back his covers to step out of bed, springs creaking.

"The bastard is up again."

"Hey, Polak—can't you sleep like a normal person?" The inaccu-racy, or the intent, of the slander—he was not sure which had been the more injurious. Cautiously, he'd slip out of the room and, with overcoat on, make his way through the narrow hallways and down to the first floor, feeling for the latch underneath the stairs—its wrought iron han-dle cool and coarse. He'd made a deal with the proprietor. For one more dollar a month he agreed to keep Austin's books safe—notebooks mostly. The owner wouldn't touch them, he'd promised. And in the milky white of those winter mornings, Austin would sit at the large kitchen table working. His drafting paper spread across the table. A compass. A slide rule. Then he was obsessed with the scientist Faraday, examining his notebooks, reading his reports on electromagnetic wave theory for radio. He was fascinated with Maxwell's question: What is light? He'd read Maxwell's *Matter and Motion* and *Theory of Heat*.

.   .   .

NEAR THE REMINGTON ARMS, mostly, and sometimes too along the streets leading to the Hitchcock Company, men lay in wait to descend upon the workers, thrusting flyers, notices, newspapers into reluctant hands, running alongside them, sometimes for up to two blocks. They were a nuisance, but Austin never refused. He took what was presented and stuffed these pamphlets and papers into the deep pockets of his overcoat. At the end of a week's time, his pockets had no room for his gloves. On Sunday mornings, early, he removed each piece of paper, unfolding, smoothing out the crumpled notices. He read them, some in Russian, others in broken English. *Lecture on the History of Russian Folk*; *Advance in Soviet Machines*; *Russian Choral Recital*; *Speak, Read, Write: English*; *History of Man*. Other postings and announcements filled the boardinghouse's entrance hallway. Newsprint paper tacked to the walls in a confusing jumble resembling papier-mâché. Someone had secured a row of nails for such flyers, and the papers hung off the walls folded inward as if fatigued, corners rustling when the door opened to a February, March, or June gust, causing the inevitable swirl of errant flyers. There were papers on the floor, strewn along the stairs, curled and shivering in the doorway, some escaping out to the street and away. Other flyers hung from strings draped off nails, dangling mobile-like and beckoning with more elegance than their unlucky pinioned neighbors.

It was Austin's habit that, when not in his shared boarding room, he scoured these walls, reading the advertisements and notices, choosing what he'd wanted, writing things down in his notebook. "Professor," some chided as they passed him entering or leaving. "Bourgeois." He didn't listen.

The flyers and notices promised a way to "pass a pleasant evening." The Russian Social Club, the Union of Russian Workers—it was a place to go, a way to avoid the boardinghouse where there was only room to eat and sleep. The Russian Social Club met in the basement of the Ortho-dox church. They held music recitals. He could belong to the chorus. They put on plays and pageant shows, organized sales and celebrated Pushkin's name day. The union offered English classes, courses on the automobile, radio engineering. He paid his dues. He attended sponsored lectures. He received the union's paper.

IT WAS A BRICK building where bread used to be made. The ovens were now stacked with books and manuals, and the pupils, all union members, sat along the old assembly-line conveyors that lay in parallel, crossing the room in broad silver bands. There was no heat in the building, just cold running water, so they sat in coats and hats. In other rooms, meet-ings about the state of Russia took place; these were often loud, one man's voice distinct over others' murmurings or grumblings. Leaving his En-glish class, Austin stood in the open door, watching the meeting in the adjacent room, listening, "workers," "society," "capitalists."

"Don't just stand there," a man ordered. "Come in."

"What's this all about?"

"For workers."

"I'm not a worker."

"Let me see your hands." The man looks at Austin's upturned palms. "You're a worker."

"I'm an engineer."

"So? That means you work, don't you?"

"Yes."

"Then listen."

He walked in, stood next to the man. The room was filled, men seated, others standing three deep along the walls. They'd turned the lights out as if for a theater performance. One man stood before the gathering, candle in hand, reciting tenets from a broadsheet.

"Why are the lights off?" Austin asked.

"No one outside can see in."

"And if they did?"

"Trouble," the man grumbled and disappeared farther into the room, lost.

. . .

To ENTER A HOUSE of women is to enter a home. He'd been in the country six years before reaching the moment when he could move from the men's rooming house to a home—a proper home, as a boarder, but still a home. Gone from those dank, stark boardinghouse hallways. Eight men to a room. Walls of cracked plaster. White chalky bits crumbling. A fine residue of white covered the splintered wood floors, gray and stripped bare, a fog of white along the windowpanes.

SEVEN DOLLARS A MONTH. For that he'd receive meals; the girls, two sisters, would do his laundry, mend his clothes, and, if needed, buy him things during their weekly shopping—paper, pencils, tooth powder, chocolate bars. Every Monday, he'd have to write out what he needed in a green ledger book that sat on a diminutive table against the stairs. Why he couldn't ask for things outright, he never did understand except that perhaps the mother didn't want him to get too close to her daughters. That, and they kept a careful account of his purchases.

IT WAS A KITCHEN of white, save for the large table in the center of the room whose checkered red tablecloth provided the room's only color. Two large windows at the back of the house filled the room with a gauzy white light. Outside, a flock of sparrows alighted from the small rectangular yard, fluttered and traced an arc of black across a window frame like a stroke of calligraphy. One girl stood at the stove in profile to Austin, the other reached for plates from a cabinet—high enough so that her foot came off the ground a little in the reaching. She set one plate atop another, the rattle of them sweet and delicate. He watched her—careful and deliberate with each, a significance in the placing as if the gold rims aligning the white plates held a power within the circle. He knew her hands first, the gesture of them—quiet and sure. Hands that matched her peaceful face, her calm and contained kind of beauty. She had a line of flour across her forehead. He imagined that if someone had told her she would've wiped it off without a thought, with no concern for her tired, spent appearance, the loose tendrils and wisps of hair framing her face. A graveness within. Quietude in her gray eyes that he, without knowing why, wanted to upset, disrupt, and cause to flash. She reminded him of something silver—regal silver with a kind of inner poise as if she had—did have—a deep complicity with herself, had figured something out and was reluctant to part with the insight.

This was Julia.

Julia, setting out plates as thin as coins. January 12, 1919. Nearly a year later they were married.

. . .

HIS PRESENCE HAD ALTERED the household, that Connecticut household of winter. There are scents a man brings: the dirt, the metallic, alkaline of tools, bleach of white undershirts. The pungency of sweat, the mildew of ponderous shoes. Smoke and shaving soap. It was never discussed, though Austin could intuit that there had been a change. The father had died five years prior, leaving his widow and the two daughters with nothing but expenses, working as a necessity and a room to let, if needed. And now the outward signs of an alteration were visible—a household of three women once again included a man. But there was also a latent shift in tone. An anxiety assuaged. His presence allowed it to dissipate like a hand reaching out to balance an unsteady table. For them, he meant security, protection, a release from worry, almost.

He was not a man of material needs. His requests were minimal. Tooth powder and shaving cream. Rolling papers and drafting paper. That is all. He stood, in profile, hunched over a small hallway table, three-legged, its half-mooned surface flush against the wall. The ledger is splayed open. A pencil within its spine.

His first list amid the commotion of morning. The constant creak of the floorboards as the sisters move from bedroom to hallways, through doorways, up and down stairs. One unrelenting flow of productivity. He'd wanted to write the list in private. He didn't want anyone to see him struggle with the words. The simplest things could bring one back to the outsider's humility—the language mostly. Had he used the right word? Was it *tooth* or *mouth* powder? He seemed to live his days then trying to decipher codes known only to others. And not simply words, but facial expressions, behaviors. He didn't know it then, but it would become a habit of his life, his way of being. But it was better to have to write out his list in the ledger than endure the humiliation of speech.

He'd held the pencil in his hand that first day, looked to his right, then left, and bent to write, the door's transom offering the same, and only, pale morning light. The pencil tip broke. Unusual for him, he who was so precise with any instruments for drawing, but in his nervousness he'd pressed too hard. He used his thumbnail to peel back some of the wood, a splinter wedged beneath the nail bed. An arc of red. Wincing, he brought his thumb to his mouth and then began again. The pencil, now jagged edged, tore the tissued ledger paper.

"You understand how it works?" she'd asked. From above he heard a step on the stairs. Julia leaned over the banister. A patient smile formed, shy, her gaze pulled back slightly. "I handle this. It's my responsibility— the ledger book, the shopping." She hesitated before fully descending the stairs.

"I was writing some things down," Austin said, his hand flipping through the ledger pages.

"I do my best to get exactly what you need, but if the store is out I get the next best thing."

"My spelling is sometimes not so good."

"I leave your bag right under the table here," she said. "It's all sorted from what we buy for the household. I put it just right here." She pressed her fingertips to the tabletop.

Soon, they had an agreement, a routine—he and Julia. Favors create a bond.

"If you get me some sugar for my tea, I'll get you a pair of shoes," he told her, still unsure how exactly he'd approach the man from work who patched together makeshift shoes out of collected leather scraps. It was

April, the thaw begun in earnest. The days were getting longer. After dinner Julia made tea. The others, Austin included, sat in the dining room with the windows blue, turning to black. At that hour the city hushed, and it was easier to hear the trolley cars in the far distance, creeping and creaking along the streets, and far beyond that the mournful bellow of the ferryboats as they moved in broad arcs along the sound.

"Really. New shoes. It will be just between us," he told her.

They had a system. During the pouring and passing of tea, they would find reason to be close, she pressing the stolen sugar into his hand, which he'd then curl into his fist before dropping it into his teacup. It was their secret. A minor transgression, but in a house with no privacy a "just between us" moment was something to be treasured. Later, Julia told him that she was surprised by what a man could make one do.

WHEN MAY AND JUNE of that first year came, they rushed from work to meet in the park. Beardsley Park. Austin waited for Julia, he always the earlier of the two because she had the longer way to walk. He paced and when he recognized her gait—fast while on the sidewalk, slowing as she stepped into the greenness expanding overnight—he took off his hat. She had once told him she liked to see his full face as she approached, stepping up to him as he extended his hand. They followed the park's outer perimeter, always moving in the opposite direction of others. Austin wanted to see people as they came toward him. He was not at ease with the idea of someone at his back. As they strolled, sometimes holding hands, sometimes not, he would describe ideas for inventions, his voice growing low and halting just in case he could be overheard. Julia had to step closer to him then, straining to hear, which made him turn his head and lean down to her slightly, their shoes nearly scuffing, shoulders touching.

He had other ideas too. A house. In time. The implication was that it would be for them and she nodded, just barely—a dip of chin and then she smiled, a quiet delight that she seemed to savor within because she was shy at the prospect of a house; it meant other things that they had not spoken of yet. He liked to lead her to a bench halfway around the park. They held hands then, she kneading his palm like a worry stone.

A HEAVY THUNDERSTORM. In early July. Austin was delayed at the factory. The force of sudden rain flooded a section of the warehouse basement and the men stayed on, trying to keep the water from damaging the machinery. In their minds, water in the gears, moss in crevices, mold within wires, and wetness causing corrosion meant days with no work and no work meant no pay. They divided into groups of five, passing buckets of water down six different lines that ran from the interior of the basement to the nearest window or door. Austin sloshed through inches of the rising water, his boots then socks absorbing the wet until he felt the chill on the soles of his feet and then the hunger too, his whole being aching for hot food. He was eager to be home, in dry warmth, but disappointment tugged at him too, sad that he wouldn't be meeting Julia for their time alone in the park, knowing that, in this weather, she'd certainly go straight home. When he was free to leave the factory, he didn't stay with his fellow workers who wanted to wait out the rain in the neighboring bar. Instead, he walked with shoulders curved forward, crouching away from the rain. When he entered the house, he was grateful for a moment of stillness and to have the sound of the downpour dulled as he stood in the front vestibule.

Julia was not there. Her mother sat alone under the grim kitchen light, twisting a napkin into a coil. The sister was out looking for Julia, who had not returned, the mother said expressionless, which had an anger of its own. He left at once and ran to the park, where he found her before their bench, umbrella in hand, though it hadn't done much good because she was soaked. The rain had tapered off just enough so that the blossoms of the linden trees could give off their soap and honey scent, the ivory yellow blooms fierce and fresh against the wet leaves. He embraced her. She was shaking. He drew his arms around her. It was the first time he'd touched her so fully and she gasped.

"You need to get warm," he said. "Come closer, I'm warm here." He could feel her chill through her clothes, along her neck and wrists. Her cheeks were both feverish and damp and he brought his own cheek to hers.

"I waited for you," she said.

"I should've come here first," he said by way of apology.

"What happened?" she murmured into his chest.

"Flood at work. We all stayed. Had to clear four inches of water out of the basement. I thought for sure you'd go home."

"You went back to the house?"

"Yes. Come, we'll go now."

"Does Mother know?" She pulled away from him, her face slick and shining white for a moment in contrast to the drab wet gravel pathway, the rain-darkened wooden benches and the trees hanging low and weighted above her.

"No. I just turned around and left as soon as I knew you weren't home."

"She surely suspects by now. Did you tell her where you were going?"

"No."

"I'll go in first," she said. "I'll make up some excuse. You should come in later."

"You'll make me stay out in this? You'll be sick as it is and then I'll be next."

"If we go back in around the same time she'll guess."

"Well, let her. We have to tell her at some point."

"She'll throw you out of the house, you know."

"So?"

"I don't want you to go."

"But it's not going to be like this forever. We'll have to tell them. I've been saving. It'll be soon."

"You say all this, but you know I worry about how they'll manage without me."

"She can let another room, get another boarder."

"But it's not near the amount that I make at work."

"They can't be your concern forever, you know. You must have your own life."

"You and me. We will marry," he had told Julia a full year after he'd moved in. It was his attempt at a kind of official proposal. Till then, it had been talk around the subject—that he was saving, what his plans were, how she might fit into that picture he was drawing out for her, with the whispers of a house. Now he'd made his intentions known.

"And how are you so sure?" she had asked, teasing and falling back from him for a moment. The park growing more crowded as the weather softened into full summer and passersby had to filter between them, turning their heads at the abrupt way Julia had stopped.

"It's inevitable," he said. "We will give each other an oath."

"An oath?" She was enraged. She was thrilled.

"Yes."

"What kind of oath?"

"An oath to live together, to be."

"Marriage."

"Yes. I will pass all my belongings to you. All my property."

"You don't own anything." She stepped beside him then and they continued on.

"I own a typewriter."

"And what am I going to do with that?"

"I have a farm. I will inherit a farm."

"But that's in Russia. What good will that do me here?"

"Will you take the oath with me or not?"

"How do we take the oath?"

"We just say it."

"And then?"

For Austin, who still practiced the old customs and rituals, marriage meant kissing the icons, kneeling together, pressing lips to the Bible. Then you were husband and wife, it was merely an oath between a man and a woman. That was all. She'd agreed to it. It was a violet evening in August. The Russian Social Club's summer dance was held in the cool basement of the stone church. She was in a lace frock, borrowed shoes with a fake rhinestone buckle; he in a navy suit and a white collarless shirt.

"A Cossack. You look like a Cossack," friends from work and the club teased him.

The heavy light of August, the late afternoon light of summer's last month, fell through the windows like ship portals. Some of the windows were stained glass so that here a circle of rose, there the blue of a star, the yellow of a leaf anointed the faces, the bodies moving.

"My cheeks hurt. From smiling," she'd told him. They'd come separately. She with her sister and he with some of the men from work. When he spotted her, he watched her among the crowd and he could tell she was struggling to keep focused. She half listened, nodding as she searched the room for him. Each, though, was aware of the other's movements— she through a handful of women gathered like a bouquet at the edge of the dance floor; he tracing the back wall to greet a just-entered friend, each smiling faintly when within each other's gaze. "My wife, *zhena*," Austin mouthed to her across the room. She blushed and turned her eyes away.

The day's mist and light rain was like an effervescence. They were eager to move into the future days awaiting them like pristine windows strung in a long row.

· · ·

JANUARY 2, 1920. We all carry dates within us, flash cards, silver-plated, perhaps engraved. We carry them in us like the memory of those long dead, tucked like the pages of a book, dog-eared. January 2. This was Austin's date. His days hinged here.

It started in rumors. Things one would hear. Nothing definite, just a sense to be watchful, aware and—to get rid of anything from Russia. Books. Newspapers. "They are taking Russians." "They don't do that here." "Yes, but they are taking them."

He ignored all the talk. The ones who were saying it were old. He thought they were simply prone to paranoia. But he started to hear things. Anarchy, socialism, communism, proletariat, revolt. To him, they had a clanking, rattle sound, like a chain-link fence in strong winds.

"Better throw out anything from the fatherland," that was the advice. He removed all the Russian books from his shelves. He still had some of them—*Science and Society*, *Aspects of Engineering*.

"THEY'VE ROUNDED UP OTHER RUSSIANS." Julia was wringing her hands. She is standing at the door as Austin walks in. The house is warm, but he brings in the cold, rubbing his hands, taking hers in his own.

"How did you hear?"

"I've heard them talking at work. They are holding some in Hartford, others in New York."

"I know. I'm not involved in any of it." He removed his hat, his coat.

"Please, do not spend these evenings out anymore. Come straight home."

"Most of the things I go to are harmless—music, English courses, history."

"It's dangerous now."

"Don't worry yourself, Julia, my jewel. I'm not a worker. I'm more advanced. They don't want men like me."

"Please don't go anymore," she says, handing him the day's late-edition paper. He reads the headline:

PLAN FOR RED TERROR HERE—Program of Organized 'Russian Workers' for Revolution Revealed—General Strike First Step—Then Armed

Revolt and Seizure of all Means of Production and Articles of Consumption
Criminals to be Freed—Blowing up of Barracks, Shooting of Police,
End of Religion, Parts of the Program.

He bristled, but hid it from Julia. He came home straight from work as she requested. They took walks after dinner, once, twice around the block and then back inside. He'd begun to look over his shoulder, stopped taking the newspapers from the men on corners. He didn't stop going to the Russian Social Club though. Here, he sang in the choir, sometimes played the zither. And once or twice a treat of elderberry liquor or someone was traveling back to Russia and could send parcels, letters, postcards home. There would be no harm in going to such gatherings. He'd long ago ended his association with the Union of Russian Workers. He didn't believe that workers and trained engineers were equal. He, with all his learning. He'd taken the courses and studied and he did not come to America to be considered equal to the mere worker, the mere assemblymen who had no design or drafting skills, no knowledge of how physics fit part to part. The workers did not know how to calibrate and compute, measure and cut to make the actual engine, gun, carburetor. Still, he read the article. The Americans were scared. He was scared. The whole country was in a panic. He practiced his English, tried to form words in his mouth without the trace of an accent. It didn't work. He avoided speaking to strangers. He placed all his reading materials in an empty canvas bag, hiding it under the bed. Just in case.

THE CITY IN WINTER. 1920. A fog shrouded the warehouses and bridges, lending an ethereal quality to the night. It was opalescent almost. The mauve sky with a dark mass of clouds encroaching. It wasn't the usual bitter, dry cold. It was damp; moisture on the air like there'd been a little bend in winter. A crack. It was snowing still. It was nice to taste the flakes on his tongue.

Austin left the Hitchcock Company and made his way through the rows of factories that dotted the shoreline. He crossed the railroad tracks into the residential neighborhoods, with their white sidewalks and storefronts of frosted glass. Here and there he could see lights on in the apartment buildings.

He was late. He could make out the others—a blurred image through the foggy windows of the church basement, all seated around octagonal tables or leaning against walls. Austin's eyes were on his step, the tip of his leather boot caught the light so that he could see the water droplets, the granules of slush forming like a string of beads. His footsteps were soft on the snow-covered cement stairs that led into the basement. The room was lit low, the green sconces lining the perimeter offered the only feeble light. The heat from the radiators and corner fire embraced him. There was dampness too. Mold mixed with tea leaves. A trace of incense, pine resin, and frankincense. Someone was speaking into a microphone.

"Kuchinsky, Marov, Matushko," the secretary read off the names, "Michailoff, Nikitin, Petrenko, Romanovich, Saloff, Svezda, Vinogradov, Vorinin, Voronkov—"

They were a sorry bunch, the aliens (that's what they'd been called) with their Russian language, all hard angles and swallowed vowels. He could see the others, their eyes sunken and gray, purple around the rims. Bruised. Some had gashes above the eye, on the brow, the bridge of the nose, blood turning black as it dried, rising over an eyebrow, along a jawline.

They were not the only ones, though he didn't know it at the time, lined up as he was, forbidden to talk. He was in the private recesses of the mind, panicked and uncertain. But across the city and in other towns along the eastern seaboard, even the cities of the plains and far out west to places he'd never go, the police squads had come for them—the Reds. Men in overcoats, felt hats. Men in police uniforms with their clubs and blackjacks. Men in black or brown suits, men doused in bureaucracy, an officious air as if ordained. They'd raided, entered, and destroyed; rounded up men in church basements, tore into social clubs' back rooms and mutual aid societies' meeting halls. They broke up New Year's Eve dances in school gyms, dances where wives in wool skirts, velvet headbands, brooches, encouraged husbands in the fox-trot—the efforts of immigrants. They stole into private parties, gatherings in boardinghouses, three to the wall. Dinner parties.

He didn't know all this yet. He had arrived late to the Russian Social Club meeting. And then the sound. It was like the sound of a thousand raindrops, like the batting wings of a startled flock. Austin had seen them first though—in the already snow-filled streets, through the still falling snow, the black figure was gliding. It was an image he was used to seeing. A sleigh. Snow. He did not stop to wonder at the incongruity; in America, grown men did not glide through the streets at night on a sleigh. That was a sight he was accustomed to seeing in Russia, not here. And then he saw the men dismount, a line of them running, their bodies held tight and low to the ground. The rush of boots on the stairs, like a crashing wave. They had filled the room. These men in uniforms, some in overcoats and felt hats.

"What is this?"

"No one move!"

"What is going on here?!"

"Quiet! You are under arrest."

"What? There is a mistake!"

"You are under arrest for alien activities against the United States government."

"We have no activities against this country." A policeman struck the shouting man with his club. The man clutched his shoulder, falling to the ground. Chaos erupted.

"Bolshevik pigs!"

"Please. Where is your reason?"

"Shut up, if you know what's good for you."

The sound of skin on skin was unmistakable. A blackjack to forehead, to backbone. Amid the shadows cast by the low green lights, within the staggered jumble of coats, arms, Austin could make out the coal black of guns.

The blow was hard, fast. He was on the floor. He could taste the metallic flavor of his own blood. He'd bit his tongue. Soon he was hoisted up with the others, all shackled now, wrists, ankles. A policeman led them up the cement stairs, every once in a while came another blow from a club, a blackjack. Sometimes too the firm press of a pistol. The shackles made it impossible to climb the stairs. They had to hop. Humiliation on a dark night.

HABEAS CORPUS. To produce the body, to present the body. To draw the body out of thin air, to produce it bruised and broken. His body was not presented. His body was in a cold, damp cell of a deep January winter.

Later, he would remember those cells the most. A block of darkness that held his body incommunicado. He learned to communicate with the other prisoners using a code they had developed. It involved series of taps on the walls.

What did they want to know? If you were a Communist. If you were an anarchist. If you belonged to the Industrial Workers of the World, the United Federation of Russian Workers, the Russian Mutual Aid Society, the Russian Social Club, the Communist Party, the Socialist Party. If you read the *Farewell Call*, *Pravda*, *Novi Mir*.

What they wanted? Names. Confessions.

He wanted to step outside his body, his mind. He wanted to send his thoughts and words to Julia. For her, his body had vanished. That was knowledge he could not handle. A compassion for her despair. His body could not take it. He shook with rage, or cold, he couldn't tell which.

He believed in the individual. He believed in the power of science too, that its laws could govern society, save society. He did not know that such ideas could be construed so that they aligned with a kind of anarchism. He was twenty-six years old, new to the language still. Anarchism. He hardly knew what the word meant. In later years, he would see. The idealism of his youth, his vanity, his proud nature—all of these things were traits that made him an enemy to himself.

The one thing he had not been told, the one thing he had not learned through the taps on the walls was the phrase, "I decline to answer."

THEY HELD HIM for two weeks. Incommunicado. On the fifth day, they came for him. The men led him through white cinder-block corridors lined with gray metal doors. No windows. He was desperate to know the time. He'd lost track of day, of night.

His hearing would be conducted over three days. He sat in a window-less, low-ceilinged room. Small. No larger than a broom closet. He sat facing the metal desk. A blotter and a green lamp sat on the desk. The lamp's brass chain rattled as metal doors slammed along the hallway. His ankles were shackled to the chair. His hands were cuffed.

A man who smelled like morning, like shaving soap, questioned him. Another served as a translator, though Austin wouldn't need him. Another man sat in front of a small typewriter recording his words.

His inquisitor leaned across the desk, elbows spread to either side. He bowed his head, sighed, and something about the gesture seemed too practiced, Austin felt. It was an inherited gesture, one not his own, a stolen gesture, borrowed by a boy. Austin looked straight into this man's eyes, the honey brown of them soft, young he'd felt. He tried to show in the gaze that he knew the man was acting.

"You understand how this works?" the man said. His voice was quiet, tired. Austin wondered if it was late in the evening rather than early morning. The man's eyelids were puffy. Large circles.

"Do you speak English?"

"Yes."

"All right then. You understand how this works. I ask you a series of questions and you answer. Got it? Good." Austin was desperate for the time. He tried to look at the man's wristwatch, but he was not wearing one. If he knew the time he could follow Julia through the hours of her day. He could tell her in his mind that he was okay. That was a light out of this trap, he'd felt. If he could only know the time he could be in sync with her, running in parallel with her life, even if, for the time being, they were separated.

"What time is it?" Austin said.

"You don't need to know the time," the man said. The light vanished, any frame of reference gone. Erased.

. . .

DAY 1: JANUARY 19, 1920

Q. *What is your name in Russian?*
A. Ustin Voronkov.

Q. *In as much as you do not believe in God, will you affirm to tell the truth?*
A. Yes.

Q. *What is your address?*
A. 116 Locust Street, Bridgeport, Connecticut.

Q. *How old are you?*
A. 26 years old.

Q. *Where were you born?*
A. Province of Kherson, Alexandriyska, Ulesd, Bokas Volost, Village of Varvarovka.

Q. *Of what country are you now a subject or citizen?*
A. Russian subject.

Q. *Are you married or single?*
A. Married.

Q. *What is your wife's name?*

A. Julia.

Q. *Where is your wife now?*

A. She lives in Bridgeport on Locust Street.

Q. *Have you any children?*

A. No.

Q. *When were you married?*

A. There was no ceremony.

Q. *In other words you were never married to this woman religiously or civilly?*

A. There was no ceremony.

Q. *How long have you lived with this woman?*

A. About one and one half years.

Q. *Why have you not married her according to the laws of this country?*

A. Because we live with her family.

Q. *Do you keep house?*

A. No.

Q. *How many rooms do you occupy?*

A. One.

Q. *One bed between you?*
A. I occupy one room by myself.

Q. *Does she sleep with you?*
A. No.

Q. *Why did you say that you were married?*
A. Because we gave an oath together.

Q. *And you state that you lived with her for about one and one half years?*
A. Yes.

Q. *Where does she live?*
A. The same house as I live in.

Q. *Does she sleep in your room?*
A. No.

Q. *Did she ever sleep in your room?*
A. No.

Q. *Did you ever have sexual intercourse with her?*
A. Not officially.

Q. *How long have you lived in the United States?*
A. About six years.

Q. *When did you arrive in the United States?*

A. August 18, 1913.

Q. *Do you remember the name of the boat you came on?*

A. It was called *Trieste*, and came from Trieste to New York.

Q. *In what month?*

A. August 1913.

Q. *Did you pay your passage?*

A. Yes.

Q. *Since your arrival in the United States have you ever taken any steps to become a citizen of this country?*

A. I intended to take out papers, but I could not speak English at the time.

Q. *Do you belong to any organizations?*

A. Russian Inspectors.

Q. *You mean that you are employed by the Russian Commission?*

A. Yes.

Q. *Where?*

A. In Bridgeport.

Q. *What factory?*

A. Remington Arms.

Q. *What is your occupation?*

A. An inspector.

Q. *Of what?*

A. Arms.

Q. *Did you have any preliminary work anywhere that fitted you for this position?*

A. I am a mechanic and engineer there.

Q. *Do you belong to any other organizations?*

A. No.

Q. *Ever belong to the Union of Russian Workers?*

A. I didn't belong.

Q. *There is such an organization as the Union of Russian Workers in Bridgeport?*

A. There was.

Q. *There still is?*

A. It seems they made it better, but the Union of Russian Workers has an automobile school in Bridgeport.

Q. *What is the name of the automobile school?*

A. The Russian automobile school.

Q. *Was it known as the Soviet Automobile School?*

A. No.

Q. *We have information that this school was run and conducted under the auspices of the Union of Russian Workers. Did you know that?*

A. I don't know anything about this. I think the soviets started it and then the pupils took it over for themselves.

Q. *You mean the Union of Russian Workers started it?*

A. No. The soviets of Bridgeport.

Q. *What do you mean "the soviets" of Bridgeport? We have no "soviets" in this country.*

A. It was called "soviet."

Q. *Have you an automobile?*

A. No.

Q. *Did you ever have an automobile?*

A. No.

Q. *Why were you interested in automobiles?*

A. Because I was in the automobile business.

Q. *Were you financially interested in the automobile business?*

A. I am interested in every kind of knowledge.

DAY 2: JANUARY 20, 1920

> Q. *Mr. Voronkov, you have been to meetings of the Union of Russian Workers, haven't you?*
> A. No. Only when they have lectures.

> Q. *You have been to business meetings?*
> A. No.

> Q. *How many lectures did you attend?*
> A. Two or three.

> Q. *What did they talk about?*
> A. About the origin of man.

> Q. *They talked about the government?*
> A. I cannot tell.

> Q. *They never talked about revolution?*
> A. I cannot know the subject.

> Q. *Are you an advocate for revolution?*
> A. I do not know.

> Q. *You have no respect for the laws of man?*
> A. I am a man. I have respect for them.

Q. *Why would you live with a woman one and a half years without marrying her if you have respect for the laws of man?*

A. We gave an oath together.

Q. *Are you an advocate of free love?*

A. Yes. We gave an oath.

Q. *You say you are an advocate of free love, that is not respect for the laws of man?*

A. I say, if we gave an oath—we will live together; get married.

Q. *You know about the laws in regards to marriage?*

A. Which ones? I would marry her by these laws at any time she demanded.

Q. *Are you an anarchist?*

A. No.

Q. *Are you opposed to the government of the United States?*

A. No.

Q. *Are your organizations opposed to any organized form of government?*

A. I am not opposed to government.

Q. *You don't believe in laws, do you?*

A. It depends on what kind of laws.

Q. *The laws of the United States.*

A. I've lived here six or seven years.

Q. *You didn't pay much attention to the laws though?*
A. If I didn't pay attention to the laws it would be a different thing.

Q. *What attention did you pay to the laws when you lived with a woman*
 for one and one half years without being married to her?
A. We gave an oath.

Q. *What have you to show for it?*
A. I passed to her my property.

Q. *Is this "oath" written anywhere?*
A. No.

Q. *Does this woman have anything to show that she has a claim*
 on you?
A. If she won't marry me, then I will see her corpse.

Q. *What is her name?*
A. Julia.

Q. *And you are here saying that she is your wife?*
A. Yes.

Q. *Have you anything against this country?*
A. No.

DAY 3: JANUARY 21, 1920

Q. *You understand, Mr. Voronkov, this is a continuation of your hearing commenced on January 19th, 1920?*

A. Yes. I do.

Q. *Do you affirm at this time to continue to tell the truth?*

A. Yes I do.

Q. *Are you an anarchist?*

A. No.

Q. *Are you a Communist?*

A. I am not an anarchist, neither am I a Communist.

Q. *I show you a letter addressed to 116 Locust Street, Bridgeport, Conn., dated January 17, 1920. Did you write this letter?*

A. Yes.

Q. *I will mark this letter together with translation of it Exhibit (1) and introduce it as evidence in your case. I show you another letter addressed to the same party, did you write this letter?*

A. Yes, I did.

Q. *I will mark this letter together with a translation of it Exhibit (2) and introduce it as evidence in your case. There is a sentence in this letter that you have written to this young woman reading as follows:*

"But there is possibility to come together although through difficult obstacles, so that we should care a fig for that dirty and stinking ceremony of marriage."

A. I wrote it. I was not feeling well. I was cross when I wrote it.

Q. *Then you were feeling cross because this young woman, when she found out that you'd be deported, refused to go back to Russia with you without being married?*

A. I offered to marry her any way I could if I could get out of jail somehow.

Q. *It goes on to say in this letter:*

"But there is nothing in the world stronger than love of heart and soul for only in it there is life and happiness, and not in that dirty marriage."

A. Yes I wrote that. What about it?

Q. *It goes on to say: "If you, yes, love me, as much as I love you, then you would spit upon all these disgustful calumnies." Did you write that?*

A. Yes. I wrote that, alas. I wrote to my lover. I did not feel very well. I know that our love was broken and in that condition I wrote it. I always offered her marriage, any kind of marriage she wants. You will find it in the letters that I offered her that. But she is my wife, you ask her. We gave an oath. She is my *zhena*.

Q. *Are you a member of the Union of Russian Workers of Bridgeport?*

A. I was formerly a member.

Q. *When were you a member?*

A. Four or five months ago?

Q. *When did you join?*

A. July 15th, 1919.

Q. *Are you still a member of the organization?*

A. No. I did not care for them. I quit.

Q. *When did you leave the organization?*

A. I stayed two months and then I left it.

Q. *On what points did you disagree with them?*

A. Because they hold on the same level workers and engineers, that is, skilled workers—this is why I gave it up.

Q. *The Union of Russian Workers is an anarchist organization, isn't it?*

A. I cannot tell you. I could not understand them.

Q. *A man of your intelligence certainly knew enough to read the basic principles of an organization before he joined it.*

A. I joined it because there were many Russians.

Q. *Don't you know or didn't you read the principles of what the organization stands for?*

A. No.

Q. *You know that if you are found guilty of the charge or part of the charges against you that you will be deported back to Russia?*

A. Yes. I do.

Q. *You said that you were a member of the Union of Russian Workers?*

A. Yes.

Q. *You stated also that you resigned as a member of the Union of Russian Workers?*

A. Yes. I did.

Q. *Can you tell me why?*

A. Yes, according to my convictions as I looked at it, I did not believe in their ideas.

Q. *Do you agree with government as it exists?*

A. No.

Q. *What is your opinion of the system of government you would like to see in existence?*

A. By name of science to obtain society.

Q. *Without government?*

A. Yes. Without government. People would be masters of themselves.

Q. *Without State?*

A. Yes. I believe it should be.

Q. *Supposing I would tell you that these views of yours are anarchist, would you then call yourself an anarchist?*

A. No. I do not consent to have any name, but if you want to call me that—

Q. *In other words you are frank in stating your opinion about society, but you do not know exactly the name for it?*

A. I cannot tell what the name would be, but the form, if changed, would mean the liberation of the workers themselves by means of science and they will improve themselves and be masters of themselves.

Q. *Your views of society are that there ought to be no government, a stateless form of society?*

A. Yes. According to my opinion, yes. There must be no government or master who will say what must be done. Only science.

Q. *These views of yours could be called anarchistic.*

A. Well, my opinions are such. Let them call me an anarchist.

Q. *How would this condition of affairs without government, without state be brought about?*

A. By means of science you can give your affairs to the people to govern themselves.

Q. *Do you believe in the use of force or violence to bring this about if necessary?*

A. No. I don't believe in force. Science is stronger than force.

Q. *Do you believe that the present form of government in the United States should be overthrown?*

A. Yes, very plainly, when the people will understand it can be done.

Q. *How will it be done?*

A. By means of science when the people will understand that they need no commander.

Q. *And no laws?*

A. I do not know how you can call them laws. They are just simply agreements.

Q. *You know we have people in the world whom we call anarchists.*

A. Yes, but I don't know what their ideas are.

Q. *They have views similar to these you have expressed here this afternoon.*

A. I said I did not know their program, my opinions are just such.

Q. *Would you think it fair from your expressions or views here this afternoon for us to call you an anarchist?*

A. If you compare what I said with what you think anarchists are, then, okay, I consent to that.

Q. *I will ask you again. Are you an anarchist?*

A. It is so. I am an anarchist.

Q. *Have you anything further you wish to state at this time as to why you should not be deported in conformity with the law?*

A. I have nothing to say. Let them deport me. But let me take my wife.

. . .

THEY WERE MARRIED—officially—at Ellis Island. Two-sentence vows. Austin and Julia held hands solemnly speaking. The justice of the peace read in a monotone voice, all the while smoking a cigar that created a cloud of milk white around them. They would be leaving in one hour. He was taking her from everything she'd known and loved. She'd re-nounced her family, her country, she'd given up her U.S. citizenship. It did not matter. Then, they were not willing to be separated.

THE NEWSPAPERS WERE CALLING it the Soviet Ark. *The New York Times*, January 1920, ran photos. A massive ship, anchored at Ellis Island on a bitter day. They stood on the pier amid the wind and ice. The sky opaque, flurries like chipped ice. The only sounds the murmur of men's conversations, seagulls crying, the moan of the boat on the day's hard air. The anchor cranking like a scream; the massive chain lifted out of the ocean, iron red with rust, calcified with sea salt, seaweed. Just moments before, he'd sat on the long benches of the waiting room, the very room he'd sat in only years prior eager to get beyond the bottled-glass win-dows whose light he knew was day in America—a country behind glass, the new country's light. Years later he would learn that there were to have been, in total, three other major raids—the Palmer Raids, ordered by Attorney General Palmer after a lone anarchist planted a bomb at the foot of his front door. The raids would be a series of roundups of supposed anarchists or Communists, men and women deemed a threat to the American way of life, men and women who may strike again—more homemade bombs, subversive articles in newspapers, party meetings. They were plotting to take over the country. Somewhere, a man named Hoover had his name on an index card: Voronkov. Affirmed anarchist. Bail set at $10,000. Deported.

. . .

MEXICO CITY
1948

HE HAS NO REAL reason to believe that this year will be any different. But there is always a "perhaps"—a habit, like a little leap of hope. It is the second day of January. 1948. The city is nearly silent at this hour—7 A.M. He steps from sidewalk to street, tracing the outline of a small roundabout. He likes the sound of his lone footsteps at this hour, the clack and shuffle of them. The press of his leather satchel beneath his arm. Its thick hide scent mingles with his aftershave—a clean, white smell. He is wearing his best—and only—suit of charcoal gray linen, slightly frayed. But it will do, it will do he thinks. His shoes are polished too, though the several coats of polish he'd applied that morning do not conceal the scuffs or the thin, worn leather.

The homes here sit behind wrought iron railings, gates and doors with black ornamental pickets like pinstripes. The sun paints lines of light along cornices. In the distance, he can hear merchants wheeling their goods to *puestos*, the open-air market stalls. They are seeking out their preferred corners, setting up makeshift stands, gathering now to smoke, talk, wait.

He pulls a wrinkled envelope from his satchel. He stops to check the contents of the envelope. It is the third time he has done so this morning. Everything is in order: Birth certificate. Nansen passport, though expired. Notarized letters from officials. Affidavits too. A postcard sits at the bottom of the envelope. *Tipo de mexicanos indígenas.* Type of indigenous Mexicans. "To my Sonnie," he'd written. "Postcard for imagining Mexico." He'd signed it "Love, from Father." It is a colored postcard, but like the Technicolor films, it has been shot in black and white, retouched with the hues and shades of Mexico—the scarlet serapes of the Indians, their wide-lipped, camel-colored sombreros, the brown of burros crossing a small brook, the milk-blue water in the foreground of the otherwise craggy terrain. The terrain consists of boulders, a dirt road veering upward through coffee trees, trees of willow and ash, and lush green ferns bowed beneath the weight of orange orchids. The boy will like it, he thinks. He'll drop the postcard after. It could be the last he'll need to send.

The empty streets, the ease of the city in the early morning meets his hopeful frame of mind—perhaps it could be different; this year could be different, he's thinking. A sudden, swift crack of a window breaks his thoughts. He sees the flash of it opening, the pane of glass reflecting the sky in first a shimmer of white cloud, then blue. The street settles into calm again and he steps back onto the sidewalk, turning down Avenida Sonora, where he can take a camion to Paseo de la Reforma.

THE LIMESTONE SIDEWALK WINKS with flecks of mica. He takes the stairs two at a time. He walks to the entrance beneath the wide, shaded portico. The glass doors before him are rimmed in silver chrome. Inside, his footsteps echo down corridors. There is a resigned, empty air to these hallways—spacious and wide, still enough to inhale the scent of dust, feel the coolness of marble. Both senses spur in him the old, familiar tightness—first in his stomach, then traveling up to his chest. He is early, but the lines already come halfway down the corridor. He can hear the requests for birth certificates, applications. Next, demands for identification. An address. A sponsor name. From above comes the boom of weighted doors slamming closed.

He reaches the head of the line. A man in a blue uniform gives him a number. It grows clammy in his hand. Up ahead the waiting room is full and appears to breathe from the collective inhalations and exhalations of uncertain men and women. Glances. Judgments. He walks down the center aisle; in the periphery the benches sit like book spines. Over the years, he's come to know the room well—its scalloped moldings, marble floors of gray and black swirls, the rows of floor-to-ceiling windows like tall glasses of water. He knows too the way the room is awash in worry: in the faces of men who sit staring into a middle distance; in the women's hands as they attend to their handmade laces; in others reading, eyes rising over the edge of a newspaper.

He settles into a place on a bench at the back of the room, taps his feet and looks at the worn tips. He hopes that they will not notice his shoes, that no one will look too closely and think him useless. That morning he tried his best to polish away the scuffs and had even taken a brown pencil to color in a bit of the tips. To his surprise, it worked quite well and he wondered why he had not thought of such a trick before. It may have worked in his favor, because well, from afar, do they now not look like a brand-new pair of shoes, shined and polished? He takes in the room. There is something about the entire building that threatens an impending scolding, as if, at any moment, he will be called out, "You there, come with me."

One hour creeps into two. The rustle of turning newspapers, footsteps coming close and fading away, whispered exchanges. His eyes grow heavy, closing for, he tells himself, just a moment.

"FIFTY-TWO. AUSTIN VORONKOV."

He feels his shoes slide out from under him. There is a bolt of cold to his throat. He is not quite sure if he is standing. He feels a little surge of blood from his lip where he's bit down. He is before the glass partition, staring at the clerk. He has not encountered this one before. The clerk has a long, thin nose. Fine light hair. Not even a strand of gray. Too young for this kind of work, Austin thinks, but then realizes, hopes, that it may work in his favor. The boy might be eager to help, be accommodating. How simple it could be. One small decree. A single stamp and a life could change, a train could pull out of the station and a border could be broken.

"Documents," the clerk says.

"Good afternoon," says Austin.

"Documents."

"Everything is in order," Austin says, patting his hand on the envelope. He passes the documents beneath the glass. His heart is racing. He wonders if the actualization of what is longed for can ever match what it is to be just within reach.

"Quite a lot of papers here."

"The letters there are written on my behalf. And these here are my inventions. You'll see that I have communicated with the U.S. Patent Commissioner. That is my oath of a single inventor."

"Not necessary. Country of origin, please," the clerk says, arranging the documents into two separate piles. The muffled patter of a typewriter fills the silence.

"Country of origin, please."

"Russia," says Austin, pressing his shoulders back, feeling his neck crack.

"The Soviet Union?"

"Russia."

"You are a citizen of what country?"

"You see—"

"You are a citizen of what country, Mr. Voronkov?"

"My wife . . . she is American."

"What is *your* country of citizenship?"

"No country . . . But my wife . . . she is American."

The clerk places the documents back into the envelope.

"My children are Americans—" The clerk rises, tells Austin to wait, and then walks past the long line of clerks seated at the same standard-regulation, blue-gray desks, reaching the end of the room and passing through a windowless metal door the color of slate.

"Shit." Austin stamps his foot, sighs. He keeps his eyes on his hands. He's come this far, might as well see it through: Keep calm, he thinks.

The clerk returns, carrying a manila file folder. He is half smiling, half frowning. It is a small effort at offering a kind of sympathy. Smug, Austin thinks. But what did this youngster know? This young chap who gets to come and sit here at such an organized desk, saying "yes" or "no." Clear-cut. Simple.

"So?" Austin says. The clerk sits down. He begins to write on a white slip of paper covered with blue lettering.

"Is it okay?"

Silence.

"I'm afraid we aren't permitted to authorize any visa for you," the clerk says, tapping the file with the tip of his pen. "D.C. handles your kinds of cases—"

"You see. I can explain about the file," Austin says. His tongue is dry. A pulsing in his neck persistent.

"Yes, you can, sir. But it doesn't help. We're not permitted to handle your case. It's D.C."

"I come here every year and I bring you people the same papers that you require. And then I'm told the same thing. D.C. It's up to D.C. Waiting on D.C. and then I'm told to return."

"We can't reverse a deportation charge. That's up to"—the clerk pauses—"Washington. I can give you the D.C. office to write to."

"I've written to that office. I hear nothing."

"It's the Labor Department," says the clerk, exchanging his pen for a stamp.

"I wrote to them. My wife has written to them. Please."

Silence. The sound of another typewriter. The clerk bows his head. He sets down the stamp, brushes a bit of hair out of his eyes. Austin sees the ink stains on the edge of his palm, his fingertips. He is not so neat and tidy, is he. Their eyes meet. Hazel—it is the first prolonged eye contact the two have made throughout the exchange.

"Mr. Voronkov, you are an anarchist. You were deported from the U.S. in 1920. This office cannot help you. It's D.C. I'm just not sure what to tell you. Deported? An anarchist charge? Don't you see?"

"I'm not an anarchist."

"That's not what the file here says."

"My children are Americans. Surely that must mean something?"

"No. I'm sorry. Listen," he begins again in a whisper, "it says that you are an anarchist. You are, by some definitions, un-American. Unfit for entrance. You'll have to wait for Washington to overturn such a charge."

"But please, between you and me, there must be someone here who can help me. Contact Washington? At least inquire—"

"We're not permitted."

Silence. He can hear a typewriter striking up from behind a row of filing cabinets that stand like sentries.

"Not permitted," Austin repeats.

"No. Look. Do you see what it says here?" the clerk opens the file, turning it upright for Austin to read. The clerk's cuff links, ring, and watch face catch the light. "See this? Clause 'd'—"

(d) That said AUSTIN VORONKOV is an ANARCHIST and believes in the overthrow by force of violence of the Government of the United States and that he disbelieves in and is opposed to all organized government.

"I can explain," Austin pleads.

"Still, our office is not perm—"

"All right, all right," Austin says. He is leaning close to the glass, can feel his cheek graze its cold, smooth surface. The row of ceiling lights shine in a line of white along the pane. How he'd like to shatter the glass, the typing like steady pinpricks. His breath fast and quick. He sputters his lips, bows his head, and steps away from the partition, arms slack and at his sides, though he feels a throbbing along his jaw and neck. He shakes his head. *Not permitted, not permitted.* He takes his first slow steps away from the partition. He is letting it settle in with each stride, *not permitted,* *not permitted.* And what is this now, but panic, the heart flutter and chest constricting, the sudden blush as if he'd come down with an instant fever. His envelope, his postcard! He looks around. Why do all these people stare so? The clerk is tapping on the glass partition. He waves Austin's envelope in irritation. Two long strides and Austin is back before the clerk.

"Not permitted," Austin says, grabbing his envelope of documents. "Well, here is what I'm permitted to say to you: I see that you are married," he continues, motioning to the small gold band on the clerk's ring finger. The clerk retracts his hand.

"You see—when you have children of your own," Austin says, "remember me and how you were 'not permitted' to help me. Remember me. Does your stamp there show that I am a husband, a father? No! So, I don't want it! You have it! Why should I want a stamp from a country that threw me out? You say, 'yes,' and stamp, and 'no,' and stamp. You are a cog! Do you realize this? A cog. You are a speck on the surface of my life! So you can have your stamps and your papers and your ink-stained, filthy fingers and when you go home at night, kiss your wife, eat dinner, put your children to bed, think for a moment if you were denied all of it, all of it—the smell of your wife, the sticky hands of your children, the earth and air smell of their hair from play outside. Think then for a moment and remember me. It is you, and all the men like you, who have caused boys to have no father, a girl to have no father. I did not make this choice! So, please."

"We cannot do anything," the clerk says. He swallows, his Adam's apple like a knot of contrition. He sits motionless.

"Please."

"I'm afraid we are not permitted."

. . .

A CITY AWAKENING. Siesta is over. The sky has grown crimson and mauve with gray plumes rising up from factories situated on the city's periphery. Lovers open windows, shopkeepers roll up gated storefronts and people emerge from narrow, dark doorways. Blue clouds lined in blood orange sit on the horizon.

Sun and dust. Broken stone. He feels heavy, his whole body turned inward. He sits down. He rises. He walks beneath the building's arcade, the marble slippery. He leans against the railing enclosing the small, manicured gardens—gardens of magnolia trees, palms. So much like those first weeks in Mexico City—how dizzying the impression for an émigré without a map. He'd come to the embassy, had been so certain then, brazen enough to believe his passage to America would be swift, secured. He is still hoping for that day.

He walks down the stairs and across the street, his brown, sorry loafers caked with dust. He draws a cigarette from his back pocket, stops at the corner to light it, watching as the little flicker of blue begins before the burn. A car speeds past, its motor loud. Over the car's fading rumble and from a window open and overhead he hears the faint voice of someone singing, a warble like that of a bird. The tightness in his chest loosens. He raises the cigarette to his lips, exhaling. He leans back against the building, one leg tucked up and under, resting against the stucco wall, its grainy surface pressing through his shirt. The last of the sun cuts a diagonal of light across his body—a man marked, a man crossed out.

For just a fleeting moment, Austin feels something like contentment, so tired he is of always wishing to be elsewhere. A respite from longing, an easy satisfaction in a small desire sated. A last inhale and he tosses the cigarette to the ground, wishing it could be the day.

He had tried to adapt as well as he could, had come to, some might say, resign himself to this adopted country of his with its bright sun, dusty roads, sepia buildings, past built upon past. A city stripped down and built up again.

But it was not the life he was supposed to live—this life, this Mexico City life. He closes his eyes and there they are—all quite clearly, going on about their lives, waking in those cold northeastern mornings when it was dark blue and felt as if night had forgotten to end, the heater clanking the children awake, he imagines. Three children, each born in a different country (Russia, France, Mexico) and all now Americans. They were walking around in streets filled with memories of his young manhood. His children, there without him. He can sometimes feel them, when younger, their small arms around his neck when he carried them in the early years in Mexico, the sound of their voices, saying Papa. How does one live with longing? He knows it. It was as if he were forever reaching, arms extended in a gesture of entreaty. Pulling on a rope, hand over hand, fist over fist, the rope only growing longer.

THE ZÓCALO: SPACE, a dusky silver sky. Steadfast buildings enclose the square. Streetlamps jeer, orange in the early evening . . . *not going to the States after all* . . . He falls alongside three older men, white hair, hands clasped at the back. One man's voice low and thick from years of tobacco. The others listen as he speaks, nodding, earnest, grave nods. Austin recoils, draws his gaze inward and down, his shoulders hunched as if direct eye contact will sting. He is not far from it. These empty afternoons of old age, stepping into evening, stunned by the throb and pulse of all this life.

Two women arm in arm clatter across the wide flagstones of slate, emerald, cobalt. A splice in his path. In their T-strapped heels and full skirts, he feels a yearning, a dull, near-forgotten burn of want that had made him falter in his fidelity; he was not a saint, he knew, could not be celibate. Long ago he'd come to know this, given in to it. Women of satin skin, women he'd clung to. He thinks of Julia. (It was always Julia.) He tries to picture in his mind the shape of her face. If he can recall even that much, her other features will soon emerge, come into focus—her steely blue eyes, how they sank in slightly, the better to see the curve of her cheekbones; the way her brow sloped gently upward to the honey hair, full and always pulled back from her face, tied into a chignon at the base of her neck. And maybe, if he thinks hard enough, concentrates on the image, he can see her smile forming, which always took a little coaxing, her lips often—and when he remembers her last—pressed together into a pout, one that masked a panic. And if he allows himself even more time, if he is lucky, he can conjure up the sound of her voice: high and sweet, like a chime, and always with that American, northeastern accent of hers, so fast and held tight in her chest as if she never quite drew enough breath when speaking. And, then, when he has the face, her likeness, her very presence quite set in his mind, he continues across the Zócalo, trying to hold her in his mind's eye. The image, though, is like quicksilver—shattered by the sounds, the night, a second's onslaught.

He passes what had once been the Aztec marketplace, the Inquisition's execution ground. A walk through centuries. His mother had given him her love of walking; how much she loved to walk in the fields of their farm. Even in those insufferably frigid days of Russian winter, when evening came at three in the afternoon. They'd walk to the road that ran along the wheat fields, barren, hard. Or even those closer, less distant winters of New England, winters cracking, breaking into spring—rain or sap on branches, the green and moss of the thaw come in earnest. Could he withstand either of those winters now?

The Mexicans are a kind people, he has to admit, though he has learned to keep a distance, slide by people, let others slide off him. He's grown into it, another habit, though if he strips it all back and really looks, his true nature, core, or whatever one wants to call it, longs to embrace the world free of any suspicion or cynicism. And back then, in the first years in Mexico City, he had been such an obvious gringo, standing out so in the cantinas of La Condesa. His pale, white skin with its bluish pallor, like alabaster. His tall, commanding countenance.

"You come here to get lost?" they asked him that first year. "It's the right country. The land of the disappeared, *los desaparecidos*. Even so tall a man, you can disappear, you can." He'd been angry at that. What right had the man to define him? He would not disappear. He would not stay in this godforsaken country.

"My stay is temporary," he had told them. "I'm going to America."

"Is that right? Where are you from?"

"Russia."

"*El ruso!* He's Russian. *Amigos. El ruso.*"

He did not like that to be known, regretted it as soon as he'd revealed it out of anger. He'd learned the necessity for vigilance—the vigilance of a foreigner. Aware, always—who surrounded him, who might be at the next table over, who lingered too long within a doorway, who asked too many questions. He did not know how else to live in the world when he was so far still from any place he could call, think of as home. Now, a city, a language has gone ahead and seeped in, and, more often than not, he knows he is mistaken for a native Mexican: skin around the eyes dark;

face, forearms, and hands a tarnished bronze; black hair graying into a metallic iron.

And now where is he? He's come out of an alley, disoriented. He doesn't know which way to go. It is shocking and in his confusion he begins, instinctually, to move not left or right, but straight ahead. *Tout droit* he thinks, remembering that was the first phrase he'd comprehended in French, those years ago on the tightly wound, cobblestoned streets of the ninth arrondissement in Paris. Hungry and in search of work, cold and bewildered by the incomprehensible streets of another foreign city. And now here he is, *tout droit, tout droit,* he thinks as he walks, laughing at himself for the sudden switch of language, not straight ahead, or in Russian, how does one say it? But never mind that he thinks, he has to now calmly do an about-face and pretend as if he were walking the other way and now no longer *tout droit* because in his disorientation, in his wanderings and his furtive, crazed walk (half run) to get away, he's unknowingly stumbled to where he stands now—before him, just a few yards ahead, sits the building he often walks twenty minutes out of his way to avoid: the Soviet Embassy. His heart nearly gushes in his ears. He sees the steps to the front door, the sheen of the heavy thick wood and the brass doorknob. He can see two figures at the bottom of the steps, hands in coat pockets, one man nodding his head, the other suddenly giving out a loud laugh. Austin freezes. He really cannot pass in front of them. He would not be surprised if his name were printed on some large banner, a kind of indictment. He dares not look in the direction of the embassy. He'll instead feign nonchalance, pass by it, pretending that he does not care in the slightest if his name is written in big, bold block letters, all in black, on a three-foot-high canvas banner like a call to arms—VORONKOV.

. . .

To see his street after the evening's wandering is a relief. He feels lucky for at least that, to see the recognizable shape of the buildings, their jagged silhouettes edging sky. The Cantina de los Remedios. Its laughter and voices fall out the lighted windows like mouths. It reaches him, draws him into the warmth, the stale, layered smell: tequila, beer, smoke, and ammonia. He sits in the way he likes, at the far end of the bar, on the side so he can see the door, aware of who walks in, who comes toward him either too nonchalantly or too directly. The clatter, rumble, and whispers bloom up from full tables, filter over those that are empty, and linger amid the few dotted with solitary patrons.

"Austinito el inventor. Buenas tardes," the bartender says. Austin taps his fingers on the bar. Its wooden surface nicked. The mirror above the bar like a strip of river. His eyes catch the ravaged reflection—a sudden recognition of self. He does not look good. He could have at least gotten the buttons on his shirt right. Has he really walked around all day, presented himself at the embassy with the shirt buttons all misaligned?

"Austin, Austin," the bartender says, grabbing his shoulder. And then to no one in particular, "the inventor who cannot invent his way out of Mexico." He is holding a cloth in his hands. He begins to fold it into a small square.

"Una tequila," Austin says.

Austin remembers how he'd first come here, still new to the neighborhood. Everyone assumed he was working for the Soviets. Then, Miguel had whispered to him, with a smile, waving his finger at Austin, "One day, you will tell me what you did that you can't get to your family."

"Nothing," Austin had said, and then, for emphasis, *"Nada."*

And it was true. He had done nothing. In fact, what he had done was follow the rules, or, at least, followed them in the way he understood them at the time. It seemed to Austin that when he looked at his life thus far, examined each year, connecting one to the next, the years were marked by a keen obedience, not unlike the bottles that sat before him in their ordered rows, the overhead light painting first one and then another bright, white arc along each successive curve of dark amber glass.

He—an anarchist? What kind of anarchist would be so compliant? What of all his repeated visits to the embassy, all the attempts to enlist the help of the correct authorities, the formal letters to the senators, to D.C., the affidavits, notarized birth and work certificates, port of entry papers—was not all this proof enough? How could these men not see the very thing that sat right before them? But then again that was perhaps asking too much of them. He'd come to know—his very predicament was a testament to this fact—that appointed clerks, all members of this bureaucracy, were only able to see what was set before them in black and white. They could not—sometimes Austin felt that it was done intentionally, a requirement of their posts and positions—read between the lines.

He sips his tequila from the thick, hand-blown shot glass. Its lip of indigo blue is curved, soothing. A spiky astringency. Next, warmth. Voices rise, then soften. He remembers Julia and the children on the day of parting. How very logical it had all seemed at the time. The consulate in Nogales had told them it would only take two months, maybe three. Julia would fight to get Austin, her husband, the father of her children, reinstated. How they believed so fully in the sheer momentum of travel, her travels, from Mexico to the United States—the train breaking through the border, from Cananea to Nogales, hurtling onward toward the northeast. Surely that and the bonds of marriage, progeny, would help to drag him in her wake. She had made them arrange their suitcases into a kind of sitting room on the railway platform. *Sit, sit, a moment of stillness please*, she'd insisted. A Russian tradition. She'd learned it from him, made it her own and practiced it with diligence, reverence. The five of them sat in silence. The train exhaled its smoke in big, rushing hisses. People clamoring, dashes on and off the train. The embraces. And still, they remained, taking pause before the journey. What to say? A forced awkward stillness. Julia cried. He distracted the children.

"And you must remember all of it for me," he'd told his sweet ones. "When I come, you can tell me all your stories, all your adventures." They clung to him, squeezing his neck. The train whistle blew, a piercing cry that frightened his daughter Vera and made her bite his shoulder. The small teeth marks lasted two days.

He can see Julia now amid the suitcases. Pausing. Always a calmness, a complete composure. She, set on establishing some kind of stability. *Two months.* He'd be on his way—in two months, now three. One year, now two . . . *I'll be with you soon. . . . And soon I shall be with you all. . . .* The letters to or from Julia, the consulate—once a constant stream that crossed and recrossed the border, on one long line of communication whose open channel was, in the first years, strong and coursing with desire and need—*I love . . . I miss . . . I pray for . . . health . . . years . . . time*—had, in these later years, frayed. Between Austin and his family lay the border, yes, with its immigration houses, guards, patrols, and posts, but also the more impenetrable gray, white light of the embassy's windowless offices, dreary-eyed clerks and paper stamped with seals.

It was those same men in offices, the bureaucrats with their sharpened pencils, their white, starched shirt sleeves, always delving into their mire of papers, stamps, decrees that kept them apart.

Two months had long passed. It is 1948. Fourteen years. It is nearly impossible to absorb how the time has passed—he still waiting for the one great invention of his life.

"I did nothing!"

"Austin, what are you mumbling about?" Miguel asks.

"I wish I had done something. I did nothing, nothing." The urge to shatter, to break, to feel the force of two hard surfaces colliding comes over him. It is the same impulse he'd felt the night of the arrest—January 2, 1920. The frustration that tore through him like something alive and malevolent, contained within and unable to act, to speak, caused in him such a rage that he'd thrown the meager wooden chair against his concrete-blocked cell.

"Well, that is an unfortunate situation." Miguel adds, "But, if you're innocent, well, I'd rather be innocent, you know? Always innocent."

"No. I disagree," Austin says.

"But truly guilty," Miguel offers, "that stays in you. The guilt lives. That is a kind of punishment."

"I'd rather I'd done something worthy," Austin argues, "something rather than nothing at all."

"So you say you did nothing. There it is. Live with your good conscience. You know the truth. And live, live! You've got a mind for invention—invent another life, a different life."

"I cannot invent myself out of Mexico."

"Well, and it's not such a bad place to be, is it?"

. . .

MEXICO CITY. 1946. 1947. 1948. The era of President Alemán. The shift within the city. It had begun. Austin had seen it. More automobiles, people, pollution clouding what Alfonso Reyes once named "the most transparent region of the air." The Americans were busy stripping the country's resources—the oil, copper, silver, labor—to meet their industry's demands, an industry that provided housewives in Michigan with brass-plated sewing needles, the U.S. military with copper sheets for bullet heads, clock gears, radio wires. In among the other Russian and Eastern European refugees, the American tourists were invading the historic center. The blacklistees of Hollywood flitted over the border too, so that the *distrito federal*, DF, began to glint, gleam from the faces of the actresses, actors, screenwriters, set designers, any of whom could be found at Sanborns. Coca-Cola bottles dotted cantina tables, and whispers about the Red witch hunts and an American named McCarthy flowed through the *taquerías*, the outdoor gardens. Men in suits and fedoras dominated the *avenidas* and one had to walk to the outskirts of the city, to the old-fashioned neighborhood of Coyoacán, to find the Indians selling serapes, or the occasional sound of horse hooves on cobblestone.

AUSTIN HAD FIRST COME to Mexico City from the north of the country, where he had been working for most of the 1930s in the copper mines of Cananea, in the state of Sonora. It was work that had lasted, had allowed him to support his family the first years they'd arrived in Mexico after fleeing Russia. When Julia and the children were granted visas to enter the United States, Austin had to stay behind, waiting until he could join them. After one year, then two, and when the copper mine closed, he, with others in search of jobs, headed for the city. The electric company, it was rumored, was hiring. That was in 1937. He did not know Spanish fluently, but knew—by that time he'd been in Mexico for six years—enough to get by. He'd been punctual and precise. He could soon read the power grids of the city. He knew the voltages coursing in currents through transformers scattered amid the city streets. It had been through the electric company that he'd found a boardinghouse in the historic center. His room had cost only ten pesos a week. That price bought a bed, two windows (for he had a corner room), a dresser, closet, a washroom, a desk and chair. It would be enough, for now, he'd thought then, saying as much in a whisper to the proprietor, one of those middle-aged men in impeccable dress—always in white shirt and black pressed pants—who had handed him a map of the city with a room key affixed to a wooden circle. Austin's room number (302) was carved crudely into the surface and dyed with red ink.

Later, alone in his room that first day, with the city blazing white through the windows, Austin spread the map out on the bed. He took a blue pen and circled three locations: the boardinghouse, the Palacio Postal, a grande dame sandstone building that sat at the corner of Calle Tacuba and Cárdenas, and the U.S. Embassy far down the long diagonal of Paseo de la Reforma.

It was a start.

That same year, 1937, another Russian émigré—like Austin, born in the province of Kherson—ambled off a boat in the Atlantic port town of Tampico. Trotsky with his Natalia. Bespectacled. Exiled. Roaming "the planet without a visa." The pictures were in the newspapers. Pale-skinned, exhausted, squinting in the white light, he stood surrounded by men in fedoras, by Frida, by General Beltrán who, Austin noted, wore a uniform, the brass buttons circles of sunlight, brass made from the copper of Cananea, zinc too. Headlines ran in *El Universal*, *Reforma*, variations on the same four words: Cárdenas, Trotsky, asylum, Mexico. The dirty Bolshevik, was all Austin found himself thinking. A whole world had vanished. White Russian officers now taxi drivers along the *quais* and boulevards of Paris, now baristas and waiters or porters at La Coupole, La Rotonde.

He had ended up in the same country as Trotsky. The man who, if not single-handedly, then certainly indirectly, caused him to wander Europe before refuge came through Mexico. The irony. Did he gain any solace from the fact that they were now both exiles in the same city? He instead felt a deep fatalism at the inkling that maybe the gods still held some sway, poking and prodding men of all stations, no matter their fierceness, nor the ferocity of their convictions. In the deepest sense though, he saw it as mere absurdity.

For several years, the boardinghouse was sufficient. His two-room home, offering just enough space. He kept his shoes under the bed—a pair of working boots, a pair of thin-soled loafers. In his closet hung one suit, a sweater and overcoat, and two button-down shirts of light blue, frayed at the collars and cuffs. Across the street, a small coffeehouse offered a buttered roll with cheese and coffee for one peso. He spent some mornings here, and within a month's time he no longer had to place his order. He simply arrived, sat at his appointed spot while the waiters prepared his coffee and roll, delivering it with a simple nod of the head. At the local market, he bought an orange, sometimes a handful of grapes, but usually just an orange. After work hours and on weekends, he began a routine of walks—through different neighborhoods and then in the Alameda park which filled on Sundays with the Indians' *puestos*, mariachis, and the city's poor clasped close and dancing.

The boardinghouse was meant to be a temporary home. The main sitting room's puckered wallpaper, the wicker furniture, peeling, the worn staircases with their steps of gray ovals, the long corridors filled with the outlines of former decorations—postcards, calendars, movie posters—all of it a reminder of men coming and going, fleeing from or stepping toward. The sparse rooms were a way to gain one's footing before the next contraction of life thrust one this way or that. If he stayed in such a place, if he never thought of it as home, he could always be on the verge. He too could be—one day—one of the leaving.

Years passed: 1937, '38, on into the forties. The proprietor retired; his son took over. Belles Artes sank another quarter inch, its Carrara marble too heavy for the soft soil as if the old water canals of the ancient city were exerting their legacy in a slow, steady reclamation of space. Cárdenas turned over to Camacho and then to Alemán. Trotsky was assassinated. The war ended. The Soviet Union bought the Condesa de Miravalle's hacienda to house its embassy. And far back the walls of his village—stone by stone—began to disappear, the foundation of childhood now intact only in memory, he now an exile of two countries.

. . .

A SATURDAY MORNING. Bright, a slight chill. The line stretches along the narrow sidewalk. Women in their floral skirts of rust, lime, black, shifting weight, hips thrust out, a sigh and slump against the brick wall. People hear about it at market stalls, word spreads through women's whispered conversations, the maids of Mexico City. A secret shared.

"He can fix anything," they say. "These Russians. From such cold climates, it is good for the brain. Makes it exact and precise. Like ice. It's in them."

These Saturdays are Austin's busiest days. The whole street has a different feel, people walking, returning from the markets with their purchases—straw bags laden with avocados, mangoes. There are chickens, feet tied with red string. Cake boxes, hat boxes too. The schoolboys are on the corner, kicking a soccer ball back and forth. The older ladies who gather each morning in the park across the street are joined now by grandchildren, plump hands reaching for a slice of peach, struggling to get a grasp of park bench. The cars glide by with a serene patience for there is little traffic. The maids of Mexico City, rising early, are either dispirited and gloomy or relieved, but several wait in line.

Already the sun is strong, even for a January morning. He will move inside to his shop soon, but in these midmorning hours he likes to work outside, a table placed on the sidewalk. The surface of it is littered with broken remnants—a wind-up alarm clock; a watch, its face shattered; a knotted silver chain; a clip-on earring, clasp loose; a pocket watch, an egg timer. These objects of the everyday. Gadgets of life and small hours. A cardboard tag is tied to each with twine. "Maria 12pm," "Constantina 12:30pm," the tags read. A powder blue telephone hangs off the edge of the table, its receiver dangling above an old cash register; silver keys like sparks in the noon sunlight. His hand aches. The palm holds a dull throbbing and, as he works, he pauses, setting down the wrench, screwdriver, to knead his tired tendons, the smashed nail bed of his thumb. Still, he likes the feel of the tools in his hands, his mind following the logic in mechanics, what bolt needs tightening, what hinge needs loosening to create the correct torque.

The sun now shines down the middle of the street, shadows underfoot. Austin scans the line—women checking watches, talking. Some stand with arms crossed, bags dangling off a wrist or shoulder. One woman bites her nails. Another opens and closes the clasp of her purse. All are in haste, eager to finish this one of many errands before launching on to the next task, and the one after that.

"The radio is broken," a woman says, setting her bag on the table. He looks to her, then to the radio.

"You see, the knob, the tuner—here, it just spins round and round," she explains.

"You use it often?" He turns the radio over in his hands.

"Does that matter?" she says.

"Not really." He shrugs. "But you know, usually a woman knows how often the things she owns are used." He does not look at her when he speaks. He keeps his eyes on his hands.

"A woman, but not this woman."

"Every day?" He looks at his nails filled with grime, grease. He is suddenly ashamed of his own, deformed thumb.

"I couldn't say."

"If I had such a fine radio, I'd use it every day."

"Can it be fixed?"

"One can tell a lot about a household from the use of its radio," he says, taking a screwdriver from his back pocket, unfastening the back plate.

"Can it be fixed?"

"Your name?"

"What?"

"I will need your name. For pickup."

"It can be fixed then?"

"Yes. In just a few hours."

"Tell me *your* name first."

"My name?" He looks to her now.

"Yes. You asked for my name. I ask for yours." There is defiance in her stance, her shoulders set square with a slight lean forward.

"Austin Alexandrovich Voronkov," he says, his eyes back to the radio.

"Your name is as long as a Mexican's." She gives a little laugh.

"Is that so? And you are?" he says, his eyes meeting hers, which are round and large, nearly black. She is very beautiful. Dark hair like the smooth gloss of a black Cadillac, the eyes intense and eager in their deep hollows.

"Anarose Luisa de Soto."

"Done in an hour," he says. Brusque. In no mood for pleasantries. The sting of the consulate's rejection still so fresh. These past few days, he'd felt the world itself was closing in on him, his sight lines narrowing to his very feet—one foot in front of the other. These repairs, simply a trade by chance. He, falling through positions, stations in life—engineer, inventor, repairman. When he lines them up, thinks of the transitions from one to the next, it is enough to cause vertigo. But he can remember how easily all this began. A Kodak camera. Next a transistor radio. Then a fan. Several fans left overnight like offerings placed at an altar, though the altar was merely Austin's boardinghouse room door—five to six fans lined up like retired airplanes, the steady cross breeze from the hallway windows enough to spur a lazy rotation of the opaque charcoal or iron blue propellers. He sets the radio to the side, writing *Anarose* on a piece of cardboard. When he looks up, she is gone.

AT 2 P.M. HE PACKS up his work, folds the table, and places his tools into the metal box. He carries the table under one arm, toolbox cradled in the other. He enters his shop, open to the street, setting the table against the front wall before locking the door and walking two doors down to his boardinghouse. He takes the stairs up the three flights to his room. Ten years already that he's been here. He never imagined he'd have such a place, need a somewhat permanent home in which to reside. Can he call it home? No. It is not home. Not that.

He makes his way up to the third floor, counting the stairs out of habit. At the twenty-sixth step, he enters his hallway and counts the remaining ten, or sometimes twelve, paces to his door. His rooms are cooler, as if they'd taken a deep breath in the colder morning air and had been holding it in all afternoon just for him, just so that he can return to a cool, comfortable place, while outside is in its usual state of brightness and dust.

He pours himself a glass of water from his still full jug and drinks half the glass in three gulps, the temperature lukewarm. He sits at his makeshift drafting table and opens the new package of paper he'd purchased earlier that morning. Once out of its brown wrapping, it has the same familiar scent of mothballs and freshly cut wood. He sweeps away the small dusting of eraser shavings that has congregated along one edge of his table. Next, he lays the paper down and it feels good beneath his hands—his palms across the cool white surface, admiring the flecks of brown pulp, some pink, as scattered and haphazard as the stars in the night sky.

The paper, for Austin, is most important. The texture and feel, the way the pencil scratches slightly across the page. The paper holds on to the lead a bit. It doesn't slip and slide so that his hand must struggle to keep the lines in place. If anyone knew precisely to what kind of lengths he goes to secure such paper—once erasing twenty pages of drafts of old ideas to preserve sheets—they'd think him mad. And, well, perhaps he is.

From out the window, the close and distant noises come—doors opening and closing, trucks spitting out exhaust, a bus screeching.

Austin's inventions. They are based on principles that cannot be seen: a belief in ether, wind, in force and gravity. He wants to harness the power of wind. He understands ether as a mode of transference. Gravity itself a power to work with, instead of against. He is still waiting for the one great invention of his life. Then, surely, he'll be allowed in, praised even. Lauded. A personal apology from Truman himself! On official letterhead! With the presidential seal! A communication from the White House. He will soon show them, they'll soon see. He knows the rules that govern induction, how to measure amperes and voltage, how sound travels on waves, and how the voice can overcome distances through a combination of oscillation and crystal conductors. That amazes him still, even during the long days of work when he looks up to find himself quite alone in the mournful hollow of night.

He sits now tracing circles with the tip of a pencil that is neither too sharp, nor too dull. The late afternoon sunlight falls in shards: bars of light along notebook bindings, lines of light thin as string imprinted on a compass leg, the table's edge. Already the drafting paper is half filled with arcs he has made by compass. It is a messy process. The lead pencil marks, the rubber residue of the eraser shavings, his hands covered with the resin of lead, the coal marks along his left palm. He draws and calculates, numbers the figures, writes out specifications for each section of the hydropropeller—propulsion turbines, the rotation mechanism. He sets down his pencil and picks up a ruler, sets down the ruler and switches it for a compass, and repeats the same exchange of instruments until he is ready to transfer the designs to a final draft.

When he needs a break he stands, walking back and forth between his rooms—immaculate rooms, nothing on the surfaces. All unblemished and blank, the better for ideas to emerge out of the space of life. In the mornings, he does not turn on the lights. He prefers to wake with the dawn, the light bright and blinding, fingering its way into the room of grays and blues. The wood floor is gray. His door is gray. The walls a faded blue. He has little furniture. A small sofa. A table he's made himself—the wood unfinished. It doubles as a work and dining table. This is where he eats. This is where he invents. The lights stay off in the afternoons too. In the evenings, long after dinner, he measures, setting numbers into equations. He likes to work as the natural light fades, as night comes on, the windows purpling. When it grows too dark for him to work, he clicks on a lamp, gold and black, a lamp he'd fixed, though the customer never returned—his abandoned lamp. It reminds him of home, the first home, Varvarovka, in Kherson province.

He will need to write to her, he knows. He runs a hand through his hair, pulling, tugging at the ends. He sighs, pacing through his two rooms. Over the years, he has pieced together their lives. By now he knows that Julia works in a bakery, that she is lucky to have any work at all. She, a single mother, raising three children through the Depression. There is still no money. Her mother helps when she can. The boys had collected scrap metal and rubber tires for the early war effort. There was Russian school at night and Russian Orthodox services on Sundays. Julia had sent letters, of course. *How it would be if you could see them dear.* They were always encouraging letters, sometimes scolding ones too—*do not fall into too much gloom, keep your mind occupied.* And she wrote of her efforts with the senators, how much interest they took in the case. In the first years apart, the letters came with notes from the children, drawings. Sometimes a letter would not reach him and so the next letter he received would refer to events he was not aware of, a cause of much confusion, and sometimes a letter he sent would take two months, others two weeks, so their communication was nonlinear, circuitous, fragmented—letters sent like skipping stones over water.

She couldn't come back to him, they both knew it. With a last name connected to an anarchist Russian—if she were to travel to Mexico, they certainly wouldn't ever let her back into the States. And the children— they would grow up to be Americans, that had been the agreement, no matter what. But, despite all this, there was a part of him that secretly hoped she'd come for him.

He steps to the window, places his hands in his pockets, and rolls back on his heels, surveying the collection of small cacti and succulents he has arranged on his windowsills. They require little care, but still he is diligent—water once a week, full morning sun, gluttons for sun, really. The aloe and agave, the ghost and amethyst plants, the prickly pear and blue myrtle. Every so often one will bloom. When that occurs, always like a small miracle, he'll sketch the flower into his notebook of faded pages—elongated petals, alongside his blueprints, numbers, and symbols. He likes the amethyst plant the best, the rounded, plump leaves like moonstones. He runs a hand over the smooth surface of the leaves and then moves his palm above the ghost plant, feeling the slight prickle of needles like iron bristles.

Out the window, pedestrians amble by, some loping, others with a vigor in their strides. One man walks back and forth in front of the apartment building across the street. The man is waiting, it seems, and Austin watches, his pacing as balanced, measured as a metronome. He cannot make out the man's face; the hat shields the eyes and the sun casts a shadow along his lips and jaw.

During all aspects of waiting or stillness—on lines, watching out windows—moments return. It could be a look or word passed in the street, a trigger. A scent of winter and snow, something clean and cold, or sometimes too the heavy, thick incense of a ceremony or a chanting, cheering, and he is back there, in the church basement. The secretary reads off names . . . *Voronkov*. The lights dim. A winter night, early in the new year of 1920. It's a point he returns to, circles around and delves back into in a second, the memory of it a hinge—of a door, of his life really. In what amount of time—it took maybe twenty minutes? The rush of boots on the stairs, the blackjacks and guns, shouts and shackles . . . *You Communist pig. Anarchist* . . . And in Russia, the shots echo through his mind, speaking to Julia, *do not look, do not look*, he'd told her. The insolent stupidity of the Bolsheviks with their dirty, filthy hands, more like animals than men, Julia had always said. Her words come to him, ". . . when I think of all our adventures and you the only person who knows as well as I, I miss you. . . ."

It's when one least expects it really so Austin is always hyperaware. He grabs the cord of the blinds, tugs it to the right to lower them, and then thinks better of it—best not to bring attention to his window. He lets out a little laugh. Ridiculous. The man is simply waiting. It is hard to shake the habit though, watching, waiting. He remembers the other windows—a church basement window, a window beyond a lace curtain, and the men that had stood on the other side of each of those panes— worlds apart. Still, he wants to see the face; he'll be able to spot a Russian in a moment—one eye lock is all it will take and a whole world's worth of animosity, suspicion, and betrayal will be exchanged. An American too, one of these FBI agents he's hearing about. Square jawed and broad shouldered. The distinctions hardly matter, amount to the same in the end, and he can nearly hear the feet on the stairs—clomping, loud and furtive voices. "He's here. This one." The knock on the door. And why not? If not now, then one day soon. Three clear knocks, a rapping on the door. Any time may be appropriate. Bang, bang, bang. They may crowd into the room, demanding, "Your name? Your papers." And what then? He has none from any country. Then it will be over and then why not? Well, fine, he thinks, I'll hand myself over instead, get it over with if they've come this far. And then what? Deported, repatriated back to Russia, a more official way of stating he'll be sent straight to Siberia. He can nearly feel his fingertips stinging from the strike of an ax on frozen wood. *Knock. Knock.* Let them come then. Fine. Take me away, he thinks, as he blinks once, twice, shakes his head and finds himself after all this time staring out the window, his arm raised halfway to the blinds, arrested in motion, the ache along his muscle, mouth agape like someone shocked into a statue. No. He will not pull the shades down, not bring attention to his window. But now he is being ridiculous, or is he? Never mind, never mind, he thinks, shaking his head, frowning, disappointed with himself for letting his mind go so far astray, to have followed such a path when he'd begun the afternoon, quite harmlessly, about to set to work; oh the places his mind goes to sometimes, to where he stands now, in silence, in the quiet of his rooms, waiting for the knock on the door that will never come. Maybe.

The man breaks into a smile as a woman approaches. She takes his arm and they dash into the doors of the apartment building. Austin feels foolish, though it takes a moment for his heart to settle, to stop racing. Is there now something like envy flooding up in him? To have smiled so warmly toward another, he thinks, wondering if the couple are lovers—most likely.

He walks into the bedroom. Small, tidy. The bed sits in the middle of the room, a wool blanket of faded stripes—orange, blue, red—lies tight across the thin mattress. The sunlight arcs along the dresser's oval mirror. He stands before it now, chest high. He opens the first drawer, feeling for the slim goldenrod envelope no larger than a two-hundred-peso bill. He walks to the worktable, and the photographs fall into his palm. He places each one onto the table, his fingers graze the corners of the photos, a task that procures a faint flicking sound, squares and rectangles in a line along the tabletop. In the first year when they believed it would be just that—one year, one of letters, telegrams—he'd kept their photographs on display. Little shrines for each image. A lock of hair tied by red ribbon, a sewing thimble, an earring. No longer.

Here, Austin and Julia, the largest of the photographs, square, a thin rim of tarnished white. Seated side by side, unsmiling, holding hands, torsos inclined. Faces set squarely toward the camera. Julia's hair is off her face. Two plaits swept down over her ears. She stares out at Austin now with that same direct stare—unabashed. It was what first drew him to her, a look on the stairs, a mistaken brush of hands as they passed—she going up, he down.

And here is the house on Seaview Avenue, Connecticut, 1917. A house like the others, lined in a row—white with one bay window. A three-story house with its small front yard, grass in little tufts. The final photo is a family portrait, taken later, in Cananea, closer to the time of parting. No trace of their travels, nor their impending separation, and so a poignant image. A moment captured. A family assembled. Would there be any others?

Julia is seated, hands folded in her lap. The children on either side of her. She is wearing a dark dress, a shawl draped over her shoulders. Her boots are black, ankle lace-ups with a sturdy heel, the leather dull. Vera leans on Julia's knee, clear eyes like his own, her bobbed hair adding a modicum of insouciance to her young gaze. And the boys: his Aussie, still in breeches, and his Sonnie, chin tucked, eyes peering up and out, not without reservation because, Austin remembers it now, the youngest boy had been frightened, scared of the black box with the draped sheet, the folds cascading like some black ghost. The flash of the bulb, the way it exploded light.

He looks at himself now. How confidently he stood, lording over his family, a proprietary hand placed on Julia's shoulder. Had he done that of his own accord or had the photographer instructed him to do so? It was certainly not his gesture. Or, then, maybe it was. The proud callousness of youth, he thinks. He'd learned now, knows, that one owns nothing. Possessions—whether things or people—all an illusion. How easily the language upheld the fallacy—"my wife," "my children," he'd said at the embassy. He shudders to think of the white marbled walls, that floor. The nasal-deep voice of the young clerk, "We are not permitted."

A backhand sweep and the pictures scatter. The click and flutter of them as they fall to the floor. His palms press against the table's edge, banging the wall once, twice. The day's clouds pass over the sun and the room grows dark and then light, and then dark again. In periphery, he can see the branches stretched across the window, full and pulsing on the little wind. A bus passes, exhaling its exhaust through the window. Below too, men and women walk past like the steady flow of days. He wishes, longs to be one of them.

The floor is littered with the photographs; white squares facedown. He sighs and he picks them up—first one, then another. He stares into a younger self, and he can tell by the eyes, his eyes, that he had been a happy man.

He'll write to her now. He puts the photographs back in the envelope, years falling through hands.

They'd fared better than most. That he knew. Lives broken, but still lived. They could, after all, do just this—write to each other. To look at a map and point to where each resided. Others had no geography, lost to each other and the world. After everything, a name, an address, a place to be found—these were precious, fortunate things.

And yet.

He is a man who can calculate the mass of a water glass, the circumference of an apple, the velocity of a pencil's descent. He knows the seven kinds of energy, can measure the potential and kinetic energies of an object at rest, an object in motion. He knows the formulas for entropy, inertia. He can tell one how light travels, sound. His world, days are a landscape of equations. He can build a radio out of wire and magnets. He can disassemble a clock and make a metronome. He knows Ohm's law, Fourier's law, Newton's laws. He knows energy could neither be created nor destroyed.

He sits at his table again, picks up his pen this time, a clean sheet of drafting paper that he's folded into quarters. *Dear Julia*, he begins. He is finding it hard to write more, to find the words. *Dear Julia*. That is as far as he can get.

But there are other letters that he can write with no effort at all.

Commissioner of Patents
Washington, D.C.
United States of America

To Whom It May Concern:
Be it known that I Austin Alexandrovich Voronkov, applicant for
citizen of the United States of America of Bridgeport, CT—my
present, temporary residence being Avenida Sonora, Mexico City,

D.F., Mexico—have invented a new and useful boiler fire box surface by way of increasing the conduits, or tubes. The following is a specification:

DRAWING NO. 1 *is a full perspective diagram.*

Below, NO. 2 *and* 3 *are cross-section drawings of the water conduits, tubes, attached to the front face of the firebox by phalanges with metal joints, described here in* NO. 4, 5, *and* 6.

NO. 7 *is an oil burner atomizer, and illustrates how the flame embraces the water from the conduits.*

NO. 10 *shows two additional, parallel conduits.*

I claim therefore that such improvements to the boiler firebox allow the steam to move rapidly through the boiler pipes using less fuel consumption.

Inventor's full signature
Austin Alexandrovich Voronkov

OATH OF A SINGLE INVENTOR

I Austin Voronkov (American), Ustin Voronkov (Russian), Vustin Voronkov (Ukrainian), who applied for citizenship to the United States of America in the county of Fairfield, in the town of Bridgeport, state of Connecticut, born in Selo Varvarovka of Ukrainia, Russia, hereby swear that I know of no other invention or device that works to such a degree. The above-named petitioner, being sworn and affirmed, deposes and says—that he is an applicant for a citizen of the United States of America and his

present, temporary residence is Avenida Sonora, Mexico City,
Distrito Federal, Mexico, and his correspondence address is lista
de correos, D.F. He hereby believes himself to be the original, first,
and sole inventor of the hydraulic propeller described and claimed in
the annexed specifications; that he does not believe that the same
was ever known or used before his invention or discovery thereof, or
patented or described in any printed publication in any country
before his invention or discovery thereof.

> *Inventor's full signature,*
> *Austin Alexandrovich Voronkov*

. . .

GRAN HOTEL DE MEXICO. Its sidewalk café filled, bustling. The sun gleams off the dusky lens of sunglasses, the blade of a knife. The patrons gathered today are the same as usual. The requisite table of lawyers in their white, starched shirts and dark eyes. Two tired American women, in matching orange espadrilles, wide-brimmed sun hats and binoculars, sit over glasses of *agua fresca*. Behind them are American businessmen. Cuff links, watches, briefcases. They've pulled several tables together, the surfaces littered with coffee cups, half-eaten plates of pastry.

Austin walks beneath the hotel's canopy, its shade like a hallway. The American businessmen are unmistakable. It is in the way they take up space, not just with a body, but with a presence that announces itself like a ship berthing in port. To be so lucky, Austin thinks. To know so assuredly one's place in the world.

He sits down adjacent to them. One man has silver hair. The other is

the younger of the two, shaven, smooth. The sun is strong on his forehead and he repositions his chair to avoid its direct blaze. He is closer, can
hear their conversation—something about refineries, labor, stock shares.
He listens. He orders a coffee, a glass of water. He opens his satchel and
removes his papers and notebook. Why he feels nervous, Austin does not
know. He has done this so many times before, and his confidence has
waxed and waned, though today he is feeling more bruised, more shy
than ever, hardly able to place his order. They will think me ridiculous,
surely, are probably now noticing my shoes, he thinks.

He waits. A lull in their conversation. His chance comes.

"Excuse me. I can't help but overhear," Austin says, leaning toward
the men's table. It takes a moment for the men to realize he is speaking to
them. The man with the silver hair looks at his shoes, or so Austin thinks,
and he flinches, shamed. He tucks his feet under his chair, hoping the
man does not spot the scraps of rubber he uses to reinforce the soles, soles
as thin as newspaper.

"Please, will you allow me to—?" Austin says, rising half out of his
chair, his voice wavering.

"Of course," the man says. Bemused smiles, an exchange of furtive
glances. They think he's a Mexican. He'll be a story they can bring back
to their wives, some curio. He can hear it now, how they'd explain him,
describe him—this stranger inviting himself to their table.

"You work in American industry, correct?" Austin asks. He sits
down at their table.

"Yes. Copper," the man says, raising his glass to his lips. And then, as
if on second thought, he sets the glass back down. He folds his arms
across his chest.

"I thought so." Austin nods. Silence lingers and then he begins with a
lie. "It is quite a coincidence I come here and sit next to you today." Years

ago he would have felt a prick of his conscience. But now, after all the years, he feels his situation allows him to resort to the occasional, sometimes extended, stretch of lies—all white.

"Is that so?" the man asks.

"Yes. I sit here, listening to you talk—forgive me—but I think to myself, well, I must speak up."

"I'm all ears," the older man says, this time raising his water glass, drinking full, sloshing the water around in it a bit. He dabs the moisture at his temples with the coolness of the glass.

"I am Austin Voronkov," he says, extending his hand. The silver haired man does not move. The younger man rushes in to offer a cautious, feeble handshake.

"I am an engineer," Austin explains. "I know the work you discuss. I think I could be of use to you."

"You could, could ya?" the man asks, smiling now. He sits forward, elbows on the table. Complicit smiles, a wink even. "I'm Russell Becker," he says, offering a fleshy palm, damp from the glass. "Let's hear it."

"I earned my degree from the Ukraine Polytechnic. I was senior inspector for Remington Arms Company in Connecticut. An engineer with Anaconda, a foreman in Cananea. I am looking for work. With an American company."

"And you don't work with Anaconda anymore, I take it?"

"I had to come to Mexico City." A pause. Austin coughs. "For work."

"And did you find it?"

"I do repairs."

Silence. Russell Becker sits back and Austin follows their exchange of glances.

"And I have applied for several patents. For my inventions," Austin says.

"All you engineers are inventors, aren't you?" Russell Becker says.

"Where are you from, Austin?"

"Russia."

Silence.

"Austin. Odd name for a Russian."

"It has gone through manifestations," Austin says, with a tired, resigned smile.

"Is that so?"

"Ustin. That is my given name. The Americans, though, they change you."

"You're not a Red, are you?" Becker leans forward, his brow lined.

"No. I am married to an American. I applied for citizenship. I was born in Russia and came to America." Why did these Americans always assume that he was a Bolshevik, a Communist, just because he was Russian? They killed my mother and father, the dirty Bolsheviks, is what he wants to say. They were joking, it seemed, but there was a fear too. He knew that look—a sudden bristling, a closing in of one's shoulders, the end of direct eye contact and a wish to finish the conversation. It is something Austin has gotten used to, though abhorred.

"And so you want a job with us?"

"In any capacity. Perhaps on the American side of the border." As soon as he utters the words, as soon as he hears their laughter, louder than their previous chuckling, as soon as he watches Russell Becker slam his palm down on the table, glasses jumping from the impact, he regrets what he has said, and laughs now too, feigning bemusement, hoping to hide what had been his quite earnest plea. But he cannot disengage himself from the request. The words have been said. The question asked. He will have to ride it out, and find a way to simply endure.

"The American side?" Becker says.

"Well, that might be difficult to arrange," the younger man says. Russell Becker finishes his glass of water, wipes his hands on his thighs. "Listen—Austin is it?—we can't really help ya, I'm afraid," he says.

"You might just take a look at my drafts here." Austin reaches for his satchel, removing his designs, searching for the copper mine cement block lifter. He stands up, moving the plates and glasses out of the way, smoothing out the papers across the clear surface. He can hear his heart beat in his ears. He is flushed.

"You see here," he begins. "Of course, you need a hoisting crew, but it will work quite well. It can lift heavy blocks. And this is my patent letter," he says, handing the paper to Becker. "You see, I've had correspondence with the United States patent commissioner."

"Let's take a look," Becker says, examining the drafting papers, the letter. Austin watches his face, the slight frown of concentration.

"These here grip the concrete. They can expand with the crank, contract again depending on the size in need of lifting. And this one here—these are rail tongs."

"Yes. I see," he says, continuing to look over the papers. "Good, good, but we don't have use for that, I'm afraid. Have machinery that handles all this now." Becker folds the papers in half and hands them back to Austin. He pushes his chair out to rise, bumping into the woman sitting behind him.

"If you want to work for an American company, well, I think you'd have better luck crossing the border." He winks. "Excuse me," he says, and then forgetting himself, mumbles a deferential *perdón*. The younger man smiles apologetically as he stands up to leave.

"Good luck," he says with a wave like a salute. Austin watches them snake out of the café and onto the sidewalk and beyond that to the Zócalo, where they disappear amid the morning's crowds—bodies walking, halting, standing.

The *Herald Tribune* lies rumpled on their deserted table.

"JANUARY 4, 1948. 3½ BILLION ASKED FOR AID TO WORLD," the headline runs.

His coffee has grown tepid. His cold water is now warm, the glass sweating. Crossing. There were years when Austin had considered crossing the border. He'd nearly done it when living in Cananea, when Julia and the children were still with him. He takes a sip of his water, looks at his hands, remembering. A carnival used to come to Cananea once a year. He and Julia had taken the children every night. They'd never seen so many lights, he remembers. The Ferris wheel with its pink and white lights. From where they lived in the mine's barracks houses, they could see only the very top of the wheel. It seemed to hover there in the night, against the stars, only brighter, like a constellation. And he'd walk to the fair with Leo hanging off his neck. The boy liked to watch the lights come into view—one white light, then one pink, one white, then pink. He doesn't remember who loved that fair more—the children or Julia, drunk on all their laughter. They'd never really seen excitement like that. All the toys and games and rides.

Round and round on the Ferris wheel. From up top one could see far out into the desert. Austin had liked that view, at night. Looking out across the land, he remembers, was like looking at a dark sea.

The carnival was smack up against the border, the stone cement border pillars like little shrines, or odalisques. They blended into the landscape, particularly at night. Once, coming off the Ferris wheel, the children scattered. In the commotion, he'd lost Leo, who had wandered off beyond the reach of the lights. Dread. That's what he remembered of it. Dread of the worst kind. He still wonders what made Leo go off into that darkness, at four, maybe even five years old. They'd searched everywhere until they found him out in the middle of an open field. Austin had run and swept the boy up into his arms, scolding him. The boy had looked all stunned and frozen, his face breaking like children's do, crinkling up into a crying mess. That was in '32 and it was only on the walk back that he'd realized—he was in the United States. The boy had gone straight across the border.

"Simple as that," Austin murmurs now. He shakes his head, sips his water and sets it down. "Simple as that," he repeats. "Wandered off across the border."

Julia found them and had brought Vera and Aussie with her, the entire family standing in the middle of the open desert leading off into the hills. He watched as Julia gathered them all together, turning back to the fair. He can still see that image, her hair backlit by the lights—golden.

"We could keep going," he'd called to her.

"Yes, but what will we eat?"

"We're bound to find some people as we go."

"Yes. That's what I'm frightened of."

"Not Indians. I meant Americans."

"There are Apaches out there in those hills. Never mind wolves. And the sun. What will we do in broad sunlight? We'll all get scorched."

They had crossed the line back into Mexico, leaving the United States and the border behind them.

And later, in the first years without Julia when Austin was alone in Cananea. Waiting. The Mexico-U.S. border so enticingly close, a constant taunt; 1934 to 1936. Then, the risks were present: increased border

patrols, enticements by smugglers. And now the consequences still remain. He keeps a low profile with Mexican authorities. He does not have
a permanent address. He sends and receives letters *lista de correos,* general delivery. He works at an unsigned, unlisted repair shop, business
spread by word of mouth. And he makes every attempt to avoid the Soviet Embassy and its vicinity, walking two or three streets out of his way
so as not to stumble into one of his countrymen—these Soviets, his own
people when it comes down to it, one never knew if they were going to
slice your throat or embrace you, beat you unconscious and smuggle you
onto a steamship or invite you for vodka and caviar. He practices vigilance like a religion. Vigilance, reticence are his now constant compan-
ions, for he is not home; Mexico City is not his home. And if he crosses
and the Americans catch him, he'll be deported—and not back to Mexico, but to Russia, or what is in reality no longer Russia, his Russia, but
an idea put into practice. He cannot even call it a country, this Soviet
Union. Russia was a country, not what it had become.

"A country run by barbarians cannot last," everyone had then said.
Well, it *had* lasted. And under this Stalin too. No. The risks, for Austin,
too great. Shipped off to another continent. Twenty years' hard labor a
possibility. He wouldn't survive that. Not after everything. It was death.
Deportation. Russia. Death. He'd escaped once, twice might be asking a
lot. And if he did not cross at all?

THE DAY HAS SHIFTED from mid-afternoon to late afternoon. The
traffic, cars and pedestrians, thin. The waiters gather inside now. Some
are seated. Others lean on the bar. The patrons have all left except for a
few American tourists who are filtering in at this empty hour, their bags

hanging tired across shoulders, their city maps rumpled. It is time for Austin to go.

AN HOUR LATER and he is in the Alameda. It has always been his fa-vorite park. Its diagonal lanes are long enough for contemplation, but not so overwhelming that his energies are wasted, walking out all his inspi-ration. It is now close to 4 P.M., and he is walking at a slow, metered pace. His footsteps like a thin pencil trace. These walks allow him to enter a flow of thoughts. One long chain of mechanical processes. He tries to keep them steady in his mind, but beneath it, lurking, lies another idea—crossing. He cannot admit it even to himself. *Better luck crossing the border,* the American man had said.

He walks absorbed, reluctant to make eye contact, instead allow-ing the park to offer him the sense that he is an inhabitant of the city with all the aspects of the urban—buildings, concrete, traffic, and city dwellers—bearing down upon this small, central space, situated in the historic center, its poplar trees long gone and replaced now by the canopy of ahuehuetes. He is trying to focus on a design, running it over in his mind—the propeller, curve of blade, engine—but the empty spaces fill, flood over with fear. He is more on guard. A heightened sense of the park. Sounds more distinct, sharpened. Others around him, anyone, at this moment, may be intuiting his thoughts within the vacant spaces of his mind—his hidden intentions, his contemplations of crossing.

He feels a sudden movement from behind, the hurried scuff of a walk too fast and he increases his pace. With as much ease as he can muster, he turns his head to the side, a casual look behind him, though it's difficult to see. He'd have to crane his whole neck around, do an about-face and confront his follower. But he is being ridiculous. He is not sure, though he keeps walking and now slows his pace to show that he is not frightened, not worried in the least. His heart loud and thudding as the thoughts of crossing pursue him even as he tries to walk them out. He is focused at once on the possibilities if he were to succeed. Next, on if he were to be caught and then on if he were to return. To be deported, to return, to cross, to not cross, to cross, all the while meandering, one foot in front of the other along the star of the walking path, each spoke, each ray a new terrain of mind. And on such a day as he dares imagine crossing, it is as if he has nearly forgotten what he was doing in Mexico City at all. He's grown so accustomed to his routine, this starburst pathway that is etched deep into the day, as if he'd always been here in the DF, walking this same way. He is not the man who, in 1913 and with one foot in front of the other, left his village—this first time by choice, the second time in 1922 by force—and not the man who had been pulled through countries and across borders and who now remains these many years later without his family.

Sweat breaks out along his forehead, upper lip. He will make an exit, losing his pursuer, if there is indeed anyone who may care, may want to know his paths and routines, which are quite consistent and predictable, like himself, dressed in the same suit. Like an image on celluloid, pulled through the city on some endless reel. Faces stream past him. Conversations, shouts. There are more faces on the benches, heads thrown back in relaxation or laughter. The sounds accumulate as if gathered in the bottom of a well. White light comes through the trees, the heads backlit by the afternoon sun so that actual faces are dark, shadowed until he walks closer and features find their shapes again. Gazes lift from the pages of a newspaper. He can feel their eyes on him; falling away and then meandering back, away and back, like the gentle rock and sway of a small boat at mooring.

He hears footsteps behind him. Loud and soft as if his follower has a limp. He increases his pace, his whole body labored. A great strain in his joints, a heavy clampdown. If he wanted to run, lift his legs, move swiftly, he knows he will be unable. He lets the weight come. Thoughts of crossing descend, to a subterranean place within himself.

THE FLAGSTONE FLOOR of the post office is as empty as a stage. The late daylight falls in long white rectangles along the walls. He is grateful for the silence; he works to enter such establishments in the off hours. No crowds. A large crowd disturbs him. It sends a shiver along his chest, makes his knees buckle, his jaw clamp closed. Bristling, he freezes, coming to a full stop as a strange lassitude, a near paralysis overtakes him. It is not just the sight of masses moving, but more the sound. The roar and hush. It has happened to him at Sanborns, at the bullfights. He cannot withstand the bullfight's stadium crowd, the ring and the endless bleachers of people, all distinct, yet en masse. He feels something sinister lurking there—in a snippet of faces. The voices stalk him, approach low and murmuring before he can hear a whole rush of human sound—whispers, shouting, laughing—approaching him in one mass, like a large dark wave, threatening to drown out his voice, his very self. *Where are you from? What is your country of citizenship?*

He cuts a path across the open, clear main lobby. He knows the feel of the floor beneath him, the way his shoes squeak just so along the worn tiles. There is the scent of pulp and glue, perfume and tobacco. The window to the right of the door, high up with a kind of welcoming sheen, is where he'd stood reading Julia's first letter to him in Mexico City. She'd described their flat, the street they lived on. And she'd written out the meals they'd eaten, how the children insisted on setting a place for him. In the succeeding years there must have been a day when she'd paused before setting out the plate—there must have been that day, that moment, when she stopped herself. It wasn't needed anymore.

Words—throngs of them reached him in Julia's fine hand, in the children's slanted, fumbling pencil print—*I love . . . I miss . . . I pray for . . . health . . . years . . . time . . . God willing . . . home. . . . I kiss . . . eyes. You must . . . News . . . children . . . return . . . coming home . . . good faith . . .* He has read them all straight through, standing in place. Sometimes, two times over, he, lingering within the building that held their voices, delaying the moment he'd have to walk to the door, down the steps and back out into a city in which they did not exist.

The *lista de correos* window is the last of a long bank of postal windows, all outlined in a filigreed copper. The marble countertop stretches across all twelve windows. Only two clerks at work. No one at the *lista de correos* window, but someone will come. Two postal workers push large canvas carts filled with letters. A whole mass of them—thick, thin, gray, white, light pink, or pale blue. So many letters in the world and he only wants one, at most two, but he will settle for one he thinks, just one.

"*Nombre.*"

"Austin Voronkov," he says, his palms against the coolness of the marble counter. The postal clerk nods and steps to the side wall—a grid of cubbyholes, envelopes nestled in tight neat squares, awaiting pickup from others whose addresses are like his own: *lista de correos*, general delivery. He hopes for a letter, but better to trick the mind, he thinks, remembering days he'd been undoubtedly certain of a letter as days when he, almost without fail, received nothing. Defend against disappointment—one day's lack of a letter. Nothing from the Labor Department. Nothing from the patent agents and attorneys. He works instead to be disappointed, certain that no letter has arrived so the opposite effect will occur—delight, should he actually receive a letter. Disappointment. Delight. They are two sides of a coin. Like circuitry, the current of disappointment cutting a path through the midpoint, then changing—like the flip of a switch—to delight.

"Voronkov," says the clerk, "Austin Voronkov?"

"Yes. That's me."

"No letters."

IT IS A WOODEN BOX but he wishes he could remember what kind. Oak. Fir. He's ashamed in his realization that he cannot remember the wood. It may have been burl wood, much more likely that than oak. Or walnut. He should know it though. He should remember. It once belonged to his father. His father's snuff box. It is here he keeps some of his smaller drafting tools—lead pencils, sharpener, slide rule, and compass. Eraser. He removes the pencils from the box, the heady lingering scent of snuff now layered over the bitter sharpness of lead and metal. He sees the evenings when he was a boy, watching his father, a stout ashen-haired man, take this box off the sideboard and remove its hand-carved lid. His father had carved it too—the amber-handled knife, pressing with a steady intention and focus, creating notches, which became cross-hatchings for sun rays or water. The careful precision of a knife's cut. The wood's minuscule shavings he'd collect from the carving—a refuse he liked to feel tickle the palm of his hands. The box was transformed. The at one time solid,

plain lid soon became embellished with ornate cross-hatchings and ro-
settes, crescent moons. How superstitious the old man had been. It frus-
trated Austin so, now remembering the days before leaving when he'd
scowl in disgust at his father and mother's insistence that he take pause
and sit for a while before his journey. How callous he'd been when his
father had given him the box, thinking the man old, harmless, and just a
bit ignorant. Disdain for the snuff box and its symbols, significant to his
parents only, and their old beliefs and superstitions—the goddess Mo-
kosh and her hold on the grain harvest, and the lectures and reminders to
wear a belt, never place a hat on the table lest you lose money (or the bed
in which case you could become ill), to always leave a pinch of snuff for
the *domovoi*, the "he," "the other half," the "well-wisher," who might
pass in the night and thus bless the home and harvest—were the very
things he'd so wanted to throw off.

But there it is. The box beside him. A significance in that, Austin
knows. Gifts that, in the giving, were to him a kind of burden now a relic
he has come to love, the border of cross-hatchings pleasing, humming of
home, soil and snuff, incense and icons. And could he not still smell the
clove and camphor each time he opened the box?

Out the window of his shop, he can see that the evening has moved
on without his realizing it. Cars with their lights on now, streetlamps
glowing in fanned skirts, men and women walking at a more relaxed
pace, digesting dinners. He's set out the drafting papers, considering the
whys and reasonings for the lack of a letter. Perhaps the designs he'd sent
had been lost in the mail. It is something he knows is liable to have happened. The country's postal system is a precarious one at best. His work
may be stuck in a mail processing plant—in the state of Sonora or across
the border. Stranded. The designs could be sitting at the bottom of a

burlap mailbag in the Midwest or left on a sidewalk where pedestrians may now be trampling upon his envelopes unaware, leaving footprints of street dust or gutter rain, he thinks, all the while watching the passersby on the sidewalk. *Watch where you step,* he suddenly shouts out to them, as if they are representative of all pedestrians and so bear a responsibility, are culpable, for his besmirched drafts. Oh, but there is no way to be quite certain of any of this. As a reassurance he decides that he will simply send his designs again. He will mail them tomorrow because while he does not have any verifiable proof that these scenarios have in fact occurred, they do remain possible. He will vary the probability. Tip the balance in his favor and send them again. It will not hurt, he thinks, though he also understands that he could never really know, be certain of, anything. One could be certain of nothing.

He runs his hand along the drafting table's surface, scraped and worn from use. A piece of blue felt lies over one end. His tools arranged in a neat line. A few splinters of iron sit near the table's edge. He does not like to be gone from his work area for long. After dinners, he returns, looks everything over. Tonight is no different, though it's later than usual. The clocks are arranged on the bookshelf to the left. Alarm clocks, squat and round with bulbous bells, flat and large wall clocks, a cuckoo clock. All sit still and silent, their hands frozen as if in shock. On the shelf above are the transistor radios—knobs and tuners like eyes, watchful and reticent. Across the counter and along the back wall stands the honey-colored rolltop desk. The curtain of red and amber beads that separates the small back room from the workshop sways and clicks in the breeze.

His first strokes are always mere scribbles, half-rendered tracings. A few fragments of an equation. Several erasures before he can fully see how the propeller should be shaped. The propeller could tilt according to the ocean's currents, gain more power and speed and work with the current rather than against it. It is a rough sketch, repeated until he can begin the full depiction. Then, the different views. From above. To the sides. A cross section. A semi—cross section. He is working out the number of blades, the full diameter of the propeller, the blade angle and curve, the velocity of rotation, the pitch of it.

An hour has passed. He isn't sure. The street noise is ambient, not invading. He steps outside now into the colder late evening. He lights his cigarette and takes drag after drag, contemplating the sky and clouds of this particular evening—silver gray. He wonders what the children remember of Mexico.

This time of day is his own, free from disturbances so that he can enter a space in his mind, create a mental image of how steam might flow more efficiently through a pipe, or what torque might provide enough resistance for his tilting propeller. How to calibrate the copper wiring to send currents of electricity along coiled springs. When he is stumped, he returns to the fundamental questions: What is light? What is energy? What is force or ether?

There is an agitation across the street, and he can see a flurry of movement through the trees of the median. On the opposite sidewalk, a woman is running. It is not something he sees often and he turns his focus, reluctantly, abruptly from the sky and thoughts of his children to this woman. It is a light step, but apprehensive nearly, and her steps clomp evenly and then sputter, slowing to a hurried walk, then run again. He moves from the doorway and sits hidden in the alcove window, watching as she dashes down the sidewalk. She slows and the flounce of her burgundy dress settles and then, as she begins to run again, swings in one great swath from side to side. She crosses the street, and moves into the median, cutting through all its green. Soon, she is running down his sidewalk, running toward him, and in a moment she will pass right in front of him. He watches as she continues to alternate between running and walking. *Whoever it is, he'll wait, he'll wait,* Austin thinks, when suddenly she draws to a halt before his storefront, her shoulders rise and fall, she throws her hands down to her sides so that they ricochet off her hips; it is the gesture of a spoiled child. And now, who exactly is this here? he wonders. He does not reveal himself. Maybe she'll go away. She turns on her heel, walks to the curbside, pivots once again, ducking her head fast beneath the lowered gate of the shop's front door.

"*Buenas tardes,*" she calls.

Austin sits forward in the alcove of the front window. He presses his hands against the adobe walls, which offer a coolness despite the all-day sun that floods this side of the building.

"Out here," he says, walking to the door, eyes on his shoes. He is annoyed by her impudence. To come at such an hour. He sees her flinch, spring back, and, in her surprise at a voice behind instead of in front, outside rather than inside, she swings around to exit, but not before banging her forehead on the lowered grill as she steps out to the sidewalk.

"*¡Ai!*" she says, wincing, her hand raised to her forehead, walking back and forth, as if in the walking the pain might go away.

"Keep pressure on it," he says. He looks the other way.

"Why do you have that down so low? You could hurt someone."

"I'm closed."

"I dropped off a radio here—"

"A good one too." He remembers. He remembers writing down her name: Anarose, 1 P.M. "You're late."

"Is it fixed?"

"I believe I told you in a couple of hours," he says.

"It works? *Funciona?*" she says, abrupt, almost curt.

He walks to the door, passes in front of her close enough to have brushed the starched cotton of her dress, inhale the citrus, astringent scent of her hands. He raises the grill and it clatters upward, clicking into place. He watches as she furrows her brow from the sound.

"I would be here earlier, but the day—" She is tripping over her English. "We're having guests this evening. It was my fault. By accident. I lost my balance and it broke." Her words are disjointed. They don't seem to fit together. He is looking for the radio, which sits on his workbench. She is still talking. She has followed him inside.

"I forgot. It was so quiet. Very quiet. And then I remembered. And they wouldn't let me go with so much to do. Imagine? So, I climbed out the back. Through the window." He is gathering his drafting papers, placing the pile on the shelf behind him. He turns back to her.

"You climbed out the window?"

She shows him proof—a small scrape like skid marks along her upper shin, just beneath her knee.

"And now you've bruised your forehead," he says, his hand rising, outstretched fingers drawing an arc in the air, as if tracing her brow with a touch, a questioning stroke.

"Have I?" She raises her hand to the red spot above her eyebrow.

"*Un poco,*" Austin says. It is the longest he has ever spoken to a customer, he realizes.

He sets the radio on the table. He reaches down for the cord and plugs it in. He is moving too slowly for her he knows. Static blares through the shop and they both jump, his forearm grazing the back of her hand, a delicate but calloused hand adorned with a tarnished silver ring.

"Perdón," he says, lowering the volume, moving the dial through first a man's voice, then more static, guitar, drums and horns. His cigarette is still burning and the ash now drops on the smooth top of the radio. He wipes it off and then looks at her.

"It works."

"Yes."

Silence.

"¿Se puede?" She picks up his pack of Faros, leaning against the counter, using her arms for balance. She sighs and reaches down to rub her shin. He can smell a waft of orange blossom. A bright, slightly sweet scent.

"I am closed. So, if you don't mind," he looks outside to indicate that she should leave. He does not like when someone lingers. It's not a rudeness, though some have mistaken him for that; his evasion is his protection. He keeps an arm's length lest they ask questions, figure him out, bring the Soviets or the FBI to his door. He cannot have come this far only to be sent back. That would not happen to him—kidnapped, questioned, killed. The dirty Soviets with their questions, these men and their power, the Americans too really: *What is your name? Where were you born? What is your country of citizenship?*

"No, no," she says, frowning, arms at her sides, a little dumbfounded, looking to the right, then left. "I will take the radio and go." She gives him the ten pesos for his work.

"A light though?" he says. He feels bad suddenly as if he could himself feel the sting of his unspoken rebuke.

"Sí. That would be nice," she says, the radio under one arm. She brings her cigarette to her lips and he strikes the match, lifting his hand to hers, hovering for a moment as the light flares and then settles.

"Gracias," she says, turning to go. She carries the radio under one arm, balanced on her hip. He watches her leave, his gaze drawn to her waist, the curve of her upper back.

He lights another cigarette, gathers up his satchel, and closes the door, pulling the grill down and locking the padlock. He can feel the city at his back, hear the far distant sirens, the subtle whir of evening traffic. He double-checks the lock and then turns to find her still, smoking in front of the next storefront, the radio set at her feet. She takes one drag of her cigarette, her other arm wrapped around her waist. Like him, in those moments just before her arrival, she is staring up at the sky, the shifting clouds, immense and laden in all their now cobalt and gray hues. He walks up behind her and he can nearly hear her exhale, the anxiousness that she'd come with has disappeared.

"I thought you were late," he says, stopping next to her on the sidewalk.

"Ready to go back," she says, throwing her cigarette to the ground. They both watch the last of its embers fade.

"You sound like it's a performance."

"Isn't it?" She faces him.

"Life?"

"No. A party." She sighs, then reaches for the radio at her feet and sets it on her hip once more. Her eyes meet his, somewhat startled, he thinks, pulsing and pleading in a way Austin finds, in spite of himself, alluring.

"Here. I will carry this for you," he says, taking the radio from her.

"Gracias," says Anarose. "I am just down here. Thank you," she says again, nodding. He follows a half step behind her.

"Don't thank me. Just practical," he says.

"Thank you," she repeats. This time it is a retort, her hint at defiance. "Thank you. Au-stin," she says.

"Yes. Anarose."

"You remember it?"

"I try to learn names. When they are offered." He keeps his gaze straightforward.

The streets are filling up again. People are on the sidewalks ambling through the night. Cars pass. Some with headlights on. Others waiting for real darkness. They walk by homes with doors the color of violets— deep purple and blue.

"I am just here. See. Look. *Mira*," she says. They have stopped now beneath a stucco wall behind which sits a kind of hacienda—a fine large home of wrought iron and glass, limestone. "They're all arriving," she says, peering around the edge of the building. He steps out to the corner to look, but she stays behind, hidden.

He knows the house. He has passed this corner several times. He knows all the houses, all the buildings in this *colonia*, but none of the occupants. Until now. He watches as the cars pull up. Fords mostly. A few Cadillacs in their colors of evergreen, cornflower blue, opaque canary yellow. Some park, others drop off men and women, each carrying a gift. The older women are in black skirts, pumps. The younger women wear flowered dresses, large skirts of crinoline and taffeta, scarves over their heads, bags like small pill boxes. He can hear their distant laughter.

"Nice. What is the party for?"

"Petición de mano."

"Who's getting married?"

"Me," she says, and then begins to laugh. "No. I am only teasing. It is the daughter of the family." She peers around the edge of the wrought iron railing and then pulls back again to stay out of sight. Austin remains at the corner, watching the guests arrive.

"Come. We will need to go around." She waves for him to follow as she approaches a narrow passageway between this home and the row of homes that sit behind it.

The alleyway is dark. Water and grease combine to stretch lengthwise like a black vein. It smells of soap, onions, and gasoline, lemon and orange peel. Water is running somewhere. He follows her, stepping around box crates, a withering bed of pachysandra, stacks of terra-cotta tiles. The 7 P.M. sky is a rivulet of sapphire between the buildings. They stop in front of a dark window under which sit two wooden crates.

"I will go in. You pass me the radio," she instructs, placing her hand on his upper arm for balance.

"Here?"

"Yes." She has stepped onto the crates, still holding his arm as she lifts her skirt slightly to raise her leg up and over the windowsill before she disappears into darkness. Then, a whisper:

"*¡Un momento!* "

"Not going anywhere," he says. From over the high wall that runs along the back of the house comes the sound of laughter, a few discordant notes from a guitar. Austin stands very still, listening. The bright brassy trumpet announces the song before shifting to a muted, mournful cry, the laughter quiets, and the jangle and strum of the guitars keep a latent 4/4 rhythm beneath the gentle, crooning voice of the singer. Of course, Austin thinks, live music. She did not need the radio at all.

He hears her footsteps clatter across the room, a door softly shutting, and then her return.

"Now. I'll take it." She holds her arms out the window, waving her hands. The anxiousness, the haste is back. He hands her the radio. Her hair is mussed, the tendrils fall down her neck, her tortoiseshell combs are crooked.

"There is mariachi," Austin points out. "Why do you need the radio?"

"For the grandfather," she says as if it is a fact known by all of Mexico City. "He listens day and night. He will not behave without it. They need him to remain *tranquilo* or else the party will be ruined. We place him in the corner and he listens to his bolero, *corrido* all night. Here, quick, I will need it now," she says, waving her hands again.

She takes the radio from him and whispers thank you. Then, she is gone.

Austin walks back and forth in front of the window as if she might return. Of course she won't, he realizes. There's no need now. He can hear the murmur of other voices, faint and fading along the alleyway. From the street, cars creep past, someone is calling out a window, a dog barks. Night arrives first here, in these hidden alleyways, dim and shadowed save for the squares of yellow light that pour out from back windows.

ANAROSE. A maid of Mexico City. Ubiquitous, unknown, dropping into his life with her radio. The complicit way she had looked at him— they'd both been revealed in this talk of life like a performance. Did he like the look of her face? The inquisitive eyes, the wonder in them when locking with his own? They seemed importunate, asking: Who are you? Where are you from?

LATER, NEARING MIDNIGHT, Austin returns to his rooms. He tries the front door lock with its stubborn maneuverings. He slips on the floor, just waxed. He begins his ascent up the stairs, counting out his footsteps in his usual way. The overhead lights on each landing cast a sad orange hue in the stairwell. The windows are open on each floor and from outside he can hear cars swoosh past, the nervous pedaling of a night bicyclist.

On the twenty-sixth and final step, he opens the door to his floor. The long hallway stretches empty and remote from one window to the next. Suddenly, he hears a faint brush of fabric, a sleeve against pant leg. He spins around. A man stands on the landing below. He is beneath the stairwell window, slightly askance from it—just enough so that one half of him is in the light. Austin can only make out the full lip and quite a large indent in his chin, like a thumbprint. He wears a fine, tailored suit. Deep charcoal with white stripes—faint, as if drawn by chalk. In his front pocket is a silver pen and a slim red leather notebook.

"You are here for me?" Austin asks.

"Are you Austin Voronkov?"

"Yes." Austin steps slowly back down the stairs and he too now stands beneath the window. They are face to face. "Can I help you? Who are you?"

"You must know who I am."

"I have an idea."

"You know why I'm here."

"Perhaps."

"I have some questions for you. Certainly, you know why I'm here," he says, cocking his head to the side and taking a step closer to Austin.

"I'm not going to cross, if that's what you're insinuating." Austin feels his chest expand, holding his breath. The drum of his heart in his ears.

"We can never be sure. But you've been thinking of it, haven't you?"

"How do you know?"

"We're aware of these things so there is no use not admitting that you've at least been contemplating the act."

"Fine, then. Yes. I've contemplated it, but it does not mean that I will do so."

"All well and good, but you understand, the bureau will still need to monitor you since your word is not enough to assure us that you won't do it," he says, all this while taking out the red notebook, the silver pen the length and circumference of a cigarette.

"So tell me," he begins again, "in your contemplations, are you maybe thinking of trying to go through the desert in Sonora? You know those towns quite well up there."

"How do you know that?"

"We know you worked with Anaconda, in the copper mines. Several years, in fact. You would know the layout of Cananea, Nogales, the entire state of Sonora, no doubt."

"I have other plans—"

"Which are?"

"If you must know—"

"I must."

"I have my inventions."

"Your inventions. These are all well and good, but if these inventions of yours don't allow you in, if the government decides you are still unfit for entrance, if there were some kind of deterrent—"

"There will be no deterrent."

"No?"

"You wouldn't do it! Haven't you and all your superiors, you men in power, haven't you all done enough?"

"We do our jobs. Our job is to be aware of any activities that may be deemed a threat."

"My inventions are not a threat. They are for my family," he says. He is silent for a few moments, watching as the man scribbles down notes in his slim, red book. "Aren't you people supposed to keep a low profile, not make yourselves known? What good does your watching me do if I can see you, know that you are here?"

"It's a precaution. Preventative measures, you might say." He is still writing in his book and Austin can hear the click of the pen in the otherwise silent stairwell. "You do know you've been accused of anarchy and as such your activities and any relations you may have with the U.S. are always subject to the strictest of scrutiny? In our view, anything you do is a threat."

"And so what is it you want from me? What do you want me to do?"

"It's not so much that I want anything, per se, it's more that I was sent to verify, that is, to confirm leads on any suspicious behavior, any un-American activities, below the border."

"Meaning?"

"Well, for one, your desire to cross the border into the U.S., thus breaking the law and becoming an undesirable alien element who may be a threat to the American way of life."

"Look here, don't you see, don't you people see, if I were truly a threat, an anarchist, as you so insist, I would defy your laws and have crossed the border years ago. I would cross now if I were truly an anarchist."

"Is that a threat?"

"No. I'm just trying to reason with you, to make you hear my side of the story. Is there anything else you want?"

"No. Not right now. I was just sent to make you aware, as a kind of notice so that you'll know we are watching you."

"I see, and now you are a threat to me."

"No. I wouldn't call it a threat, merely a warning to make you aware of our presence."

"I am aware. How could I not be?"

"If you do attempt to cross the border, there are consequences."

"I know the consequences quite well, thank you." Austin's heart is racing faster now. "And why not write to me on official communication? Why come here and bother me so?"

"Am I bothering you?"

"It feels like a taunting."

"No. I'm just here to assist, to help you realize your predicament."

"What about my family? Have you thought of that? What are they supposed to do? What is Julia to do?"

"We know all about her."

"You do?"

"We watch her too, you know. Can't be too sure what her activities are. After all, she has a last name connected to you, and we cannot forget that she did go off to Russia with you. She may have been influenced."

"Influenced?"

"Yes. Propaganda. She was exposed to it, you see, the Red Menace."

"She's done nothing wrong!"

"Still, we must watch her, you understand. America is no longer a safe country."

"You don't touch her!"

"We know she writes you letters. Several letters in the first years apart, though it seems that they tapered off a bit and now, maybe once a year, twice a year. Isn't that right? That's all she can do because, well, linked to an anarchist Russian—if she were to travel back here, it would be risky for her. Who knows about the children, right? Of course, they are older, but back when they were little, I wouldn't have attempted it. She wouldn't be able to afford it too, isn't that right? A young mother working to raise three children alone. How would she ever have the means to travel back to you in Mexico? So, it's just the letters. We need to monitor them."

"We can do that. It isn't against the law, to send letters."

"No. But, again, all your activities are a threat, you must understand this, Mr. Voronkov."

"And you? Can you tell me something?"

"If the information is cleared."

"Cleared."

"Yes."

"What is your name?"

"Jack."

"Your surname?"

"I do not have clearance to give you that information. Good night, Austin, or should I call you Ustin?"

Austin takes the stairs back up to his hallway door. He pauses and turns to look behind him. No one is there, the stairwell now empty and still.

FIRST, HE CHECKS HIS DRAFTS. Then, the notebooks along his book-shelf. The papers in his drawer. All untouched. He will find a place to hide them, he thinks, folding the drafts in fours now, lunging toward his dresser, turning it on an angle in one full jerk. He stuffs the papers behind its latticed backing. Next, he remembers the loose floorboard beneath the window, and he runs his palm across the floor, his fingers grabbing hold of the wood's edge, bent back now like a broken limb. Sweat breaks out along his neck, brow. The air in his room is too stuffy and dry. But he will not open the windows. They should remain closed, locked.

His pulse is racing. A strain at the back of his throat. He must settle down, try to sleep. He begins to undress, washes, pulls back the covers to his bed, all the while attuned to every noise. Unsure if a floor creaking is outside his front door or from the room above, if the rattle of the glass is from the wind or someone trying to get into his rooms. The pipes creak and moan. He lies still. Thoughts. Images. They cloud in and then fade. A constant stream of words . . . *deterrent, preventative measures, precaution, threat, anarchist.*

How dare they send this Jack to interrogate him! So smug and certain. His knotted-up neck, the red notebook like an insult. He was a man who had a talent for—to Austin he even seemed born into—a life of easy transition, as if his joints were overoiled so that he could slip quite easily and without effort, entering locked doors, falling into and out of cars, traveling through towns and villages, across borders.

Anarchist. The word. It lingers. He knows it intimately, almost like a lover. He knows its connotations and contexts. It is a Greek word. *Anarchos*—without rulers. It is true he'd subscribed to what he now knows to be the more philosophical basis of anarchism, a kind of wish for utopia. Any man of true reason, a man like himself, would understand the beauty and sense behind the ideas, the simplicity and elegance of it—individuals could create a pact among themselves, make simple agreements to behave humanely and fairly toward one another, create a civil society based on mutuality and exchange. It is sound. It makes sense. Or maybe not—too simplistic? Too ideal?

He turns on his side and back again. He rubs his palm across his tired eyes. But no, he was never someone who would create bombs in the basement, deliver dynamite to the front door of a senator or congressman. If he looks at the truth though, if he sorts out his beliefs in science, well, when it comes to that, then he is certainly against rulers or any governing body. He has always felt science to be the true ruler and longs to be in a country in which he can explore and experiment with his ideas and inventions at will. He'd accepted laws, but deep down his firmest, strongest belief is that even science trumps government. It was not something to state outright. They'd seized upon it, he remembers. *You have no respect for the laws of man? I am a man, I have respect for them. . . . Are you an anarchist? No. . . . Are you opposed to the U.S. government? No. . . . Are you a member of the Union of Russian Workers? Yes. . . . You don't believe in laws, do you? I don't know how you can call them laws. They are simply agreements. . . .*

HE IS CROSSING the border. He is embarking on the passage, but the dream consists only of the approach and the aftermath, never the actual physical breach. Instead, he is up north in the Sonoran desert, in Cananea, waiting. The border quite near. He is conscious of the emptiness around him, and then the far-off sound of voices, men's voices, overlapping—*country, citizen, government, anarchist.* The voices gather, growing louder, and then it becomes not just voices but a sense of being watched, not by any one person, but a network aware of his movements, able to see his inventions. He is holding his satchel close to his chest, all his drafting papers safely inside. He is alert, wondering just when they will step out of the invisible.

He staggers around, trying to find his footing, though his step is light. He feels unmoored, as if he were floating, as if whatever had tethered him to the universe had snapped and he felt a falling within, still gripping his satchel. His papers are now scattered along the ground, left to a wilderness and to anyone who may take his ideas and pass them off as their own.

Then, silence.

His next footfall, heavier now, and he is in Varvarovka, walking down the main road that runs through the village. The earth is frozen. The road uneven. Underfoot, the grooves made by wheels of carts and coaches are as hard as steel train tracks. The sun is gone. A bleak light fills the wide sky. The houses sit still and in their familiar rows, thatch-roofed. One or two let out a trail of smoke from chimneys. There are no sounds save for the wind. No animals mewing. No cows lolling. No shouts or voices or singing from an open window. No clank of scythes from the fields.

He approaches the church, searching for people, but finds only a broken, cracked bell. It sits like an old anchor, rusted and cumbersome. He walks into the fields that lie barren, leading to the horizon. He can feel his legs growing heavy, dragging and ponderous. He sees a woman in the near distance, walking, more pacing like a feral animal, wringing her hands. He knows it's Julia, though he cannot see her face. It's more in her behavior. Her gestures, manner. He keeps walking even though his legs are weighted. He calls to her but no sound comes. She does not hear him. When the woman turns, the face is darkness, effaced.

He wakes with a feeling of damp on his brow and chest. He sits up into pitch black. Rising, blinking and unsteady, he uses the bed as a guide. He walks to the sink and turns the tap, which, no matter how many times he's fixed it, screeches and hisses like a cat. The cool water on his wrists feels good. Then the splash to his face—brow first, cheeks. He sputters his lips and stands upright. He can see his face in the glass, eyes glistening in the darkness.

How strange that in his dream Julia should be in the Varvarovka that no longer exists. The images linger. A disquiet in his mind. How icy and barren his home looked. Could the dream be a segment of his life as it might have been, taking place elsewhere?

Julia, Julia my jewel, what has become of us? Do you think of me as I think of you? I am ashamed I do this still, after so many years, fourteen years, time that is nearly enough to forget a face, but I remember yours, do you remember mine?

· · ·

ST. PETERSBURG, VARVAROVKA
KHERSON, ODESSA,
CONSTANTINOPLE, PARIS,
MAZATLÁN, CANANEA

1920–34

HE SAT BEFORE A MAN who smelled of morning. They twisted his words around. He didn't understand then. But time brings clarity even in the confusion and murkiness of the present. If only he'd understood. They wanted him to be something so they made him into it.

They called him a Red, an alien, an anarchist, Communist, Polack, Bolshevik, pig, commie, un-American. It's what they leave out that matters. Husband, father. Of course, he was not yet a father, but how did they know. Others were. He soon would be.

KHERSON. IT SITS ON the Dnieper. Like in Gogol. It's close to Odessa, but Odessa is on the Black Sea. Kherson is close to the Black Sea, but

farther inland. When Austin and Julia traveled back to that continent—
Asia—the boat took them first to Riga. They had to get to St. Petersburg. Then, from St. Petersburg to Kherson. There were no trains. They
waited three months for one train, and, even then, they could not be sure
of its destination.

HOW DID AUSTIN REMEMBER St. Petersburg 1920? He cannot see a
whole city. Instead, there are just moments, rooms, views out a window.
Like flashcards. There is the divided room they shared with other deportees now returned to Russia, the one stove between them. A midnight's commotion on the floor below as the tenants fled to Finland. In
the morning, the others fell upon their abandoned belongings—the
pianos and desks, bureaus and tables divided for firewood.

And then there are the memories of taste. The way he'd gotten accustomed to, some days longed for, the moldy taste of oat coffee. The
meager coating of plum jam on black bread.

Three months for one train. It would be going south, to Kiev, he'd
heard.

"Where is this train going?" he'd asked in the railway station, Julia
by his side, he holding her wrist tight.

"Nowhere. A train to nowhere," someone bellowed.

"To Ukraine? South?"

"Yes."

"No," someone else shouted.

He told her not to speak. He too was frightened to utter a word lest
his bourgeois accent be recognized. His own voice was his enemy. Hers
too. It happened once and silence fell like an anchor amid the jumbled

mess of suitcases, rucksacks, tied bed linens, icons, kettles, leather and felt boots.

THE TRAIN TRIP TOOK a whole week.

"How can a country be run by barbarians?" He heard that often enough on that train ride. No one believed the Reds would win, that their revolution would last. And he began to believe it. He cared nothing for it all—politics, civil war, red, white. To hear politics to Austin was like hearing a dirty word. He simply didn't want to live in a city where he could be shot on sight, where he was scared to utter a sentence, always whispering in broad daylight. As far as he knew, others were going to their summer homes, country estates, waiting it out. They could not stay there in St. Petersburg. They would go to his family. Then, as he overheard, the Reds had not gotten that far. Not yet.

WAS IT RIGHT TO be back there—in Russia? Where else would they have gone? And he'd no idea what they'd encounter, and he'd thought of turning them straight on to Paris from Riga instead of heading south. But at least she was getting to see his country, which he was proud to show her, the space, the sheer vastness of all that land. The civil war was tearing it up, but he and Julia looked out train windows into the birch forests, the trees iced, the ground sloping, meandering, curving hills and flat plains of white as far as one could see, and the country was indifferent. That nature could be so peaceful when the people of its land were killing each other, he thought.

"What a sad country this is," Julia said again and again.

. . .

THEY TRAVELED WITH no documents. By marrying him, Julia was no longer an American citizen. Austin was stateless, but, as far as he was concerned, they were Russian. Only Russia no longer existed. It had been stamped out. The most he could hope for was that no one searched them. They had no papers. Later came the Nansen passport—in 1922— but then, on that week's train trip, they had nothing.

Paper is stronger than one realizes.

IN RIGA, he'd sent a postcard to his mother and father. How to write such a postcard:

"I've returned from America," he managed to spell out. They never did get it. Instead, Julia and Austin arrived unannounced. His mother slammed the door in his face. She didn't recognize him and when she did she burst into tears and still slammed the door in his face.

"Shock," people whispered, as a kind of searching explanation.

THE FARM WAS in Varvarovka, province of Kherson. A day's walk from the station to the village. Their feet were swollen from the walking, making the leather tight, confining. The swelling did not go down for two days.

The house was smaller than the house of his memory. It seemed dwarfed. He had been unsure whether he had grown or if it was time that had been the distorter—time and distance. The world of his childhood had taken place in larger rooms, surrounded by larger furniture and windows. The wardrobe that stood behind the table, the sideboard under the front windows covered with lace—both once loomed over him. Stalwarts of memory.

He had not expected to return so the reunion was all the sweeter. He looked to Julia. She smiled at him as if imagining him as a boy. It was a tender smile. Her home was with him, it seemed to say. This American woman.

The first evening. A meal. Ham, cabbage soup, eggs, bread and butter. It was the only food they'd eaten for three days. They ate in silence. He did not want to ask about the others, his brothers or his sisters. He could tell in the silence, in the furtive glances between mother and father, that there had been loss. It seemed best to wait. To eat, sleep, rest.

The next morning, they learned that his sister Katya had died of spotted typhus. His brother Cornelius, an officer in the White Army, had shot himself rather than forfeit strategic information to the Reds.

AFTER THE WINTER THERE is the thaw. Wetness, water. The streets and lanes are mud, fields too. The snow dissolving, soaking into the ground. Here and there bits of green emerge. Buds. There is the gentlest hint of pink as if the bare brown branches of the cherry trees had blushed.

They heard the sloshing, suckling footsteps first. Then, the voices. Brusque shouting. He'd heard about the other homes, searched, looted. How sometimes they took the man of the house into the woods. Up until that moment, they lived in a relative state of peace, could even pretend at times that they were safe, free from any harm. Soon, the rumors of other lootings, Bolsheviks, the Reds dragging people to the commissar increased. Once, he heard the faraway ricochet of shots. It was a new sound. He kept walking then, faster. He never mentioned it to Julia. She was pregnant with Austin Jr., and he did not want to upset her in such a state. He didn't speak to the rest of his family about it either.

They came then. In the early spring. 1922. The mud of that season, in the midst of the thaw, was thick and slick. He heard the sloshing first. He drew the curtains back from the window and he could see their faces, coated with dirt, the earth staining their uniforms, their brows and hands. One of the men was eating an apple. Julia stood at the basin, scrubbing clothes on a washboard. She'd heard the sloshing too and a look passed between them he would never forget. It was as if they both knew, had been waiting for this moment and he'd thought then of all the ways they could've left, all the ways they could've been already gone from there.

They were at the door. A loud knocking. Then they crowded in, four in total, their bayonets pointing. A strong scent of onion on the men, that and a chill blast of air—the Russian spring. They looted the whole house, what was left. Bayonets were thrust into icons, destroying the "beautiful corner." They tore curtains, the lace shredded, hours he'd stared at that lace as a boy. Tables were upturned. The wardrobe fell to the floor, books were spilled, splayed open. Austin's notebooks, engineering books, automobile textbooks. Nothing went untouched. The men with their bayonets.

"They'd cut the air if they could," a common phrase, he was now a witness to it.

He was ordered outside. He expected them to make him kneel or bring him to the forest. Instead, he was forced to stand, watching them ruin the house.

.   .   .

HE REMEMBERS THE FEEL of water seeping through his felt boots. The chill of the April morning as they stood beneath an opaque sky hanging low over the hill that led to the church, the hill which held the last remaining patches of snow and ice. Above, a flock of birds—geese, sparrows—flying in interlocking V's with a grace and ease in strict contrast to the clatter of furniture, all the splitting, splintering wood. Plates, cups shattering.

One of the men emerged from the ruined house, his bayonet slung over his shoulder. In one hand he carried a book. He walked up to Austin and Julia, stood before them turning the pages of what Austin could now identify as an engineering manual. His dirty hands, earth beneath fingernails, his thumb purpled and black the color of plum was tough with calluses, his hardened fingertips pulled at the pages, opening the book at random, tearing the thin paper like onion skin.

The fields were fallow. The horizon like the horizon of the ocean, endless. The man was turning the pages of the book. He sometimes licked his fingertip—a too-dainty gesture for a man so gruff. The thin paper crinkled in a breeze. He looked to Austin. Then to Julia. Back to the book. It was in English. An engineering manual from his courses in America. The thin pages caught in the breeze, rustling like one hundred accusations.

"Spy," the man said in Russian.

AUSTIN CAN SEE IN his mind's eye, the leaving, the long walk to the commissar. Julia on the cart, his footsteps alongside the wooden wheels creaking every third step and his boots making a sucking sound as his soles sank into the mud. As he walked, he could see quite quickly what was before them along that road—more homes raided and looted, some already burning.

"Julia. Do not look. Look to me, to me. Do not look."

Bodies lay on the ground, blood trickling out of a mouth, mixing with the white snow and mud. All the while the geese traced their V's in the calm sky, and in the far distance he could see smoke rising from a stove in some home that still sat within its place of peace.

He heard his mother sobbing, but he could not look behind as they'd left them. Gun shots in front and behind, but he could not look. If he did, he would have to run to them, would have been shot, and what of Julia, he'd thought, his footsteps alongside the wheels, she seven months pregnant. He focused forward. He set his mind to it. His eyes on his boots, one foot in front of the other.

NOW, HE DOESN'T CARE what people say. His life, he knows, is proof that men's lives are ruled by chance. It was chance that saved him, saved them.

HIS BACK WAS TO the wall, a wall pocked with bullet holes, his body standing where other bodies had fallen. They were not allowed to lean against the wall. Instead, they held each other upright, shoulder to shoulder. Julia's hand in his grasp, squeezing. He could feel her shaking. Five men gathered in a small half circle at the end of the line began addressing each person, asking questions. A bayonet tip scraped the ground, a scratching noise that grew louder as the men proceeded to first one person, then another. The commissar drew closer now, and one man collapsed out of fear or shock or a deep panic. Julia leaned up against Austin as the men passed their gazes over her. To Austin now. One, two steps and beyond him to the next man and the one after that. Then, a look back. A flicker of recognition. The commissar retraced his steps. He was in front of Austin now, Austin who kept his gaze on the ground, knowing that an eye lock was an easy provocation for a bayonet or bullet.

"Look at me," the commissar demanded. Austin lifted his gaze, met the commissar's stare.

"Bring them inside," he ordered.

AUSTIN STOOD BEFORE the commissar's desk. He could see the outline of absent icons that had once cluttered the walls with their gold, black, and bronze, now rectangles and squares of white. The one room smelled of pine and smoke and ink. Men in a corner were laughing. Julia leaned on him. She could hardly stand.

"Please, let her sit. She is pregnant," Austin said in a whisper.

The commissar came in, looking first to Julia, then to Austin. The gaze lasted a minute.

"Ustin!" he said. His hands fell hard on the desk, the paraffin lamp trembled and its light flickered a moment before settling. "Ustin, Ustin," he kept saying, smiling. And then, to the men standing idle in the corner, "Bring her a chair, then go. Leave!" Austin could not get his mind, his thoughts to catch up with this new, drastic shift in tone.

"You don't remember me. It's okay, it's okay," the commissar said, "I know you. That is all that matters. Ustin Alexandrovich Voronkov.

Village of Varvarovka. You went to America." He slapped Austin on the back. He moved fast, with energy that frightened Austin. And then a face emerged out of the fan of wrinkles now settled around the eyes, the coarser skin of the high cheekbones, the broad brow. Distant shots broke the joy of recognition. Austin could think of the wall only, the bullet holes as he stared deep into the shifty black pupils of his childhood friend.

CABBAGE SOUP, PORK, POTATOES, raspberry jam. And tea. Vodka. A feast—a meal worthy of reunion. He'd believed they were being led to death and then they threw them a party. It didn't matter to the commissar that Austin's brother was a White officer, that Austin was in fact a kind of enemy. He was a private landowner after all. No. He'd just been pleased by some memories of childhood.

They slept on good clean sheets. All the while, Austin cautious, believing his friend would change his mind, luring him into some trap and that, at any moment, he'd be led to execution. He was shifty and besides, Austin didn't remember any of his memories, though he pretended to and thought, many times, of what he recalled when he recognized Austin, what images came up for him—some kindness bestowed, an afternoon of unbridled joy, an adventure in the forests or fields. It was distinct enough though, a memory that makes a life turn on a dime, a memory that meant—when one skins it all down to the bare bone—well, the difference between life and death.

They covered them in rugs. Austin and Julia took a train to Odessa under rugs. That way, they would avoid the gendarmes searching out anyone attempting to flee across the now closed borders. A ridiculous idea, Austin thought, surely they'd be found. They held each other tight, one rug after another piled on top. Under woven rugs—they loaded them onto the train. The discomfort for poor Julia, terrified she'd lose the baby through that train ride. Hours of must and cold. And then the man who knew, the one who had been bribed to smuggle them out, collected his rugs and they were loaded onto the dock in Odessa, where they would be safe in the port city for the time being. Enough time for Julia to have her baby. A week later, they boarded a boat to Constantinople. With their newborn, they sailed down the Bosporus, gorging themselves on pistachios and apricots in the bazaar. There was little else to eat.

They were greeted by other Russians. Exiles, refugees, émigrés. These words had not yet stuck. They were not yet uttered. It was only 1923. For the time being, they were still Russians. They would return. "A country run by barbarians cannot last," they said. They said it in the streets. In the markets. In the rooming houses where countesses didn't clean—"Why should I clean? I'll be going back to Russia soon."

Everyone had something to sell. Emeralds stitched into corsets. Pearls among a child's toys. Rubies sewn into coat linings. Rubles stitched into an astrakhan hat. Silver spoons were ubiquitous—the easiest to smuggle out. It was impossible to go back. After a year, two, there was despair. The White Army disbanded, any hint of counterrevolutionary talk and one could disappear in the middle of the night. The language began to shift and soon it was no longer a crime to refer to themselves as émigrés or refugees. He now belonged to no country. It was not what he had planned for his young family, his firstborn son. To be stateless, unwanted just like his father. It was his fault at the unknowing boy's expense. How many other children were caught between countries? An entire generation without a known fatherland. It pained him to think of it. They would return to America. He made a promise to himself and to Julia and to their young son.

PAPER IS STRONGER THAN one thinks. Papers, documents don't define a man, but they lived in a mire of them. Nansen passport. Work identity, birth certificate, country of origin, ration stamps, postcards, telegrams, newspapers, degrees. The list like a litany, a memorized chant. His days revolved around papers. But no amount of paper means a country. And Russia, their Russia, his Russia, that had vanished. He had left it the first time with a secure sense that home would always be there even if he never expected to return. It was different when he realized that his home as he'd known it had vanished, that it existed now only in memory. A whole world. A country. Poof. Gone.

He wrote to his mother and father. One year, then two, and he was near certain that they were long dead. Starvation most likely. Or they were shot. One or the other. Word spread fast in the villages. People did not forget. They had a son who was a White Army officer. And then Austin returning from America with an American wife. It was easy to point the finger at them, to say take them, take their land, they are the real traitors to the fatherland.

THEY FOLLOWED WORK like water. Paris did not embrace them. The skies were often bruised yellow, mauve, and, should it be about to rain, charcoal gray. It was impenetrable, this pearl of Paris. He stood outside the language, living on Rue Daru, in the garrets of an apartment building, six flights up, the plaster façades the color of bone.

But he'd found Russia in the bistros of Paris—a hub of memory and argument held within the gleam of brass, hovering over the glow of orbed lights, lingering amid the small marble-topped tables of La Rotonde, La Closerie des Lilas. He would often gather around the old White generals who pushed salt and pepper shakers to map out their military machinations, maneuvers, wracking minds and memories of what would've happened if they had approached from the hills, across the river, in the morning, no, at midnight, in the late afternoon, through the fields or woods.

THEY DIDN'T MAKE THE U.S. quota system. 1924. 1925. 1926. They were not among the 2 percent allowed to enter the United States. Whether he'd ever be let in was a different matter.

HE SEES HIMSELF THEN. The demitasse placed before him, the cubes of sugar, the stray espresso foam staining the rim of the cup. The red door of the apartment on Rue Daru, entering and leaving each morning, that comes back too. He can almost hear the resounding click of the iron lock, which allowed one to enter first along a narrow corridor and then to a small courtyard before walking the steep six flights to their attic apartment—two diminutive rooms of yellow and white. Julia with Aussie and their new baby girl, Vera, waiting for him.

Walking up the stairs, down, his hand rises, like an instinct, to the front inside pocket of his overcoat, feeling for the crude booklet, the corners thick and splayed, the three staples rusted. Gray. He worked then for the Renault factory. His booklet and working papers were gray. It was a hefty fine if one was stopped and found with no papers. A whole week's worth of pay. By then, he'd had his young family to take care of. That gray booklet, all those papers—he was obsessed. Inspectors stood in doorways of Russian émigré hotels turned to rooming houses, destined to become final dwellings for some, and in the apartment houses filled with one- and two-room shared apartments. It was easy to stop the workers, most on their way to the Renault factory, or to seek out the cab drivers who lingered at the corner tobacconist and who scattered upon the approach of an inspector.

SOME NIGHTS, NEIGHBORS DISAPPEARED. Loud knocks at early hours and then a struggle. The next morning, no one spoke. It was as if it didn't happen. One could hear the whispers though, "They've kidnapped him. He was working with the ROVS. He was a member of the OGPU." At night, the cabaret across the street sold vodka and wine and conversations revolved around counterrevolution; the Whites were still fighting, there were plans. Everyone had plans. Fights broke out, drunken shouts, glass breaking, once a chair broken along the cobblestones. After a year, he received two letters from home, one from his mother, another from her sister. They were censored, stamped, torn in half, held together by string in some cases—it seemed one could not get away from surveillance: "The village is in a terrible state. Hunger is everywhere. We haven't eaten meat since Easter. Some walk around dressed in rags. Train lootings, bandits and robberies are rampant. Live well, be good where you are."

SOON, HE SEES WINTER OVERCOATS and boots stacked on the sidewalks. He learns that people were heading to South America. Some to

Paraguay, to Chile. They would no longer need their furs, overcoats, felt boots. Others were heading to Mexico. Two months later, they decide to follow, and they too will sell their winter belongings on sidewalks, their china, fake paste jewels, crystal trinkets, pots and pans, kettles, scarves piled in boxes.

ONLY MEXICO WAS ACCEPTING. They were told that they could live there and work and then enter the United States. It would, at least, be on the same continent. How much he'd wanted only to be with her, to love and live, raise a family and enjoy the things they'd do, the people they'd become in a good country. But perhaps they should have stayed in Mexico, all of them together, living at that lighthouse, growing up by the sea—Mazatlán, the place of the deer, the Aztecs' name for it. He doesn't like to remember it. The lighthouse. The time there held a preciousness, lived within him like a secret that if divulged one too many times loses its significance, tarnished by the repeated reverie.

They lived in a lighthouse. He knows those days as the happiest of his life, when possibilities were open still and when he could provide for them all, his young ones, and his Julia. They'd fought through a country disassembling, had lost two homes, two probable lives, he waiting for the third one to turn over, wondering if it ever would.

What did the lighthouse in Mexico look like? There was the sea, for one, and it was on a cliff . . .

. . .

MAZATLÁN, CANANEA, MEXICO

1927–34

THE CLIFF WAS ON top of a hill, which sloped down to a rocky beach. The hill leveled out to a flat plateau from which one could look out over the ocean. And the lighthouse was built of stone, lichen, and barnacles on the outer edges nearest the water. Windows ringed the cylinder; to stand inside was to stand within a bracelet of light, the wrought iron staircase curling upward like a trail of hardened smoke. The constant ocean winds washed over the lighthouse, some days weak and other days fierce, gusting, but always washing over the lighthouse, windows shaking in their frames, the door shuddering too. The howls and whistles, the clanking of the chains in the wind. And at this lighthouse in Mexico, a long cement walkway led to the front door, bordered by small steel pillars. A chain was strung between as a kind of railing, the ground strewn with a thick layer of white and gray pebbles, darker, sea-stained rocks, and shells the color of sunset—rose, violet, peach. To walk on it was like stepping on broken shards of bone china.

. . .

SHE STANDS AMID THE billowing sheets, shirts, pinning clothes along a line made of hemp twine, one side affixed to the exterior of the light-house, the other end tied around the base of a palm. The air is dry, the wind from the ocean choppy. A boat drifts close and away again; its white wake like a scar. The smell of brine in the air. The scent of the sea's ero-sion. She bends and reaches, straightens and stretches. She places a palm at the small of her back, aching, the flutter and float of her stomach as she draws a hand across her belly. It seems she has the ocean in her, the slosh and splash of it. In her, her third one.

"Julia, Julia," the call comes. She watched him leave that morning, and then later saw him, Austin walking a straight path along the coast, the two little ones weaving behind him like the tails of a kite. And now they return, coming up over the dunes, far up the hill. They walk up the sand and rocks to the brambles, the seaweed salted white and dried, crunching beneath their step. They disappear and then, after the long hike uphill, they are near. She can see the tops of their heads.

"Mama, mama," they call to her, running, their hair tousled, wind-blown. And he comes up after them, his wide, wicked grin on. He is like a child. It is like returning to a town or country long loved and long missed, the familiarity welcomed.

He is a handsome man. A solid head, the brow strong and high, a kind of fine sheen to his skin—sweat, sea. His black hair tinged with streaks of charcoal now. There is a thickness and certainty to his beauty. It strikes a certain, resonating note in her, like a solid bell chime. This day she will remember. She knows to savor it and she works to memorize the way the light is, so white and blinding in the heat, the breeze from the ocean warm. His eyes too, rising up from the sand to meet her own. Look how he smiles. She watches them, her hand raised to her brow, blocking the sun's rays, shielding her eyes. In that moment, he kissed by the sun, the white flash of his teeth, the ease and heft of his walk—this, she will remember.

THEY SEEMED TO BE in no country, alone for miles on all sides. No borders, nationalities. No decrees, politics, beliefs of fervor. No panic. No disappearances in the middle of the night. No fear. Austin is calm here, relaxed. They are at peace in this loneliness, and it is a joy for her to see him contented in his work, his mind at ease.

It is hot and white all day, the grasses dry like hay, the color of sand, and the palm fronds brown and shriveling. She can hear the slow crawl of insects in the grass. She knows the scorpions lie burrowed and silent under the rocks and she warns the children. Every now and then, the slither and rustle of the large lizards frightens them, but it's the silence they should be most scared of, she tells them. They find the smaller lizards in the house, sunning on the windowsills, devouring the bananas. Once, one made its way far up to the top of the lighthouse.

They are far from what they know. It is not their landscape. So tired then of always moving, traveling. But they stayed there a year. They lived in the lighthouse.

. . .

SOMETIMES SHE SEES IT in a dream, intact. Other times only the children come running toward her. She can hear their voices and laughter carried on the wind. But he does not come. She can only sense him, she waiting. She may see the furtive flash of his eyes as they look up from the ground to meet hers. Then, she wakes. Some mornings his presence is so strong, he seems to hover over her, follow her. These years later she can no longer distinguish what was dreamt from what was lived. Dream and memory have merged, more braided like the individual strands of a rope.

So this is it, then. Two lives. They live two lives. The life in their minds, the life at hand. And in that shared place, the landscape of the imagination, they continue to love each other; they live.

. . .

ON ANOTHER DAY OF that year, he fixes the lighthouse. He climbs up the wrought iron railing, swirling upward.

"There are bats up there," she tells him.

"They're sleeping now. It's daylight."

"Be careful," she says, staring up at him, nearly dizzy from the height of it, her neck craned, looking up. She can hear his step clanking up the stairs, tools in tow. She takes Vera, now four, and Aussie, six, outside and down to the shore. She is walking slower now, the baby growing, she getting rounder.

The lighthouse was abandoned before they arrived, the keeper dying a year earlier with no one to claim possession. No keeper's son, wife, or daughter. They found him at watch, the light still blazing like a second sun, the radio tuned, he slumped over in his chair. It has not worked since.

"How would you like to live in a lighthouse?" Austin had asked her that first month in Mexico. After the old keeper had died, and, when in town, Austin had volunteered. As an engineer, he felt confident he could handle the equipment.

"What? Here, in Mexico?" she asked.

"Yes. A lighthouse. In Mexico."

. . .

THEY USED TO LIE on a wide bed, their room golden, spherical, like the world. The ocean surrounding them on all sides. She hung a white sheet. It divided the circle of the house in two, like an equator. The room seemed to breathe as the light grew dim, then strong, pulsing like a heartbeat. It was always windy, the windows shuddered and the sheet rippled.

If only they knew then to stay there. They lived in a lighthouse. They had no car. They were marooned. Over the rush of the ocean, the wind, and the seagulls, they can hear the sputter and clank of Mitchell's truck, its plume of smoke over the hedges, zigzagging along the land, flat and wide. And in a cloud of hazy dust, it comes barreling out to the coast. She can still see Mitchell, at the wheel, smiling. His long, lean face, all sunburned and freckled, his hair a shock of white. Mitchell the expat by choice. They met him at the market.

"I am never going back," he'd always say of America. And Austin and Julia would look at him dumbfounded, for that is all they wanted.

He drives them to the market—Julia in the open back, the baby now a month old and asleep in her arms. Aussie and Vera riding on the crates. Mitchell and Austin up front, arms hanging out the windows. She will always remember the drive to the market. The hazy heat, humid and moist, sulfur on the air, and salt. One would never think they were so close to the ocean. All the land around is dry and cracked for miles. The movement of the truck speeding down the roads creates a breeze, her hair whipping wildly around her face. She can hear the low rumble of Mitch-ell and Austin in conversation. Sometimes serious. Other times lewd, Mitchell mostly lewd. She ignores it.

Mitchell strolling through the market is a giant. He is a foot, some-times two feet, taller than the Mexicans, Austin too. But they smile wide when they see Mitchell. "*Señor* Mitchell, *Señor* Mitchell," they call out. He strides through. He shows them what to buy. How to buy. Everyone knows him.

"Bargain. Always bargain. If you don't, they are insulted," he says to her as she stands in front of a man and woman, staring at her blankly.

"No, no," he says to her. "Give it back to them. Start over." She tries again. This is how she learns to bargain. Soon she is buying flour, corn, peppers. There are eggs. Chickens. Straw hats and bags. Animals for sale. Goats and pigs. The Indians selling dried herbs, flowers, medicinals. Donkeys tied to the posts of their tents. The white canvas flapping in the breeze. Rows and rows of sunflowers, *girasoles*, like gold from a distance.

. . .

WHEN HE GETS LIKE this there is no stopping him. His mind fixates on a problem. And his mind works like his hands, tinkering, taking it all apart, reassembling the pieces. He will spend all day up there. Sometimes she can hear him talking to himself, muttering under his breath. It's like a fever has taken him. He won't eat. They tell her it's from being alone, but they're alone together up there, so high above Mazatlán, above any other person or family. It's just them and the sea, the storms, the birds and boats that might happen to pass by. Their only contact is Mitchell and the days at the market or the long walk down into town.

She keeps busy. There is so much to be done. Making meals do, stretching them out until the next market day, until they see Mitchell again. The sand gets into everything. Always a track of it in the house, in the sheets, sometimes in the food—the tortillas she makes are granular. She takes the children for walks on the shoreline. They collect shells.

AFTER EVERYTHING, she doesn't mind the being alone. It's a welcome solitude. They know this will not be forever.

"I think we should stay here," she tells him.

"Yes. But the work won't last. And it's not a proper place for them."

"I know. But I don't like the leaving."

FROM THE MARKET they buy seeds.

"I will plant a garden," she tells him.

"No use for that, rain will wash it away."

"I will plant a garden," she tells him. She must keep boredom at bay. They will have squash and maybe peppers. The children will help her.

The day she plants the garden is warm, clear. The sky so blue, pulled tight like the canvas on a drum. Austin is up in the lighthouse. She can hear the clank of his tools. She is digging into the ground with a shovel, the baby on the blanket beside her, Aussie and Vera watching. The ground is firm, with a topcoat of pebbles, the larger stones underneath. How rocky the ground is. When she hits a stone, the three of them kneel and dig with their hands, taking out the rock. The dirt gets moist as they dig, filled with worms and larvae, ants. The dirt is under her fingernails, in the children's hair, on their faces. Oh, the washing she'll have to do later.

The day nears noon, the sun blazing, the only cool from the ocean's winds. She is sweating, her handkerchief tied around her head is soaked through. She's removed her blouse and stands only in her cotton shift dress. The sun feels good on her bare arms. Every once in a while, she turns in the direction of the breeze and lets it dry her wet face, salt stained. The children are tiring.

"Aussie, Vera. Go sit down now and watch Mama," she tells them. She pulls the seeds from her pocket, each wrapped in palm leaves. They fall like marbles into the palm of her hand.

"How is it going down there?" Austin asks. It's his first appearance of the day. She sees him leaning out, his torso hanging over the balcony. The children shield their eyes and look up. She does the same.

"Fine. I'm going to plant now."

"The water will wash it away. You don't listen, but it is true."

She ignores him.

"Papa, there is no water."

"Not now, but with a storm—just wait until the next storm comes."

She listens to their exchange as she places the seeds into the ground. Vera and Aussie run around the house, staring up at their father. They tire and walk out to the farthest edge of the plateau, where it drops off to the hill and then far down to the sea.

"Be careful," she yells to them.

"We will," come their voices in singsong. She can hear his footsteps clanging down the iron staircase. He is hurrying down like she tells him not to, so fast he moves that he might propel himself over a banister. She hears the front door open, and can feel him watching her.

"What? What is it?" she turns to him, angry. But he stands there, with that little gleam in his eye, smiling, a pleading smile that both teases her and asks for forgiveness. He knows she cannot stay angry long.

"Julia, Julia, my jewel. Why do you not listen to me?" She ignores him. He walks closer to her, following in her footsteps as she bends to place the seeds in the ground.

"Don't step on my seeds with your big, heavy boots," she tells him, pushing him away.

"Well, if I do, it will not matter. You'll see. The storm will come and ruin it, not me."

IT CAME WITHOUT WARNING, no gray clouds hovering on the horizon at sunset. Even at night the clear sky held no sign of the early morning hours' torrents and squalls of water.

The winds thrash the house, the shutters spring open, banging. It feels as if the lighthouse itself might break off into the sea. Austin springs out of bed, frightened. It takes them a moment to realize it is only a storm. He runs up the stairs to the light. She runs to the windows, grabbing for the shutters. Wooden and splintered, they nick her hands. She manages to get both closed and place the plywood across the windows. The room is lit by candles and the shaft of light from above. The floor near the windows is soaking. She is wet through. Vera and Aussie stand at the edge of the circle of light, blurry-eyed, barefoot.

The next morning is like the previous day's—cloudless, tranquil. She is sleeping now. They are sleeping now. She wakes first, slipping out of bed, her feet bare and the floor cool, still damp. Out the windows the sea is calm as if last night's tumult exhausted it. It's appeased, serene. The air cool, but tinged with a heat that will grow, edging over the day's hours.

The shore is littered with the storm's refuse, seaweed clinging to the sand like a residue. Wood has washed up on the shore too. Later, Austin will collect it, dry it out in the sun, maybe burn it for a fire or carve it into something of use.

She steps outside and all seems cleansed, bleached. The cement walk is still damp under her bare feet, no longer chalk white, but a dirty gray. It scratches the soles. Branches of the palms are strewn across the pebbled ground, the burned grass, like garments along a bedroom floor. She turns to look back at the lighthouse. Disheveled. It seems as if more paint has peeled, like the earth dried and cracked. Shutters are blown off, glass shattered.

He is right about the garden. Flooded. The white seeds are like beads unearthed. She finds them in the crevices between the rocks, floating in puddles of water, in the tufts of grass. She begins to move quickly. Her feet sink into the muddy ground, her footsteps making a sucking sound. The ground is cold. She shivers. Goose bumps. She gathers the seeds and steps into the garden and the dirt pushes up between her toes, soon her heels are stained brown, her ankles. She tries to replant the seeds, placing each down in a divot, scraping the earth back, removing portions with her hands. The dirt smells of clay, pungent and fecund, a moldy smell that almost reminds her of spring, those last days of March when the mornings were chilly but the earth had a give to it, the crocuses peeping up behind the back of the house. She misses the seasons. She tells the children about winter, and they look at her wide-eyed. They cannot believe a world of white.

. . .

"It looks like a diamond," she says.

"Yes. It does, doesn't it?"

Austin lifts it out of the crate and the sun glints off it, sparkling, triangles of light across his face, forehead. The prisms, staggered steps of glass, smooth cut, surround the lens, which is concave like an enormous crystal eye. The Fresnel lens, shipped from Paris.

"It's like cut crystal," Julia says. Vera reaches out her hands to touch it.

"No, no. We cannot smudge it up, it will dull the light," Austin explains, and he crouches down to her, holding the lens upright. "Do you want to know something?" She nods, smiling.

"This light. Ah, well, we will see to the other side of the world."

"No, Papa. That's impossible."

"Well, if you don't believe, I'm sorry for you."

They carry the lens up the staircase, two steps at a time, Julia at the bottom, Austin holding the top. There are five hundred steps in all. They stop at each landing. She's stopped counting, her arms ache, quiver; soon she no longer feels them.

When they reach the top, the day is ending. After the work is done, after mounting the lens, they sit.

"It will shine, reach farther. The light will reflect off the prism."

"But how does it create more light?"

"Light moves in waves like the ocean."

That night they light it. They've brought the children up and the glow of it, like a chandelier, falls on their cheeks, reflects in their eyes. And the beam, a band of whitish light, reaches far out over the water, cuts through the mist. It seems to burn a hole in the dusk's horizon and then disappears.

. . .

THIS HAPPENED LATER. In the copper mines of Cananea where Austin had found a more secure job as a mine foreman. 1934. After all her letters—to consulates, senators, to her mother and sister—a telegram arrives. How she's not sure. But she envisions it on the course there, Connecticut to Mexico. In a sack, on a train and perhaps another, crossing the border, getting on a truck bound for her. It's a wonder to her how such a fragile thing as paper, prone to tears and other destructions—fire, water—can arrive, bearing a message. Paper is stronger than one imagines. It has a power. Sometimes she's not sure what has more efficacy—the blank page, what is yet to be written, or the page filled with words like the telegram she received.

One letter and we will travel distances.

VISA APPLICATION ACCEPTED.
COME HOME.
LOVE MOTHER.

THAT NIGHT, they do not sleep. They lie awake and stare out the window at the mines, hearing the clatter of the copper carts in the distance, echoing off the hollow land, seeing the flicker of fire in the hills.

"You must go," he tells her.

"You will come with me."

"If they permit me."

"They will permit you."

"Perhaps."

"What do you mean by 'perhaps.' They must and they will."

"They've reclaimed you. We now belong to two different countries. We are foreigners to each other." He chuckles at the thought. She can feel the tears slide down her temples into her hair, which is spread out on the pillow.

. . .

THEY ARE DRESSED, she in her navy frock, hat. He in his gray suit, a white shirt, stained brown at the collar. It will do. Mitchell has come to take them to the consulate in Nogales. It is a two-hour drive and they leave Cananea in the blue of morning. The horizon is rimmed in white. It is like they are traveling into night, but they know it is day. In an hour, the sun will breach the horizon, golden and full. The heat will come and the haze.

A MAN BEHIND THE glass tells them Austin will not be permitted.

"Deported once. It is difficult. I'd listen to what the senators have told you—if there is a chance at all, it is from the other side. You, Mrs. Voronkov, can go back now and work from there to bring him in." They look at each other. Austin raises his eyebrows, questioning her.

"Maybe this is so, Julia."

"I'm telling you, it's your best chance," the man says. She stands silent. Later, all she can say is how much she doesn't like the leaving.

SEPARATION COMES QUITE SUDDENLY. One day you are as close as two people can be. The next, a line is drawn and you stand on opposite sides, regarding each other across an expanse that is barren and unknown. To look at him reminded her of all the ways she'd miss him. That whole rest of the day, wandering through the dusty streets and the long drive home in the blue of encroaching evening, she felt far from him as if they'd already taken the first steps away from each other and her stomach was hollow. The gnawing had begun.

. . .

"My things will greet you," he says, referring to his truck of belongings. Somehow, they think that if he sends parts of himself— clothes, shoes, books, drafts, and notebooks—he will follow.

"We must be positive," he reminds her. "Dream, imagine that it can happen, that I will be with you and it will be." She smiles at him, through tears. She still remembers the green of the truck, army green, the color of a glass bottle. In a few days' time she will unload it on the other end, un- pack his things, hang his clothes, shirts and pants.

And wait.

He is smiling. He is composed, serene. He will not let himself be any- thing but, for her sake, for the children. They all know his moods too well and can sense the smallest register of panic—a flicker across the eyes, the crooked way he presses his lips together, the arch of the eyebrow.

The train station is a crush of bodies—animal, human. They had stood in the gray room of the train depot, surrounded by people, by the dry scent of newspapers and wood and metal. It was as if they'd already left, Julia saying "My stomach feels hollow." Women, men board the train, crates of chickens. People are hanging out the open windows. Tears.

They'd taken the Mexican Central Railroad line, connecting to the Southern Pacific in El Paso. The train cars, the large white lettering on the smooth black surface—new trains. They stood between the *X* and the *I*. The train started and she jumped, the steam from the engine was like a giant's sigh.

. . .

MEXICO CITY
1948

IN THE EARLY LIGHT, dawn still, Austin is up before 6 A.M. He can see out the window a sliver of the moon, not yet faded from the night sky and hanging like an eyelash. He feels the sheet over him in his small bed, the stillness of his body in the still morning, seeing if he can perhaps lull himself back to sleep even if for just an hour. He lies on his back, staring at the ceiling, also painted gray, except for the areas where peeling paint reveals a deep-sea blue green, and if he squints his eyes in a certain way or stares long enough so that his vision blurs, the successive curls of paint look not unlike a flutter of butterflies. He next tries lying on his side, legs outstretched, legs bent in fetal position. Neither position works. He rolls onto his back once more, this time bending his legs so that the sheet drapes off his knees creating a white peak, like Iztaccihuatl, he thinks, the white woman.

But it's no use. He is fooling himself. He will no longer be able to sleep on this morning and even though his eyes are drooping, and one or two times do actually close, he wills himself to sit up. And then, blinking, he returns to a horizontal position. Ten more minutes I will lie here awaking, he agrees with himself, listening for the usual morning noises of the boardinghouse, though because of the very early hour, the walls emit no sounds and Austin feels at once as if he were on an enormous ocean liner, adrift on calm waters, he the only passenger stirring in his berth. Soon enough though the pipes begin to gurgle, the faucets open, toilets flush, and the crack of windows opening procures the morning's din. Footsteps above. The creak of a bed. Someone has dropped a heavy object. Someone has turned on the radio. Someone is singing. Another is shouting, but he cannot tell if the shouts are of joy and exclamation or of anger and hostility, but for the most part these noises may as well be the sounds from the structure itself, its inhabitants ghosts of bygone days, he the lone one anchored to his own time, or so he thinks for, in the years he's lived here, he rarely encounters anyone in the hallways or on the stairs. It was as if all the boarders had come to some mutual agreement that no one person will be exiting his room at the same time as another. In this way privacy is upheld, but so too solitude and its first cousin loneliness.

When he rises, he walks first to the window, peering through the blinds. A feeling of disquiet, but he is not sure what is causing this sudden, early-morning unrest. His thoughts still vacant from his near sedated sleep. He is now searching for last night's worry, the idea that had vanished, the thing he should be thinking about, gnawing over in his mind. He watches the leaves in the breeze, can feel the morning air through the glass. Soon the evening returns, in pieces only—his shop, Anarose running, her radio, the window. Then he sees darkness. The full details begin to emerge, hazy still. The return to his boardinghouse, the stairs and then the unpleasant recollection—Jack. But had it truly happened? Could it have been a dream or could there now be this man named Jack watching him? If not at this exact moment, then is he in the vicinity, waiting? Has he a room in the adjacent building? As far as Austin knows that building is vacant. Could he be lurking within alcoves and alleyways? Austin remembers hiding his designs and looks around the room now, half hoping to find nothing, a confirmation that it had all been some terrible dream. He isn't so lucky. The drafts sit where he'd hid them, strangled by the lattice bracing of the dresser like evidence of an awful crime. He tries to clear his mind, shake such suspicions away, but it seems Jack will now be something to contend with as one contends with the weather—rain or wind.

Preventative measures . . . consequences . . . Jack knew most of his story. Austin had to admit he was impressed. They were good at their jobs; that was certain. Thorough enough, trained to focus on the detail, and, despite the discomfort, was he not curious to find out just what other kind of information Jack had on him? Austin had lived with the knowledge of his past, his travels, his struggles, internal and alone, and to speak of it with someone who knew, if not intimately, then on a purely factual basis, made him uneasy, yes, but also oddly comforted. Linked. Connected as if a line had now been drawn between himself and another. This will not deter him, though. He will proceed as normal if more on guard, his suspicions heightened. He'll just take more precautions. He will go to the post office as usual. Certainly, there was nothing wrong with that, a man going to the post office, the *lista de correos.*

He is dressing in a rush. He wants to beat the early traffic and lines. He leaves his rooms, satchel beneath his arm. The bright morning. The sky in its vast continents of distinct white and blue. He decides on an alternate route. Despite the early hour, the street traffic is thick. The sidewalk wide and pedestrians moving in staggered lines. He dodges the oncoming people while those behind him speed up and pass him, his peripheral vision extending farther than usual. *A reminder, a warning only*, Jack had said. Well, he can send a letter still. That will not be considered a threat. *All your activities are a threat. . . .*

THE POST OFFICE IS swarming. People stand before the windows and long lines trail out into the main lobby. All the voices create a mass hum and he tries to shut it out. Focus. His heart racing, the beating loud in his ears. He keeps his eyes on his feet, cannot look up to absorb the sight of all this movement—a crowded chaos even if the people stand orderly enough in their lines, patient or impatient, fidgeting or quite still.

He takes a deep breath and delves in. First, to the counters, finding an unoccupied one with space enough to lay out his designs. He will mail one set to the patent commissioner. Another set he will send to Julia. He takes a blank piece of paper from his satchel. *Dearest Julia, my jewel*, he begins, *Dear, you must do as I say. Forgive me for asking this of you, but it's of utmost importance. I am sending, herewith, an envelope that is to be sent to the Patent Commissioner. I implore you to please mail this on my behalf. It is imperative that this is done at once. I can't tell you how crucial it is to my well-being and to yours and the children's. Tell no one. Speak to no one.* Too alarming perhaps, he realizes now, reading over the letter, but, well, he can no longer protect her from what is transpiring. She'll have to do it for him. He will have to trust that she will send them on his behalf. It is all of his hope, he is availing himself of it, placing it all in her hands.

He thinks of calling to let her know the letter would be on its way. He's been through this before—days of calculating the cost of a phone call. He knows what he needs to do, skipping both breakfast and dinner for one day, though if he does call there is no guarantee that she'd be home to answer, and if she is, what will he say to her that he hasn't already written in the letter? It would be a waste. He knew this line of argument, had spent years on the back and forth of it and all the thought-of calls had been aborted, he hungrier and in need of a meal.

HOURS LATER, AFTER LUNCH and an unsettled walk through the Alameda, he returns by bus, dust now filling his hair, a thin film of it along his brow, but walking down his street, he is relieved that he has at least succeeded in mailing off two sets of designs. It is growing colder as the late afternoon heads toward evening. Outside, the streetlights are glowing in amber orbs, awake in their oblong pools of light, spilling through the window so that Austin now walks through these before stepping behind the counter and through the back curtain. He sits on his chair, first in a kind of relief that he has made it to the post office and back without running into Jack. He had not realized how fast his heart was racing until now, the exertion having its aftereffects, waves of exhaustion come, little surges of heat.

He hears the gentle clink of the shop door's wind chimes, which announce customers. The opening door causes the beads of the curtain to sway, clatter lightly as if a cat had walked beneath. Austin rises with a start. He steps through the beads, which settle behind him now, clicking in a lazy way. The wind chimes above the door rotate in a slow, steady circle, menacing in its orbit. And it would not be too far off the mark, he would not be surprised at all to see Jack standing in the doorway, sauntering through the shop, looking at the clocks, standing there pulling one off the shelf, examining it, turning it over in his hands before placing it back in its original position.

At first he tenses and then softens. "Anarose?"

"Sorry. I did not mean to frighten you." Her cheeks are flushed, her smile tentative at first and then easy and wide and latent beneath her lips.

"How did you get in?" Austin runs a hand through his hair, still dusty from the bus trip. Anarose searches him, her look imploring.

"The door was open."

"Open?"

"*Sí.*"

"I was certain I locked it behind me."

"No." She shakes her head. "I have a clock," she says. It is matter-of-fact, mechanical. But there is a pull in her words as if the vowels had become more weighted, like stones sinking to the bottom of a pond. His eyes feel tired, slack. He is embarrassed that his jacket is so crumpled and wrinkled, sweat dry along his skin, hair disheveled surely. A man in a frantic state.

"A clock?" Austin says.

"*Sí.*" Anarose nods. She is framed by the front window now purpling into dusk. There is sawdust on the floor, on his shoes. He steps forward. She smells of the evening air, cigarette smoke, dried leaves. There is deference in Austin's movements, the way he leans back on his heels and then reaches above Anarose's head, pulling on a string. Light fills the shop. A metal washer swings like a pendulum and hits her temple.

"Sorry," he says, reaching to touch her forehead and then thinking better of it, dropping his arm to his side.

"It's okay," she says, rubbing. They tread around each other with caution.

"Show me the clock."

"*Sí.* I have it right here." She turns to her canvas bag, abandoned on the floor behind her. "It just stopped. Worked and then one day, nothing, *nada*." They both stare at the bag. She bends down, removing the clock.

"Sometimes it's just a simple winding," Austin says, taking it from her. He sets it on the counter. The clock is cool to the touch. One firm press and the back opens. Gears, springs, an eerie silence. The gear teeth are like a cat's, a dull sharpness that bites through the minutes, invisible and unknown. Taking the gear full in hand, he tugs at it, but it's old and stubborn and the teeth leave small indents in his palm, pink and white like a baby's bite. A copper spring clatters to the floor—a lost part and the clock could remain forever broken. The hands are paused, like the long arms of a dancer.

"If the winding doesn't do it, we take it apart. Gears first, ratchet, hands."

"Please leave it for now. I will return. I can come another day," Anarose insists.

"No. It will be just a moment more," he says. A grimace and he snaps a gear back into place. "Nearly done," he says, setting the clock upright. The hands ticking back to life. "There, works," he says, looking up to meet her eyes. Neither moves. It should be a natural progression. A simple exchange of service rendered. A polite transfer, she then walking out so that he can close, pull down the grate, lock the door. But this is not what happens. Austin, hesitating and then deciding to at least do something, steps around the counter. Anarose takes a step back, now placing the clock in her bag. Austin still stands, at a loss. To stay may invite Jack, and to work in his rooms is impossible now too. He is a hunted man. Watched. He could walk, simply walk throughout the city in circuitous routes never to be found or followed. He takes his satchel, and then in an awkward, hesitating way, they are stumbling to the door, excusing each

other, "you first," "sorry, no you," a strange, nervous dance set to the
ticking clock—loud and full in the surrounding silence.

OUTSIDE, THE NIGHT IS COLDER. Leaves fall from the trees, blowing across the sidewalks and spilling over into Calle Colima. They walk
out of the shop, Austin locking the grate, and then breaking off, first one,
then another, Austin falling back from Anarose, Anarose now hesitating,
slowing to wait, until they are in sync so that on the last stretch of the
sidewalk, Anarose is next to Austin.

"*Gracias*, Austin," she says, her arms wrapped around her bag. They
walk close, bumping shoulders once, twice. The feel of her in periphery is
warm, curious. It is awkward for him, walking side by side like this. He is
not used to it. A gust of wind makes some leaves scatter, rustle along the
sidewalk. Fords and Cadillacs are crammed with people. Taxis. On their
way to destinations unknown, but they will all be going somewhere for a
good time, borne away on the night's promise, still early at that hour, laden
with laughter, music, life. At the corner people mingle, enter and leave
the small café, which, as they draw close, pulses with music and lights.

"I invite you for a tequila."

"Now?"

"Yes. A thank you for helping me the other night."

Austin does not respond, but walks next to her still, wondering if he
can allow himself to go. He looks over his shoulder.

"Come. Just right here." She swings around to face Austin, her teeth
flash in a car's headlights, beckoning with her wide, warm smile, her
eyes glistening in the moving light as she ushers them both through the
door.

It's an open-air café. Small tables sit around the periphery of the courtyard, huddled like worried young women eager to dance. Some are angled or overturned, some are tucked into corners. White lights arc in loose garlands, dipping close to the dancers' heads. The lights click and swirl in the wind. Glass hurricanes shield small flames from the breeze. Austin steps to the edge of the staircase, watching the string of lights swing toward Anarose, she raising her elbow as if to shield herself from a blow, the bulb grazing the inside of her arm. To Austin her whole body seems on delay, she pressing her lips to where the light burned, the soft place where she places her perfume, which he can smell now, an acrid scent, yet familiar. He lifts the lights for her to dip underneath and he feels comic, a nervousness in his smile as if he has forgotten how.

"Lights," he says, feeling foolish, his cheeks hot, wondering what exactly he is doing here and why. Anarose bows underneath his raised arm and looks back up to him, once, twice.

Out on the floor, couples dance. Some sway, tracing small tight circles. Others hold a distance, the better to practice the slow formal steps of the *danzón*, heads turned away from each other, dignified, proud. Every once in a while, a man thrusts his chin down over his shoulder as if regarding the ground with disdain. His partner in opposition. The tendons in her neck shining. Then, on a beat, they meld and are off again once more.

The crowded place, though not overwhelming, makes Austin nervous. He knows this place. He had come here in his first years at the boardinghouse, to sit and mingle among the people, watching the dancers, drinking. He no longer comes. He hasn't been here in years, he came to feel contempt for the dancing couples, it was no longer a place for him. He looks back to Anarose, who is at the bottom of the staircase, voices behind him in English, the words grind and cut over the music. Her hand flutters to her necklace, twirling the fine, silver chain around her index finger before letting it drop to her chest once more.

The maître d' nods to them and leads them through the clutter of tables, zigzagging. Anarose is looking over her shoulder; she wants to see where he has gone to, though he is only two steps behind. Heads turn, men mostly—a sudden hush, a halt in conversations. Anarose feigns indifference—that, or she is simply oblivious, walking with her easy grace, confident in her beauty and not as if all those eyes were stealing something from her, as Austin feels now, a secret shed, discarded.

"Bueno," the maître d' says. He's pulled out two chairs, his hands turned up in offering. Their seats face the dancers, some gracing their table's edge, a woman's bare back taut and unapologetic. Anarose falls to her seat, the maître d' holds the back of the chair, pushing her gently forward. She sets her bag down and the table wobbles. He takes his seat next to her, his satchel on the floor near his feet. He is silent, looking out across the dance floor, to his hands and then to her face. Her eyes are darker in the light, black lines drawn in perfect arcs along the lid, the under eye. There is a momentary trace of sorrow, dissatisfaction in the way she suddenly rests her chin on her palm, now looking over the floor. Just beyond the pulse and lilt of the dancers.

"Amazing dancers, aren't they. I have come here before, just to watch. I love dancing though. Sunday afternoons are good too. Then, they have the rancheros. Do you know the rancheros?"

"Yes."

"Always mariachi, but the rancheros, such stories," she says, pausing, and then looks to him. "Tell me, Austin, you are Russian?"

He does not answer, just looks at her—a hard stare. Austin should go home, but he wants to stay.

"Well, you either are or you aren't."

"I am from Russia, but I'm an applicant for U.S. citizenship."

"You are Russian then. The shop. It's busy all the time, long lines every time I pass. You have built up a reputation then. How long have you been here in the D.F.?"

"I am waiting to go to the U.S." The waiter skirts the edge of the dance floor, takes their order of two tequilas and leaves them. Austin can feel her watching him. Her gaze travels to the dancers and back to him.

"Ah, we're all waiting to go to the U.S." The waiter returns, setting the glasses on the table with an abrupt little slam. Austin takes his first sip.

"Tell me, what is it you have in this satchel of yours?" She smiles and in one movement sweeps down to lift the bag to her lap.

"Please leave that." He reaches for it. She is laughing, leaning back, holding it close to her chest.

"So heavy. So many notebooks," she says, pulling away from him, opening the satchel, teasing as she looks inside. "What is all this?"

"Designs."

"For what?" She takes out a notebook.

"No. Leave it all be." She is flipping through pages now, diagrams and margin notes.

"What will you do with these? Ah, I see. I know. You will make your big fortune, right? Like an American. Dream big," she says, her smile large. "Well, you can hope. There is nothing wrong with that." Her gaze is fixed on him. She turns back to the dancers and then in a softer voice, directed into the middle distance: "And one day you will forget all about old Mexico." She smiles, setting his bag back down on the floor. She lifts her glass of tequila, clinks his and takes a sip.

There is a pause in the music. It shifts from a slow, meandering ballad to an allegro, the guitarists strumming fast, hands banging the box of the guitar. Austin's hands are on the table, fingers splayed, palms wide as he leans back in his chair, his smashed thumb darker against the white table-top. Anarose is not looking at his face. He feels her beside him, his leg pressed against hers. She does not move. He shifts away even though he likes the warmth of her limbs.

The music slower. The lilting chords of the *danzón*.

"You know how?" Anarose says, standing up. Others have begun to dance around them.

"A little." He shrugs and follows. Her hands are tentative in their touch, eyes on his shoulder. Austin squeezes her palm, little pulses. The light strings sway, bleeding streaks before his eyes readjust and each bulb takes shape again, pearled and gleaming. Warmth here in the crook of his arm. How strange the automatic, instant clutch. He'd like to stay here, holding on to her, as if he'd discovered something lucid in the state of their embrace, the way his hands hold her, the solid flesh of his palm against her shoulder and curve of her lower back, and likewise the way her palms hover slightly before pressing to his chest, her fingers now clasped within his own. It is a hold permissible, his palm squeezing hers as if to quell whatever he is feeling brimming up within her—a response of instinct. He feels the dip in the small of her back, guiding her by this subtle ledge. A man cannot live so many years without touch. The body unable to withstand the missing.

They are in sync—light, yet full, bodies and music in concordance. The other women are certain, their dignity often mistaken for haughti-ness. A breeze makes skirts flutter. As they guide their partners, men's forearms flex, like little gasping breaths. Beyond the lights it's darkness, the trees lining the courtyard like black shadows. The leaves rustling, branches tapping, lights clicking—all create an alternate current of sound in contrast to the strumming guitar, the singer's vibrato. Near them a couple dances, a command over their limbs as if they've stepped into the music like clothing—the flick of a foot, the bend in a wrist. Austin glosses over him at first. It is only a vague sense of familiarity within this out-of-place context. The gestures. The jaunty way he crosses his legs. The fidget of a hand when talking. Austin keeps dancing. His body calm, his heart though, frantic. He is surprised by his ability to feign composure. He can manage well, he can handle this. It was as if the moment had already happened, as if he knew, had been through this very scenario before, the moment simply existing in a near future he'd finally come to meet.

"Austin, what is it?" Anarose looks over her shoulder. "Do you know someone?"

"*Sí.*"

"Who?"

"An acquaintance."

Anarose's arms fall away from him like a shawl. Austin's neck is strained.

"No. Don't stop dancing," Austin says, and he takes her into his arms again, wondering if she can feel his pulsing, racing mind, if the body gives it away. Jack is standing next to a woman in a doorway. The music ends. Austin's arms go lax. They stand like adversaries. The band begins the next number, all horns and brass. It is loud. Austin grabs her wrist, his face now tense, but trying to stay controlled, inconspicuous lest Jack spot him.

"I need to go," he says.

"Now?"

"Yes."

"I will join you."

"No. Stay here, stay right here." He is harsh, curt, he puts his hand out, a dividing line. She looks at him perplexed, uncertain. "You must stay right here," he says.

He is only half aware of the bodies moving around him, his own step unsteady through the dancers. The perfume, smoke, briny smell of hard liquor seem to encapsulate them all in a small, fetid cloud. He returns to his table, finds his satchel and then heads for the back entrance, down a dark hallway and out into the evening. He walks straight away, walks as fast as he can without making his hurried pace look too conspicuous.

WHEN HE TURNS DOWN his street, he continues straight past the boardinghouse, walking directly to his shop. He is lifting the grate now, inching it up. He clicks the door open and feels his way to the back room, the lights off. He will stay here and wait until morning. He stands in darkness. He takes a rolled-up canvas in the corner and lays it out on the floor. He removes his jacket and sets it on top of the canvas. Then, the pillow from his chair, curling up into fetal position, the floor firm and cold beneath him.

After twenty minutes or thirty, he hears the rattle of the door, the breaking of a lock and then the chimes. He clamors to stand, his back pressed against the wall. He tries to steady his breathing and then there is silence and only the loud pulse of his heart. He tries to listen for more movement, but the front room is still. He watches for a trace of light and shadow. After ten minutes, his legs cramping, his shoulders ache. When he can stand it no longer he bounds through the curtain. He stops short.

"How did you find me?"

"We put two and two together," Jack says, leaning against a workta-ble. Calm, composed, with a satisfied look.

"What do you mean?"

"It makes sense, you see, a man like you, a man such as yourself—good with mechanical things, an engineering mind. Of course you would do repairs. Tell me, Ustin, do you have any associations with Commu-nists down here?"

"No."

"You're certain of that."

"Yes."

"You do know they're all here."

"Who?"

"The Communists."

"I am here because Mexico is the closest place to the U.S."

"Right. Well, you should know that several so-called Americans are here in Mexico City and her surrounding environs. Hollywood types, you see, those avoiding subpoenas by the House Un-American Activities Committee. Heard of it, have you? I was assigned to a few of them before you came along, before we grew suspicious of your activities too."

"I have no activities."

"That's what you say, but I'd be careful if I were you."

"It's the truth."

"I think contemplating crossing the border can count as activity."

"Why now?"

"We have our reasons."

"I've lived here fourteen years and you come now. Why?"

"We know your kind is thinking about infiltrating the U.S. It's our job to keep people like you and your kind out."

"What is my kind?"

"Anyone who is suspected of subversive activities. That, and there are new developments."

"What do they have to do with me?" Austin watches Jack cross the floor to sit in the windowsill, torso twisted slightly so that he faces outward. His raised leg swings in and out of the streetlamp light shining through the front window. His ease, his nonchalant demeanor angers Austin, the impudence, thinking he can come here and persecute him with these accusations. It is unconscionable.

"You've been on our radar before, and due to new developments, we've been advised to keep an eye on you. You're a perfect candidate for illegal entry so I'm here to ensure that you won't try something funny, or at least warn you not to do it. Of course, crossing the border is more difficult now than it was years ago, but you have your connections, Sonoran smugglers maybe? And besides, you've got to see it from our perspective. How are we to know what you might do with these inventions of yours?"

"What about them? You'll soon see. Once they are patented, I'll gain admittance to the U.S. and join my family."

"I'm not so sure about that."

"Why do you say that, why would you say such a thing?"

"Again, it's my job to make sure people like you don't enter the country and that means taking all means necessary to ensure that it won't happen."

"But my work is good, it's useful."

"We know. Quite useful too."

"Thank you."

"The steamship engine. Now that is some good work there. It's been reviewed several times. We've flagged it, you see."

"You have?"

"Yes. We are impressed with it."

"But it's mine. Surely, you wouldn't take my idea—"

"We use whatever is useful, whatever we can if it helps us do what we need to do."

"And what of me?"

"Well, we can appreciate your intelligence, your inventions, but we can't trust your activities and motives, even if we do find your skills to work in our favor."

"I see. So you will take my ideas and use my inventions to your own ends, to the U.S. government's ends, and you'll leave me, my family, in this dastardly state? And what about the individual, the man himself?"

"I work for the U.S. government and will protect and serve her in any way I can, and again if it means keeping your kind out, well—. But, listen, I'm not going to get into theories or pretend to philosophize with you about the individual and the pursuit of happiness. This is how it goes. It's the way it is, you see."

"You have no feeling. You are an unsympathetic individual."

"I'm trained not to have feelings. It's what you might call a requirement of the position."

"To lack empathy."

"If that's what you call it."

"Yes. Empathy. Write that down in your notebook," Austin says under his breath as he turns to pace back and forth. This is all too much for Austin, who now finds that he is gnashing his teeth, his hands are clenched and he begins to glean an understanding of what is happening. Could they have intercepted his designs, prevented them from getting to the patent commissioner and then stolen them for their own ends? The bastards! It was an outrage, that they could do such a thing, a betrayal of the postal system and his rights to read his own mail. He feels certain that it is un-lawful, to treat a man so, to confiscate his work and tarnish his reputation. No. He will set it all straight. They will soon see. He will take an action of recourse, yes. That seems a fine way to handle things, to get him out of such a trap. Yes. An action of recourse, the word, *recourse*, like a refrain. These patent agents and embassy clerks, damn them, all in league with miscreant men who will outright steal his ideas, the scoundrels. They will soon see. He will simply go by other means, he'll go above their heads, all their heads, to the ambassador. Why has he not thought of something like this before? It is brilliant. He will write to the ambassador! That is a man who will clearly see his predicament, who will surely be a man of reason.

Dear Sir Ambassador,

I am a trained engineer and applicant for American citizenship and herewith are my inventions along with an oath of a single inventor, declaring that I—and I alone—am the sole inventor of the enclosed. Be so kind as to review my inventions for sea and air travel. It has come to my attention that these designs have been stolen by a branch of your government and are thus deterred from getting into the right and just hands of the U.S. patent commissioner. I write to you with a plea, requesting that you mail these designs, under embassy authority, to the U.S. patent commissioner, thus preventing unlawful confiscation. I congratulate you on your discretion in these matters.

Yours sincerely and humbly and with my trust in your good and gracious services,

Austin Voronkov

Inventor

Satisfied with this decision Austin finds himself seated now, staring into the evening which seems to have proceeded forward in brazen unawareness of Austin's predicament. Jack is gone. He steps outside, the later-hour sidewalks almost haughty in their stillness. Well, it was just like them really, just like them and all their cronies. They would do that, show up unannounced, torment a man, and then casually walk away to leave a man wondering about his own mind, left now with a little inkling that perhaps his mind truly was fraying, his very hold on reality exhausted, no longer working in the same way. Oh, but enough! He will not allow himself to go so far astray with such needling thoughts. Surely the authorities will know how to handle such a situation, best to, as he's done, write to the ambassador at the U.S. embassy. They will act on the behalf of an applicant for American citizenship. Yes. He will write to them directly.

. . .

HE IS NOT CERTAIN what day he noticed the car, a taxi parked across the street, two doors down from his boardinghouse. It may have been Tuesday of last week, or just as easily Wednesday, or it may have been there all along and only now has he begun to pay attention. How he could've missed it baffles him and he is angry with himself, to have not been more aware, watchful. The curve of its hood, rising just above the median's plants, glimmering in the sunlight. He begins to test the taxi. He wakes late at night and again early in the morning, peering out the window to find it still. But no one is ever in the car. He has never once seen it pull in or drive away. The driver most likely is somewhere else then, melding into the street activity, watching.

The car's presence is a disturbance. He is unable to concentrate, the image of it parked across the street burns into his mind. Sitting at work before his papers, rising to look out the window, to pace and return once more to his desk. Rise, peer, pace through the afternoon. It means nothing, nothing, he thinks, but when the car vanishes, it is as if a migraine has lifted.

It returns two days later, parked across the street with one tire up on the sidewalk. The insouciance, he thinks. In his notebook he begins to keep an account of the car, searching for patterns within its presence and absence. He has, these last few weeks, turning into a month, examined the street with more scrutiny, the waiters in the café, their shifts, comings and goings, the deliverymen, the men selling tortillas, anyone he may see more than once, watching them pass by the taxi, seeing if anyone will open the car door. The rhythms of the street, the bus schedule with its timed stops dispensing the regular passengers, on the lookout for the unfamiliar, searching for a pattern, a repetition, some link. The street moves and breathes from the point of the taxi. He fills his notebook with a kind of code, a daybook record:

> *Tuesday, 3:00 a.m., taxi.*
> *6:00 a.m., taxi.*
> *Waiter A. Café opens. 8:00 a.m.*
> *Bus arrives. 8:20 a.m.*
> *Waiter B. Work. 9:00 a.m.*

"The taxi is not marked," the boy says.

"No license?" Austin says, annoyed with him.

"No." The boy shakes his head, shrugs his shoulders.

He had paid him to inspect the taxi. No identifying markers, no way to trace it. Clever, Austin thinks. The taxi is an everyday image, able to blend into the city, innocuous, but he is on to them. As a precaution, he continues hiding his designs—more papers stuffed into the slit in his mattress, pressed behind the lattice woodwork of his bureau, beneath the floorboard in the corner of his bedroom, wedged within the medicine cabinet door.

A TUESDAY. He is leaving the boardinghouse and steps through its narrow front door and out into early gray. No visible sun yet. It's still hidden. Anarose, her back to him, stands on the edge of the sidewalk. Arms crossed. She spins around at the sound of the door.

Austin freezes. She calls his name and takes a step closer.

"I came to make sure you were okay," she says. "I haven't seen you in a while."

He looks to his left then right, trying now to remember which route he'd taken the day before. He's been diligent about varying his walks. At the corner he can see a taxi, unmarked and unknown. He does an about-face and continues in the opposite direction.

"Are you not going to speak to me?" Anarose says. She has stayed where she is, watching him. "Where are you going?" she asks, following him now. The early sun breaks through a cross street. It's in his eyes now and it is hard for him to see. He ducks into a back alley, tension along his face, grimacing. He feels her two steps behind him, and he tries to conceal his own weary affliction, hiding it like an addict. The taxis line the avenue ahead. He tries to look without staring too intently. His glance grazes over the taxis, searching for the unmarked one. Just to be sure.

The threat is soon multiplied, surrounding him, one after another in long rows that line the avenue, each probable. The people on the street, in the park, entering and leaving, the taco vendors, all an assumed link to any parked taxi.

"What are you doing?" Anarose says. "Won't you stop and talk to me," she says, her steps sputter and falter until she is in sync with him.

"If you want to speak to me, you must walk faster. Please."

"You must tell me what is going on."

"I don't want to involve you."

"Involve me in what? What is it? Are you in some kind of trouble? Are you?"

They are rushing by a few early risers, newspaper stalls, crossing to the next street. He can feel Anarose next to him, her steps struggling to keep up. He stops, looks to her. He can feel an onlooker now, hates to have eyes on him. He walks to her, takes her wrist, and brings her to the next side street, her feet dragging compared with his long, bounding stride.

"Austin, tell me what is going on," she says. They have stopped now, the street noise hushed in the cold shade of the buildings, the narrow alleyway and the sound of trickling water and his short, quick breathing drowning out the city.

"Look here, you simply need to know this," he says, his stare fixed on the ground, his voice low. "If you come to the shop and one day I am not there, you must promise me something."

"You are frightening me."

"Please, just promise me," he says.

"Tell me—why did you run off from me that night at the café?" she says, shifting and then taking a step closer to him.

"Take my designs to the U.S. ambassador."

"What?"

"You must take them to the ambassador!"

"The ambassador?"

"Please." He brings his eyes to hers now, pleading. "You must tell them that they are designs by an applicant for U.S. citizenship. You must give them to the ambassador."

"But I don't see what good—," she says, her eyes wide, anxious.

He breaks from her gaze and turns from her, brusque and quick, as her words trail off, he continuing to walk. He feels foolish now to have told her. How could she understand? He hardly knows if his suspicions are correct, if he can trust his own instincts, and now hearing her slow steps behind him he realizes she can never know what he has known and the city pulses in on him from the sides of the buildings, the taxi tangled within his mind, and her look of fear, her confusion, alarm. It makes him want to protect her and flee from her both, and within that back-and-forth he wishes to slip once again into the vast city, anonymous and alone.

"What's the use of you getting all involved in this?" He stops and shakes his head, arms at his sides.

"I don't understand any of what you are saying. You are frightening me. If you want me to take the designs to the ambassador I will. I don't see what good it will do—"

"You promise me?" He looks up to her now.

"Yes, yes, I promise," Anarose says.

She is staring at him, nodding vacantly, wary. How could she ever know what he has known, he continues to think as he walks beside her, eyes to the ground, their steps now slower, his heart's racing settled, even and steady as they amble on, the city enclosing him, trapped, he filled with fury and shame and a sudden longing for his first years in Mexico City when solitude was a solace even in the ache of loneliness.

THEY HAVE WALKED ALL the way to the Alameda. She stops, falling back to sit on a bench. She beckons him to do the same.

He feels a reprieve, his breathing settled and calm. He looks around, feeling Anarose watching him. He can hear her telling him to sit calmly, sit still. "Do not upset yourself," she keeps saying. He'd hardly known what it was to sit and watch the passersby, he always walking through the park.

The early sunlight comes and goes, the clouds drifting and dispersing. He sits back, eyes closed, and he can feel the sun on his face—the warmth and pinch of it and then, as it hides behind a cloud, the darkness and cool of shade. It goes on like that, back and forth, the sun burnishing his eyelids, then a swath of chill, until he falls into a gentle, lilting rest. He can feel Anarose get up and hears her footsteps drift away and a few moments later come back. She blocks him from the sun and then he feels a brush along his cheek. He opens his eyes to see her before him, marigolds in her hand.

"You offer me a bouquet of death," he says.

"What?"

"The marigolds. They symbolize death."

"Yes, I know, but you say the strangest things."

"But it is the truth."

"They are lovely just the same."

"Where did you find them?"

"A few dropped along the pathway. Left over from the markets, I think." She twirls them in her hand and brushes them across his face again. He looks at her, bent forward, her hair around her face, the flowers drawn close to her neck. She is smiling and then it vanishes as their eyes meet. He looks away, opening his satchel, removing a notebook. She sits down now, rummaging in her bag. She pulls out an apple and a green paring knife, trying to peel it.

"Here. Give that to me," he says. He takes the knife and apple, holding both firmly in his hands, and, in one even motion, he peels the skin, coiling. She laughs and then cuts the apple into pieces. She offers him a slice before eating most of the apple on her own.

He begins to draw lines, arcs.

"Oh, you with all your measurings and these drawings. Look at all these marks, all these equations. They own you, you know that?" she whispers, slumping back into the bench. He watches her now, her profile and pouting lips. Could he relinquish his fight, let it all go, simply stay here, live in Mexico City, allow gravity to do its work? He turns from her, unable to let his thoughts settle on that idea. It feels like the deepest form of betrayal—not only of Julia, but of his very self.

. . .

THE LETTER ARRIVES ON a Thursday in early May. A thin rectangle of blue, postmarked from the United States. The handwriting, a fine, legible print, is not in a hand that he recognizes. It is clearly not the letter he is expecting.

On this late afternoon he had walked through the Alameda, across the Zócalo and hurried into the post office, near closing hour.

"Voronkov," the clerk had said, "Austin Voronkov?"

"Yes. That's me."

"Letter," he said, and then had dropped the thin envelope on the counter, passing it toward Austin with a nudge of two fingers. He did not pick it up at first. He stepped back for a moment, looked down at his shoes, behind him once, twice, and then stepped forward to make sure that it was indeed addressed to him and not some mistake. He placed his palm across the letter and slid it off the counter, slipping it into his pocket. He wouldn't open it here. He'd wait. The letter resting in his coat like a heartbeat. He left the window at once as if he feared the postal clerk, realizing his mistake, might take it back from him. Ridiculous, he knew. Was it not addressed to Mr. Austin Alexandrovich Voronkov?

He stands now in the middle of the lobby. Hands at his sides. People passing him—bumping him. Why do they have to come so close, sideswiping him in such a way? He then nearly propels himself toward a corner, hand over his coat pocket as if such a gesture will be able to mute what shouts within. He can wait no longer. He removes the letter from the front interior pocket of his blazer. He tears open the back flap, but not before reading the address—known by instinct and yet remote, like a language one used to know. He wavers back and forth between the two extremes of near and far as if he is examining it beneath a telescope, aiming to get it all into focus, though his eyes are now blurred by tears.

> *Dear Father,*
>
> *I wanted to write myself so that you'd have it from me and not indirectly from mother, but I'm writing with very good news and can only hope that you actually do receive this letter. You know, we are never sure when we send things off to you and simply cross our fingers and hope for the best. But the good news—I'll be coming to Mexico*

City for six months. Father, I'm so happy to write to you with this
news and mother is overjoyed that I'll be going. You will just have to
wait a month and I'm sending this early to give you warning and to
prepare yourself. In the meantime, sending much love and I will
write again once I arrive, which will be on or about May 15.

Love,

Vera

Words written—facts. For two, nearly three minutes he cannot move. Austin lingers on the name and what it is about to do. Vera. Arrival. It is difficult to contemplate. She'd written it herself clearly, she'd stated that. Vera, his daughter, will be coming to Mexico City. His mind races in all directions. He tries to gather his thoughts, focus them, but thinking of Vera now, he sees a young girl, wondering how she can come all this way by herself. He is wracking his mind to race up to her years. He folds the letter, following its two marked creases. He slips it once again into the envelope and inserts it into his front pocket. He leans against the wall, staring at the people traversing the lobby—some halting before moving on, others performing a dramatic about-face, still others a relaxed pivot as if they have misplaced a thought and had to step back to retrieve it. After a few moments, he draws the letter out once more.

May 15. My God, he has no idea what day it is. He looks up for some sign of a calendar. Of course he knows it is Thursday, yes, but the date. Is it nearing the 15th? It seems just a handful of days ago that it was the first so the 15th, well, that is surely near, isn't it? Or maybe it has passed, he thinks in horror. But no, that's impossible. When did she mail the letter and how long had it taken to arrive? One never knows in this country, one just never knows. He scans the envelope for the postal date, difficult to read from the faded ink. The date must be written somewhere in this official building. He cannot find a single calendar, not even a polite little triangular cardboard calendar, quietly indicating the month, day, and year. Ludicrous for there not to be a calendar in a post office. He starts back for one of the postal windows, passing the line, excusing himself among the customers. *Just need to know the date*, he mutters to himself. *The date*. He hears himself asking, his voice coming to him loud and perhaps too overexcited so he checks himself, speaks softly again.

"Excuse me. Sir. Can you kindly tell me the date? I know it's Thursday, but what is the date?"

"May 12."

"May 12."

"That's right. May 12."

"Thank you." Okay. It's May 12. My God, May 12! She will arrive in three days. There are so many questions he nearly falls to the ground, his mind spinning. But now he has to get a hold of himself, calmly go about the rest of his days as if her looming arrival is the most natural thing in the world and not an occasion that to him sounds off in his mind like a trumpet, so that as he leaves the post office his thoughts stream ahead in counterpoint—at once tranquil and meandering, the next moment a blasting explosion of joy.

. . .

THURSDAY TURNED TO FRIDAY. Friday to Saturday, Austin's busiest day. Then, Sunday—long and spacious Sunday. For Austin, most Sundays lay before him in long vacant hours filled by a well-ordered routine that had not been disturbed since his first months in Mexico City. He would rise at 6:12 A.M. Not at 6 A.M. sharp. Too inhuman an hour. He would then set the water on to boil. As he waited, he took his aspirin bottle from the shelf above the stove and removed one pill. Next, he'd search for the X-Acto knife in his rectangular box of tools, cutting the aspirin tablet in half. He'd learned the precise pressure needed so that as he pressed on the knife, one half would not, as it often did, project across the room, falling into a crevice behind the counter, where, if he were to ever peer down with a light, he'd find a series of half-moons that had never risen, trapped amid dust and cobwebs. He'd then take a spoon from the sideboard—one of three spoons in total—crushing the half tablet with its curve. A fine powder. The chalky bits left, which he'd stir into a glass of water, drinking it on an empty stomach. In twenty minutes, the dull ache in his hands would disappear.

When the water was ready, he would make his coffee and a cup of tea and drink from each intermittently. He now preferred the dark, rich taste of coffee over the more mild, barky flavor of his tea, but he didn't give it up. He would then take both cups—cups of clay, an indent the size of a thumbprint on the handle—and, sitting at his table—for drafting, for eating—place each cup in front of him. His papers in the early morning light, white like alabaster. He drank from first the coffee, and, as the tea grew lukewarm, the tea. The morning continued caught between sips. In an hour, two hours, his drafting papers would slowly fill with his arcs and equations and notes scribbled along the paper's perimeter. Sundays would continue like this for hours. Then, he'd rise, a bit stiff in the legs, and take his late-afternoon walks in the Alameda.

Though on this Sunday, he is now in a bewildering situation. He reads the letter over as a reminder. A reassurance—Vera would be coming to Mexico. He reads it sometimes once. Most days two or three times.

It is too difficult to fully contemplate. How will he get through the next few hours, never mind the next few days? How will he contain himself, this expansiveness? He feels as if he is standing in sight of the ocean. My God, he hasn't seen the ocean in years! But never mind that now. Her pending arrival lifts his spirits, which are rising and threatening to float away. He has to check himself, do a kind of mental pivot and not forget his looming predicament. He aches for a walk. To walk and dwell on the idea of Vera's arrival. Where will she stay, for instance? He can assemble another bed. But he must remember Jack. He cannot run into him with all his taunts and persecutions. His presence sits in his mind like an irritating head cold, a faint pressure that he cannot locate, but that always makes its presence known—when he looks up from his work, when he turns his head too violently, when he yawns. And now all this sudden excitement. How much easier if he can simply sit before his papers, unaware of coming evening, disappearing within, drifting along on his ideas, for who knows what such hours preoccupied with other thoughts may force him to give up—a solution to a design issue?

It is already the in-between hour. Daylight descending, evening rising. He stands before his desk now, the window a gray square silent and still in periphery. His paths out in the city awaiting him. He wonders in a ridiculous moment if the Alameda would miss him. He dresses now, is somewhat grateful for a place to go, even if it is only the cantina down the street. A plate of food with each tequila purchased. He doesn't mind eating alone now. An old, forgotten self abhorred it. On Sundays in particular. Sometimes those afternoons the first years in Mexico City return to him in all their dry and brittle hours. Now, he has learned to contend with eating in solitude, he's resigned himself to it.

He stares into the mirror, shaving. The stubble along his jawline the color of iron. His eyes though still hold their sapphire blue. He draws his hand along his chin. In the Sunday afternoon's near silence he can hear the lonely sputter of a truck, the dripping faucet.

He dips the razor into the basin. In the mirror the window's reflection, and within its frame, the sun is the color of tiger lilies. He draws the razor across his face in careful, even strokes. The blade is sharp, cool. His thoughts without his realizing it turn to Anarose—drawn, like stepping toward a place of warmth. A moment of sun along an arm. A pocket of possibility, something to mull over every now and then. A palliative. She'd surprised him so, she with her broken clock, her scent, her smile. Determination, bashfulness too as if she'd thrown something to him and then had been unsure of herself, clamoring back to fetch it. He had to admit, she was distracting. In her red, T-strapped shoes, in her yellow blouse with blue flowers. Light material—silk, crepe. Something as soft as a petal. The slight flush to her cheeks, the dampness along an eyebrow.

When with Anarose, he'd taken an almost guilty pleasure in the fact that he could, for a moment, forget the years' yearnings, but it came with a price he knew. His vigilance lagging and his ideas vulnerable to anyone free to intuit his thoughts, to Jack and his persecutions, his seeming omniscience, watching. And then a flood of remorse—if he did not continue his unrelenting pursuit to get back to Julia, to get to America, what purpose would the years have served here? For an instant he feels them crumble in his hands . . . *In your loneliest moments, know I have them too, that I long for you to be with me, dear, and oh the children, they long for you as you long for them. . . .*

THE CANTINA'S TURQUOISE doors hang off the darkness. He does not like to use his hands to press them open. He's gotten one too many splinters from that action and had offered to sand the doors down, polish them too, but Miguel would not have it.

"What's the point? Anyone coming here will not feel the splinter when they leave." True, Austin thought.

He uses his shoulder to step into the cantina. Empty, save for the regular domino players with their shouting or laughter, the crash of wooden chips. The scent of onions stronger. Glasses white and clear, clinking as the waiter walks, balancing the tray, arms pulled in close to his sides.

Austin sits at a small round table in front of an open window. From here, he can see the bamboo trees that sway in the night. It is darker out now—navy, intense. The breeze with its insistence of a chill. A table erupts into laughter like plates clattering to the floor. Large platters of food line the bar. There is fruit salad, chopped papaya and watermelon. Beans and peppers. A small bowl of cilantro. Tortillas in their covered earthenware dishes. He has his first tequila and then rises to wait in line behind the others, workers mostly. Austin is careful to take only one serving, knowing he will return, ordering a second glass, taking two servings when no one is apt to notice.

"Austin," he says his name like a reprimand. Austin recognizes the voice at once. It can be heard over murmuring, quiet conversations. It is the same loud, grating voice, slightly gravelly, veering on a metallic abrasiveness. He stands in the narrow green frame made by the open jalousie doors.

"I will sit with you, if you don't mind," he says. Austin does not move. He feels he should leave now. Without a word, turn and walk fast down the street, across the avenue.

"I will get a plate of food first and then I will join you," he says. Austin turns to go back to his table near the window.

Jack joins him with a full plate, piled high with double servings. He sits hunched over his food, stabbing with his fork, taking large bites.

"Starving," he says as he delves in for a second bite. "You know the good establishments, don't you?" he says, mouth full of food. Austin shrugs his shoulders.

"I at least benefit from that. I appreciate it, let me tell you. Difficult to know which place offers the best food. You fit right in here, don't you? Tell me, you found work okay here your first years in Mexico?"

"I operated a lighthouse," Austin says, addressing no one in particular. Eyes on the ground as if the question came from the air.

"Lighthouse, copper mines, repairs," he says.

"I have learned to be versatile."

"Where was this?"

"Mazatlán."

"Mazatlán?"

"Yes. You know it?"

"A fishing port. Lots of activity there."

"Yes."

"Not easy work, that. Lighthouse work."

"I managed."

A table erupts into laughter. Austin shivers from the suddenness of it, and then the dying out. Silence. He can hear other voices far in the distance, a word or two wafting over the low walls of the back of the restaurant, settling on the night air.

"Two months, wasn't that what they told you and Julia?"

Julia. Her name had fallen between them—weighted with absence.

"How did you know?" Austin says.

"We have our ways of finding out these things. A mutual decision of course. Wise, at the time, considering the circumstances." Jack sits across from Austin. "Certainly, she can't come back. Of course, I don't blame her," Jack says, leaning forward, his eyes focused. There is a long pause. Jack is waiting for Austin's response. Austin sits still, unyielding. He will not give anything away. He will not divulge, forfeit his curiosity, but he does want to know exactly how much they know. He sighs. Looks around. "I am glad to run into you. I usually don't come here, but I am glad I did." With his other hand, he reaches across the table, and shakes Austin by the shoulder a bit. His hands are firm and strong, like marble. "A marvelous coincidence that we should meet in this very place, in such a large city, don't you think? What are the chances?" It was a phrase that lingered in Austin's mind, Austin knowing full well that Jack and his people had arranged it.

"Of course, I know most of your details from your file. Amazing what happened to you. I guess you don't like to think of it too much, too difficult to recall all of it—such a chaotic time, why go back to a bad time, right? And here we are again, after the Reds, mostly in Hollywood now, but before, it was you people, Russian immigrants. But as I interpret it, you thought you'd just set up a life in the Ukraine, isn't that right? Live a fine, simple life farming whatever it is you farm there—wheat, rye? I don't know. To have traveled all that way only to realize you are unwanted there too. A civil war will do that to people, Reds versus Whites. And we know your family were landowners—at the wrong place at the wrong time, it seems to me. Oh, but from what it sounded like, Julia would've followed you anywhere, really, even if you were off to Siberia, right? Who could've ever predicted this Stalin? Brutal. What's going on there now, just brutal. The labor camps. I wouldn't want to go back there. But Mexico—after everything, this country must've seemed like a paradise to you. I know the aim was always to get to the States, but now, though, well, I bet you think the worst the two of you ever did was agree to part. In this crazy time, you just can't do that. I know you think your inventions will get you in some way."

"If you don't prevent it."

"Why do you think we didn't allow you entry in the first place? It must have been hard, though, having them leave you, but then again I suppose you've grown accustomed to doing a lot of leaving in your life."

"I was to follow her. In two months they said. Two months!"

"But all that time in Cananea—Austin, I am surprised you never tried crossing the border. It's right there."

"No."

"And so you're telling me that you never tried, never even stepped across?"

"No."

"Why not? It was much easier then. Sometimes even a mile away from the border port of entry, people going back and forth right under the noses of the border patrol, smugglers at your beck and call. Of course, I suppose you had a reason to be fearful. I can't blame you for that. No country. That'll make you feel vulnerable in this world. Like you're standing outside without a coat your whole life."

"I must go," Austin says, rising. He is looking out the door.

"Now? Right this minute?"

"I just now forgot something."

"No you didn't. Don't forget I know your routine. Almost as if it were my very own. Like clockwork, really. Right about now, you'll go to the Alameda, wandering, walking, and then in about an hour, two hours, I'll find you at work, drafting." Jack says all this while glancing at his watch and then looking back to Austin. "I am right, I see, by the slight blush across your face."

"You have no right to speak to me this way."

"I'm merely taking notice."

"How dare you come here and disturb me like this."

"Careful, don't get so hot tempered. You must see that there is a reason why we keep your type out."

"You cannot begin to understand my type."

"I know what I see. I know what your file says."

"You know nothing."

. . .

CANANEA, SONORA, MEXICO

1930–36

COPPER CAN BE TRICKY. In some lights—a morning's blue before the sun, the violet gray of evening—it can be dull and opaque hiding in a guise of stone, rock. The sun rising, setting will reveal copper's brilliantine surface—sometimes a sheaf of copper as thin as paper, deposits of it spread across the surface of a rock face. Other times, it's in boulder form. The scent is briny, cloying, during the smelting. The solid softens. The smell never leaves.

Austin worked in the copper mines of Sonora. In the mining town of Cananea, which, before it was a mining town, was a land of Apaches. *Cananea*. The Apaches' word for horsemeat. A land of copper too. Rich in copper. The great quarries rose-hued in some lights. A scarred earth, copper emerging out of rock and dirt, reddish against the camel-colored dust. The quarry like a canyon, steps carved into ore. The embers burned in the hills at night. Carts of molten, smelted copper gliding along the quarry paths, carts rumbling like far distant thunder, carts blazing like torches to a ritual, beacons with no messages to impart—no signs of safety or of conquest.

The land beyond the mines is wide and empty, a craggy terrain. There are solitary nopals or agave cacti, a yucca plant's spiky leaves black beneath a cobalt sky. The fragile wooden barracks are humbled by the otherwise barren, desolate land and the open, empty sky stretched tight above the Sierra Madre, the Sonora River, and the neighboring towns of San Pedro, Naco, Agua Prieta.

COPPER IS APHRODITE'S ELEMENT. No wonder it's a place that can break your heart.

Then, in the 1930s, the lands were owned by several California copper capitalists, the ones whose families owned homes in the hills, the hills where the Chinese grocers delivered crates of tomatoes, green beans, cigarette papers and tobacco, molasses and sugar. The mining town barracks sat on the outskirts of the mines, far, but not so far that one couldn't see the molten copper at night, the carts of blazing embers along the hillside. The blue flames the hottest, burning to white, then blue, then amber, orange. At night, one could stand on the mesa, a mile off from the pit, with its ridges like the seats in an ancient amphitheater, watching the wooden carts follow paths to the right, then left, then right and left again, slowing slightly at the narrow turns.

"Stare long enough and it's like one is staring at beads of fire on an abacus," a fellow engineer had said when showing Austin around.

AUSTIN HEARD ABOUT THE work on a trip from Mazatlán to Hermosillo. In 1927 the companies had begun to send out labor agents wearing placards—to the city, the coast towns, the farmlands, to the places they knew—to find the immigrants and migrant workers, the Yaquis and the farmers, all willing and in desperate need of work. The placards read: "Electricity. Running Water." The men walked back and forth in the train depots passing out flyers.

They built a home there in the land of Cananea, in 1930. In the two-room barracks house. A shack of raw wood really, filled with splinters. He'd sanded it down, but the splinters were endless—on the porch, along the beams of the slotted wooden railing, the stairs. The children always with a fresh white bandage wrapped around a thumb, a heel. The interior was shadowy and dim. A meager light came from the small saltbox windows in the morning hours, a light that grew stronger, more persistent as the day wore on. They got to keeping the door open—Julia's idea. It lets in the most light, she'd said once to his concern about danger.

"No one comes around," she'd told him in response.

"True." He couldn't argue with that, but in her voice, the "no one" echoed. She'd missed her family, her first home, and in this open space, during those long hours and the lingering weeks, there was time for the stillness that allows loneliness to enter, reflection too—enough to absorb the distances; the ties to what was once home stretched far and thin, nearly severed.

SHE WROTE LETTERS. She wrote every day. Sometimes two in a day—letters to her sister, her mother.

"What do you write from one day to the next? You know they both read them anyway so there's no need to write to each one separately."

"Oh, you'd be surprised the thoughts that flit through my mind when you're off digging for gold."

"It's copper, my dear Julia, copper. The best conductor of a little something called electricity."

"Yes. I know, I know."

He made her a desk. Two planks, smooth and sanded, balanced across bases of wooden milk crates. She liked to write with the door open so that, in the periphery, she could see first the shaded gray of the porch and then the way it gave onto the whiteness of the Sonoran afternoons.

We deliver ourselves through letters. He understood that soon enough. She was writing herself out of Cananea, out of Mexico. After she and the children had left and he'd been there on his own, six months, seven, he walked around in what he could only decide was her discarded solitude, like a garment tattered from overuse. He couldn't deny her that loneliness—he gone for sometimes up to two weeks, required, as the foreman, to stay at the works full through, the children at the company's school all day. Some weeks he was let out days early due to an equipment problem, lack of labor, but he never knew before leaving just when he'd be back and so the good-byes now linger in his mind as stagings, intimations of the larger, future parting even if he was only a mile away. He was always stunned and awkward with her tears. She, tense, tight, hands wringing. They seemed to be both standing in awe, overwhelmed by the chasm of sorrow that seemed to crack open within her.

"A letter travels so easily. Why can't we?" she'd said one night. This, after he'd been home for a few days. That week's inevitable parting upon them, the night darkening as the horizon disappeared into black, and with the burning copper and the stars out all simultaneous, one couldn't distinguish between land and sky, sky and land.

"I wrote a letter today," she'd begin in the silence after dinner. He'd come to wait for it, the day ending with its horizon in bands of blue, apricot, pale yellow deepening into blackness.

"To whom?"

"My sister." He knew the answer.

She sat, bending forward, her torso pressed into her thighs so that her chin was nearly propped on her knees, her forearms clasped around her shins. The yellow light of the porch illuminated the rectangle of her letter. She clasped it between both hands, and, held that way, he could make out her fine script.

It was their routine. The pauses between each letter reading a way to extend the pleasure of this small ritual, these habits of their domesticity— this, her eventual, evening reading, letters she had written and was about to send, letters to her sister who was trying to plead their case, trying to get the entire family, Austin included, reinstated.

Silence.

"And are we going to hear it?"

Cananea

September 9, 1930

Dear sister Catherine,

We are in what they call here the Desierto, which is not desert as we know it, but more a wilderness, and is it ever quiet, especially with the children gone during the school hours. If you could only know this silence. And there is nothing around. No neighbors, mostly officials, that is all. Not the neighborly kind either. The only entertainment is when we receive a letter so do please keep them coming. We so love to hear news of home and all your doings. All I have while Austin is at the works and while the children are at school are the cars that go by or any that happen to stop in front of the house.

Now that we are somewhat settled (after all our travels), with Austin as a foreman here at the mine—he does work ever so hard and they don't ask too many questions here which is a relief—I can

begin to make a case on our behalf, and work toward reinstatement.

I shall write again regarding our efforts.

Your loving sister,

Julia

Cananea

September 28, 1930

Dearest Mother,

It's now what they call the dry season here and is it ever dry with

enough dust to keep me always sweeping. It seems that I can't ever

sweep enough. How I do miss grass. It's never something one thinks

about missing, is it? Well, you'll laugh to know that I'm sitting

here and right outside the front door is a cactus.

Now, to business. I have been corresponding with Senator

Tierney, who, in all these years that we have been trying to return

back home, is the first human I have encountered. Every one of the

officials have said they could do nothing without the permission of

the Immigration Department. And now to finally have some clear

directions as to how to proceed with efforts to get reinstated. As you

know, due to the Cable Act, I now qualify for a visa and will need

to go to the Consulate here in Nogales, who in the past has not been

helpful and quite unfriendly, and suspicious of Austin. But they tell

us that if the children and I receive a visa and return to the U.S. we

will have a better chance of getting Austin reinstated. By then, I

will be an American citizen again, you see, and can work all that

much more, with more power to get him home with us. Of course,
the authorities will realize the humane aspect of this. How can they
possibly let a young mother and her three children live away from
husband and father at a time like this? No. I am an optimist and do
believe we will succeed on every front.

Your loving daughter,
Julia

Cananea
November 3, 1931

My dear Catherine:
The children are learning Spanish. How strange, Catherine, to hear
these words come out of their little voices. "Mas, mas," they ask
when wanting more food. How ever are these my children, I wonder?
There are no other Russians here so I'm afraid Austin is quite
lonely—that is, there is no one for him to speak to in his native
language as we had when in Constantinople and then more so in
Paris. How much he misses his countrymen. Even me, I cannot give
that to him, knowing only a few words of Russian, but we try to
keep up with the traditions, give the children some sense of Austin's
culture. But you should see him—with his dark black hair and his
skin darkened so by this sun, he looks just like one of the Mexicans.
I call him an Indio. He fits right in.

Your loving sister,
Julia

Cananea

November 22, 1932

Dearest Mother:

We received your letter today and what a joy it is always to see your fine print. I have come to recognize it like I would your very face. The man at the company store teases me so and I believe if it were not for his kindness, I may not get even half of your letters as the mailman, who comes delivering the mail on the burros, is not diligent and often a letter disappears.

> *Your loving daughter,*
> *Julia*

Cananea

January 12, 1933

Dear Catherine:

I want to thank you for writing such clear, succinct letters to the Senators. You should be proud—and tell mother this—that you are communicating with such esteemed men in public office. I do believe Senator Tierney, though I have never met him, is a good man who genuinely feels for our situation, and, as his letters have illustrated, is working hard to secure a way for me and the children, and God willing, Austin, to travel back to all of you. It is what I pray for most.

> *Your loving sister,*
> *Julia*

Cananea

March 15, 1933

Dear sister Catherine:

I do believe it won't be much longer and the Consul tells us that too. So we will settle for the time being and wait for word. The consul says to return in a few months' time, but I wonder if that means one to two months or several months. A funny phrase, that—"a few months' time," vague, sitting on either side of hope, either soon or not soon enough.

Just yesterday (Sun.) we went to a neighboring town where the company held a carnival. The children were overwhelmed with such excitement. Poor dears, they never have seen such color, brightness, toys and games. The border runs through this town, cuts it right in half. So close. You can see the other side, almost throw yourself over it, really.

> *Your loving sister,*
> *Julia*

Cananea

April 2, 1933

Dearest Mother:

I do wonder if you've had any word from Senator Tierney. They've given us such hope here thinking that if the children and I can come home, we'll have more of an argument and case to plead on Austin's behalf. He is just about the most hardworking, kindest man, and it's absolutely silly of them to think he'd do any harm. Oh just thinking

of it makes me furious. And they've got us so worried here at the

Nogales Consulate, with all their questions and suspicions. There is

never any rest from thinking they will take Austin away. It stays

with us always. Oh, but they must let him in. How can they not?

Where would he go and what would happen to him? But I do hope

what they say here is true. Perhaps I'll get a letter from you with

news before this one reaches you. We are just now preparing for the

rainy season and as much as I've complained about the dust—from

the dirt yes, but also from the copper smelter which is a very

particular kind of dust, lighter than dirt dust, more of a resin that is

light and diffuse and enwraps everything in a bronze cloud—I'll be

writing you mud-stained letters with raw hands from all the

washing I'll be doing.

> *Your loving daughter,*
> *Julia*

Cananea

May 1, 1934

My dear Mother and sister Catherine:

Well, what I've long awaited to write you news of has finally

become a reality. Dearest sister and mother, the children and I have

been granted a visa and very soon—I'm so delighted to tell you I

can hardly write fast enough—we'll be reunited with you. I'm due

to secure our visas at the Consulate in Nogales. From there, we'll

then take the Mexico Central Line and change in Chicago for the

New York line. You can expect us sometime in late June. I'll post a
telegram from the railroad when in Chicago.
    I only hope Austin will be safe and well here without us.

      Your loving daughter and sister,
      Julia

This is what Austin came to know: the evening readings of her letters were a buffer. They were a way for her to share (indirectly) her longing to be home, though she was not aware of it when she read openly as if she were speaking to her sister one-on-one, those words between women, words not meant for his ears. And he'd found it so endearing, the innocent way she'd read to him, her soft, warm voice filling the night, all the while he listening, aware of the significance of each line.

After a week at the mine, sometimes two, he'd return to the barracks, to their home now empty and disordered. He washed with the soap Julia made him, dry and cracked from disuse during his days away. Other nights, before dark he walked the half mile to the company's store, where the Yaqui miners sat in a row under the shaded overhead, chewing sugar and molasses cakes.

"Another letter for you, Voronkov," the storekeeper said on this night close to eleven months from their departure.

"Is that right?"

Silence.

"Tobacco. And that paper back there please."

The sun was setting and Austin walked the route he took from the company store to his barracks house, a route he knew by sensation alone, the temperature dropping on his right and the late day sun, still hot and brittle, on his left. He passed the other barracks houses and nodded to the few workers seated on the front porch, knowing he would hear the flurry of whispers as he reached his fifth step past them. He did not speak to many, only out of necessity and then it was rare—work, when at the store, a few sentences only, "Paper please," "Pack of Faros," "Yes," "Thank you." He was not empty-handed on this particular walk. He held an envelope in one hand and a package of paper beneath his arm. In his habit, he had not yet opened the letter, rather enjoyed the press of it in his palm, the envelope still sealed like a secret and its scent fresh from the canvas mailbag, allowing the walk to delay the reading so that he could look forward to absorbing her words alone and free from the eyes of others.

How thirsty he was, he realized upon entering the front door, the screen banging behind him as he walked into the room, which, because he kept the shutters closed all day, still held the early morning air, air not touched by the heat. His step on the floorboards caused the unavoidable creaks and pops in concert with the shutters tapping and closing in the breeze, a racket that caused him to drop his bag of purchases (tomato, can of beans, cigarettes) on the table and cross the room to secure the shutter as the yellow-gold light from the end of the day filled the floorboards in their isolated parallel lines. He cleared his throat and hummed as he set out the can with a little bang of confirmation, the tomato already bruised and soft on one unfortunate side, and the pack of Faros, which fell from his hand with a light clicking sound as it hit the table. Then, he turned on the radio he'd made himself—copper wire and magnets. Loud at first and then softening as Austin lowered the volume with the crude knob (a button attached to a thimble), which required the lightest of touches to maneuver.

He took the letter and his Faros and sat on the porch railing in near darkness, the faintest lip of white edging the horizon like a baseboard. He smoked one cigarette to completion and then tore open the letter, this one handwritten on thin, newsprint pages, the palest of gray pinks.

Connecticut, 1934

Dear Austin,

. . . You are in our thoughts and prayers constantly. In your loneliest moments, know I have them too, that I long for you to be with me, dear, and oh the children, they long for you as you long for them. If I had the money, I would take the train all the way back to you, though I know, it's as you say—if you can hardly support yourself, how would you be able to support a wife and three children, and you are right—they shall grow up as Americans. After this, after everything, that is the least we can come out of from this dreadful situation. I do hope you are eating well, that you are occupied and that you stay strong in mind and body. I write to the senators and congressman almost weekly. . . .

He folded up the letter. *Eating well.* Eat? Was he hungry? Some days he could not tell. Of course he was, he had felt moments when his stomach growled. He would make something—the beans, slice the tomato. Still, he sat, the letter folded and tucked into the front pocket of his shirt. He took another cigarette from his pack, smoking, the sound of his exhale loud as any voice. *Write to the congressman weekly.* He could see her poised over her desk as she'd been here, the frown of concentration, the indents, half wrinkle, and perhaps she sat with hand on her chin, wondering at how best to make these men in power understand, to write the human element of the story and not just the facts—black and white, with dates and accounts, countries and borders. What did it all mean? Nothing.

Inside, he placed the letter with all the others in a crate under the bed. A whole pile of them—some in pencil, others in her tight script, and still more typed front and back so that it was difficult to read, the print from one side showing through beneath the other as if she couldn't quite say enough and so her words fell over and under each other, tripping almost in a hurry to say, *I miss, I miss.* It was as if the words, like the ones she'd sent from Cananea home, now did an about-face and started pouring out in the other direction, as if she'd suddenly realized—horrified— that home was not where she was now, but with him and she'd maybe regretted the leaving now that it was taking so long for him to come.

It was now close to a year.

Cananea, 1935

Dear Julia,

I can imagine what a surprise it still is to your mother and sister to have you back—their long lost Julia, "my Julia," and in addition three children they've never seen before. I am quite happy they are out of this wilderness. It is not the place to raise children. However, I am lonesome without you all, my dear family. I miss you to the point of it being unbearable. I only hope the children aren't too much trouble for you. Children need a father. Then, they are good. Aussie—he's as you state. Too boisterous, yes. Really, he is one restless fellow. I just remember that I was not a penny worth better when of his age, but I do love him. If he's too much mischief, please correct him and sometime overlook him and suggest to him right manners. Oh, that rolling ball Leon. He is a real pet of mine. All the fun I had with him. While, Vera, my dearest baby girl. I know that she loves her daddy greatly. Well, tell her dear to be happy and that I will be soon with her. . . .

The border was close—a mile beyond the mine and one could stand before it quite easily, as Austin stood now after a long walk. The hand-painted placards were driven far into the ground with a black line down the middle, "U.S.A." written lengthwise on one side of the line, "Mexico" on the other. He'd been as close as this many times.

"It's easy enough to cross," a fellow foreman had told him in the first months after they'd left. "A few years back, in the twenties, much easier. Cows, all the cattle too, grazing back and forth across the line." He'd said this fanning his arm through the air, an easy back and forth to denote crossing.

"Yes, but I'm not cattle."

"I bet some days, though, you wish you were."

"True, true." Laughter. But he was Russian. That identity was vanishing, just like the country itself. It was 1934. The Americans still feared the Red Menace, the border guards on the lookout for any Reds coming up through South America, intent on revolution. It no longer mattered that he was a husband and a father. The world did not care. He stared across the border. It was not just that he felt Julia across that line and the children too, a two-thousand-mile line stretching west to California's Pacific and east along Texas. He was there as well, or a version of a self, his other, parallel self, that industrious, proud man who was granted his visa (such a small thing to want after everything), the man who escorted his wife and children aboard that train and then sat with them in the leather banquette seats as it crept out slow and steady from the Cananea station, picking up speed onward to Nogales and breaking fast through the border so that they didn't even know it when they'd crossed it, not until they'd reached far into Texas with its skies as big as Mexico's. He saw the man who watched that big sky country fill up with hills, as the train kept steady toward the smaller skies of New England. And when he liked to think big and stretch his imagination far to cross every boundary—real or imagined—he'd see himself living that other life, certain of his position, living without any fear, these images running alongside him, streaming and stretching back and forth across the line the way we carry our past with us, our futures too. He'd be that man. Not this one—the one in Cananea: the border a separation; the place of closest connection.

THE SECOND ANNIVERSARY OF their departure. Austin lay asleep, his heart pounding not in fear but in expectation of an arrival, his whole being open to the moment he'd embrace them, see their familiar faces. He was damp with sweat, disoriented as he woke at 5 A.M., his eyes adjusted. He lay hot under the covers save for his shoulder exposed to the chilled, early morning air. From the front room, he could hear a floorboard letting out a familiar crack and he threw off the covers, sitting up, still expectant, eager. His heart raced and grew loud in his ears as he listened for more signs of their presence. This time the humming was louder and he was certain of it, knew the melody, a children's nursery rhyme? His feet hit the floor, tingling from the cold. He was certain that it was their voices he heard in the next room over. They must be near—there, beyond the door. Julia's humming, the quiet absorbed play, the soft click of blocks. He was smiling so hard his cheeks hurt. Tears sprang to his eyes. They'd come back to him! She'd gone and done as she wrote in one of her letters. *Take the train all the way back to you.* In an instant, he would embrace them, but he was walking such a long way and still he could not step over the threshold. He could hardly bear to open the door, to see their faces, knowing eyes. Yes. It would be them for certain. He could see the cool, milky morning light from under the bedroom door and his stomach growled as he realized the hour—5 A.M., drowsy, empty.

He pushed on the door and took in the front room. The small, square windows placed at shoulder height let in two long beams of gray-white light.

"Julia," he half whispered. He cleared his throat and then called her name once more. This time louder. Where had they gone? He stood in the center of the room, turning around. A minute passed. He retraced his steps to the bedroom, and then back in through the front room, to the porch, their voices trailing him like tracers. Turning around, he stood in the frame of the front door, looking into the small barracks house—the light through the windows, the air holding on to a stark, steadfast silence. He stepped back outside and moved to the porch steps, shaking the voices from his mind, yet trying to hold on to that joyful certainty of having been near to his family. The dream lingered through the now-tarnished morning of their absence and when a moment of it came back—murky, incoherent—the infusion of feeling was one that he could only recognize as joy.

By 7 A.M. the sun had changed the light to a soft amber glow. He remained standing, watching the day begin to arrive, staring, near-catatonic as the gradual, incremental sorrow sank in, intruding on his day, wanting to stop time, but knowing the minutes would keep coming and soon it would be hot and the heat and white sunlight would take him far from this moment, their presence, the dream, all still fresh in his mind and the hours of the day waiting. Friday. The workday ahead, the interminable weekend—two concrete blocks of days he'd have to chip through with a chisel. He would feign it though, pretend to fall in with the raucousness toward the evening, playing cards, drinking tequila with the workers before they traveled back to their remote villages, where they'd eat big meals, and stroll arm in arm on Sunday with a sweetheart. He was sitting now on the porch and found himself occupied by the efforts of the ants that busied themselves on his windowsill. He laughed in what he knew was a bitter, tired way, in awe at how the little creatures lifted and carried crumbs and sticks, tiny heads holding high a load twice their size—nature's engineering.

IT'S EASY ENOUGH TO CROSS, he heard the foreman's voice. But he had not crossed the ocean twice to end his days with ice and a pickax, languishing in a labor camp. And to stay?

THE CONSULATE IN NOGALES is a low-roofed, single-floor structure. One room in front. One room in back. It is almost always closed. He'd gotten a ride with a group of migrant workers. He'd had to sit in the back of the truck and so arrived with a fine film of dust on his face and in his hair. He stood outside the consulate, combed his hair—one, two strokes along the left side, one stroke for the right, his part now visible. In the reflection of the window, his face blurred as his focus shifted to three men crossing the street. He could just make out their faces beneath the brims of hats, neckties cinched tight around starched collars. Eyes concealed in dark shadows, mouths moving as they conferred. He placed the comb in his front pocket and turned to face the men, who were upon him, close enough for him to see the lines etched deep into foreheads, along the corners of their still-moving mouths. They passed him and walked into the consulate. He followed, a little reluctant, a little cautious, pausing to check his reflection in the door's glass before walking from the bright day into the dimly lit room.

HE WAS SURPRISED NOT to find the three men he'd seen enter. Surely, they'd be standing at the front desk, but they were nowhere to be found. He wondered if he'd half imagined them, when, as he approached the front desk, he heard men's voices in low, secret discussion, the suit sleeve of one of the men now visible through a half-closed door. The man made eye contact with Austin, looked away, and then closed the door. He turned back to the room, a single ceiling fan turning slow and apathetic above the clerk at the reception desk, a Mexican family sitting on wooden chairs lined along the front window. Why had the man looked at him with such a strong gaze, and then shut the door so abruptly? Not a good sign, he thought, as he took a seat beside the family. Not good at all, he thought, sitting on his hands and leaning forward a bit in his chair before sitting back to take a less anxious pose, shoulders pressed into the back of the chair, legs outstretched, one crossed over the other, in repose. A confident posture. Let them open the door and shut it in my face once more, he thought. Let them see me seated here in this way.

. . .

"You said maybe a month, two," Austin said. He was seated before the Nogales consul, wondering if the man remembered him at all, remembered his Julia and their children. He'd once been considerate, accommodating then, had left them with some hope.

"I make no promises," he said now, eyes hard.

"You men and your power," Austin said under his breath. He shook his head and stared out the window.

"Mr. Voronkov, it is not easy with this anarchist charge. You must have patience."

"It has been two years."

"Anarchy is taken very seriously, you see."

"I am not an anarchist. My wife is an American. My children— You see, if I can simply enter the country, I will show them I am not an anarchist. I will—"

"It does not work that way."

"And what am I to do for them down here?"

"We can petition again, but it takes up to a year."

"A year?"

"Yes."

1936. The men in white muslin are back. White tunics and pantaloons. A red sash around the waist. Their hats wide and flat. He sees them once every month or so. They pass by his barracks house sometimes in groups of three or five. They stare at him, smoldering gazes, accusatory and patient, as if they knew a secret about him.

He'd been thinking hard, running through a pattern of an idea, the position of the hoist chain for the cement block lifter, his thoughts wandering off to his boys and his baby girl, *be good to your mother.* Telepathy. They might even be able to hear him. Did they remember the sound of his voice? "Papa's funny accent," they always used to tease him. And he'd been working all that morning, three hours or more spent at the desk he'd built for Julia, trying a new idea from all angles so that he'd run out of the last bit of paper and was forced to go out to the company store. How much he did not like to venture out on a weekend when the mining barracks were more desolate and empty than during the week. Chalk days is what they were, brittle and breaking—it was running smack into their absence and it hurt and stung like any lash of a whip he'd ever felt. And he'd run into one of the men in muslin. Hard, cold stares and silence. "What do you want from me?" he'd asked the man, and then walked away, onward toward his house.

Now, he is watching them cross in front of his barracks house, slow strides, two front, three behind. They never speak to him. Just stare. Not a blink of eye or movement of head. Nothing. He steps out on the porch, better to let them know he knows they are watching. He walks down the steps and makes as if he's mending the railing that lines the porch. Best not to let them wonder at what he might be doing inside, let them think he is a man with a house to attend to, fixing the loose boards. With his hammer he begins to knock on one of the wooden railings. Will they see that there is no nail? They watch him for what seems an hour, but it could be only five minutes. Or is it? He is hammering, sweating.

He stands tall, arching his back, and runs his palm along the banister. "Shit," he yells and looks into his palm where a long splinter the length of a needle has lodged itself into his thumb. The men are still watching. He can see them out of the corner of his eyes and all it took was one man to enter his rooms, hold a rifle to his chest and demand his papers, his inventions, taking his notebooks. His hand is throbbing, but he will not let go of his grip on the banister, he will show them that he is simply a man working on his house. When he turns around the men are small as toys, far up into the hills, hardly visible save for their shadows, which stretch sideways on the ground.

Cananea, 1936

Dear Julia,

How I do miss all of you dearly—my wife and children. When I think of the good times we had. I can only hope for a future when we are all together. I am working, and thank goodness for that—I have my work. Without it I do feel these hours would seem useless for I must say this is a lonely place. I know not a soul. All are strangers to me, and for a man like myself—rather peaceful and calm of nature—it is not easy for me to always face people I do not know whose customs are so different. I am afraid that I spend my time in the barracks house, working on my inventions. I do have a wonderful new invention—a stationary hydro-propeller for steamships. . . . I have also corresponded with the D.C. patent office. Of course, what will they make of me here in Mexico, but I've explained my situation thoroughly and can only hope they will accept my ideas. If they do, we will all benefit, and mostly you my dear Julia, who I've written on my application as a sole benefactor of any monies earned. We shall see what they write me. And I hope they will accept my oath of a single inventor. Being alone here, I had to sign the witness as God.

. . .

AUSTIN SOON DEVELOPED A series of pastimes for the weekends. He'd wander through the vacant works, closer to the border, not altogether unpleasant at times to walk within the shadow of the machinery at rest, lying quiet and unused, the smell of copper lingering, a screech of metal as wind blew dust into gears. Vultures sat atop the hoist and the cement blocks, and on his walks he stopped to watch them—their sternums pulsing, fast undulating breath.

Other days he ventured farther along the border. He was only one man, and all he need do was walk calmly across it, and continue. One foot in front of the other. All the way across the open expanse like any farmer surveying his land, and he'd walk not parallel to the border as his pathways took him now, but perpendicular, a simple repositioning of the body. And he would stumble upon a town, and as long as he spoke to very few, he would then walk to the next one over, and the one after that before finding water and food, and maybe he would take a situation, an odd job or two—fix car engines. He would save enough for a rail ticket—he would need $25 for the ticket, a month or two of work. No more. His hopes lifted like a small prop plane along a runway and for a while it was all clear before him—the sky, the ground. The border placard reached knee height and if he kicked it with his boot it would fall down into the dust and brambles. He could see that, he could make sense of it, the openness, but he stood still and before he knew it his mind was wandering down pathways, as he imagined Julia's letters to the congressman and senators, next, his own walks to the consulate, the company store, his meandering along the edge of the border, at the end of each journey, each trip he felt the weight of a heavy door like a tomb. The consulate in

Nogales, the patent officers, his ideas, all of them together formed in his mind an impenetrable barrier and he saw it as paper—a clean, white boundary filled with an incriminating fact—he was an anarchist, a threat, a dangerous, subversive element. And then he stood tall, shoulders pressed back, staring out across the border, and for an instant he was back in the cement block cell, hearing the taps through the walls, the men and their questions, an endless barrage that seemed to afflict and wound him, and he felt a terrible shudder, a quaking at the exposure, alone. He cowered back, ashamed and broken, and when he could look no more, he crouched on the ground to bury his head in his hands.

He wept, his eyes blinded by the tears. He tugged at the ends of his hair. The dirt scratched at his ankles, and the dust stuck to his damp, sweaty forehead, soon to pour down his brow and neck. The beads of sweat formed along his back, tears rolled down his face, and his heart felt dry and parched with anguish as he felt something break, a deep terrible split, like a tendon torn, his heart beating faster, a sinking feeling as if he were falling from a great height, though when he looked he knew he was on the ground, and the tearing pulled and stretched and, as much as he tried to throw himself across, he felt it all fall away from him.

A truck passed, its wheels kicking up dust in clouds of misty sparkle. Austin rose, placed his hat on his head and turned to face the road two yards from the border. The truck windows were down and someone had a radio on, the static and scratch like tangled twigs of a bird's nest. A man's voice was booming through the static. The words were in Spanish or maybe not. It was hard to tell through the interference, not on the right frequency, something off there, he thought. The voice surrounded him, in an accusatory tone, but he was not certain.

The voice trailed off into buzz and noise and then the truck sped farther off. The sun overhead was hot and bright. His jaw locked tight, his eyes watering slightly, and a stillness came over him, nearly paralyzed. His heart raced. He pivoted to look behind him, took in the horizon on all sides, the white sky above him, and the sun temporarily blinded him so that he saw blackness and then red and then light. He closed his eyes, feeling a vertigo. He stumbled, breathing hard and trying to relax his mind, struggling to gain a foothold as he opened his eyes to see the horizon slanted on an angle, tilting, as if the earth had been momentarily jarred off its axis and then back again.

The man stood twenty yards from him, a dark shadow underfoot. The sun reflected off the man's watch, the sheen of his polished shoes. He did not know where the man came from, and the barracks and the mines were a far ways off from where he stood at this lone, abandoned border placard, though he knew about the patrols—the border agents, the FBI, the Mexican police, even the Soviet agents were here. He looked behind him and across the border placard, searching for any sign of a car or truck, for any others, a horse even. Nothing. The man did not move, simply stared at Austin, and then he began to open and close his mouth, but Austin could only hear a kind of roaring tumult and then a piercing ringing, his heart seemed to flex as if it were a hand opening and closing within his chest. The man took a step toward Austin, then another, still his mouth was moving, but Austin could not make out what the man was saying. He tried to steady himself with the now-still line of the horizon. When he turned back, the man was flanked by others, they held their bayonets in dirty, rough hands, five of them in all, their bast boots in rags. One was holding a cigarette between lips, Siberian blue eyes like his own, a sapphire now dulled to white gray, and beyond them in the hills the red flags were in wait. He looked to the border and then back again. The men were gone. Austin was left alone.

. . .

THE MINE CLOSED IN 1937—the depression's victim. He heard about
work for the electric company in Mexico City. They needed engineers to
inspect the machines. They'd take him without any working papers. He
would get a recommendation from the Anaconda company, continue his
case with the more senior consulate in Mexico City, and lose himself,
find safety, in the balm of the city's anonymity.

. . .

MEXICO CITY
1948

SHE STANDS BEFORE THE French doors that lead from the bedroom to the balcony. The olive green curtains are drawn, the sun lining the edges like a frame. She is up before the others. She draws her poppy red robe tight around her waist, placing her hand on the doorknob, cool to the touch. She winces and draws in her stomach as she turns the brass handle. It makes such a loud noise upon opening and she fears waking anyone in this house full of people she hardly knows. Best to simply get it over with in one swift thrust. The light grazes her chestnut curled hair, pouring into the room in one long diagonal. She slips out onto the lip of the balcony that overlooks Avenida Amsterdam, drawing the door closed behind her.

It is a warm May morning. She blinks in the brightness. The wrought iron railing is cast in shadow along the red flagstone floor of the balcony. She leans back against the doors, her shoulder blades pressing into the glass. She places the arch of her bare foot on the lower rung of the railing, dragging it back a little so that her toes curve into the iron, cold still from the night. She pulls her cigarettes from the deep side pocket of her robe. She lights up, the smoke mixing with the air. Leaves lie scattered across the street and sidewalks like pencil shavings.

Like at home, it is here on mornings like this, in the quiet and stillness before the day begins, that she loses herself in memory. She stares down the line of windows—watery and watchful—so much like the many years that had piled up now to bring her back to Mexico. Sometimes, when she was younger and walking with her mother, she'd catch a profile, a sudden flick of a match to light a cigarette that would cause in her a reverberation, the shudder of remembrance—at first a cool memory of far distant happiness and then a burning longing. Sometimes she would keep the moment, freeze it for a pleasurable, lolling few seconds, pretending that the man was her father, and that he was merely out in the city, at work, or away on a business trip, soon to be on his way back to her and the family. She is ashamed that she does this still. After so many years. She is older now. No longer that eight-year-old with such girlhood longings. No longer she who had once—and still in the way she recounts it—been his baby girl.

She thinks again of her father. She is worried about who and what she might find. The letters he sent home always left everyone feeling guilty and sad. They were sometimes loving, sometimes angry and questioning. Why had no one come to visit him? How could they ever explain the truth? "He'd die of shame," her mother always said. They were forbidden to let him know how much they were struggling, with barely enough money to eat, never mind an extravagance like train tickets. But to live knowing he felt abandoned? Oh, it was a futile situation. She ached to think of it even now, now that she was here, really here—in Mexico City in search of her father.

These thoughts are only a few stolen moments of reflection before she will go back inside, and prepare for the day ahead. She hesitates and then tosses her cigarette off the balcony, her gaze tracing the arc of its fall.

. . .

HER ACCEPTANCE INTO the work exchange program came with Spanish lessons and the promise of secure employment as either a receptionist, if you knew how to operate the phone keyboards, or a secretary, if you could type forty words per minute. She knew how to do both, but lied on her application, knowing she'd need to use work hours to type—letters to her mother, letters to the U.S. Embassy. She sat now in the low-ceilinged, fluorescent-lit office. A phone beside her. A slate-blue desk rimmed in silver chrome with a speckled sky-blue surface held a black typewriter and, next to that, the previous girl's dictation pad set askew as if she'd left in a hurry. Vera flipped through the notepad, recognizing the shorthand. Of all the crucial things she needed to accomplish in this city, it seemed so unfortunate to her that she had to sit still at a desk, answer phone calls, type correspondence, take dictation, and cater to colleagues who, she knew, would come and go in a confusing bluster of cologne and cigar smoke. She'd be working for a Mr. Davies, whom she'd not met yet and who appeared not to be in the office. The main office door was closed and no coat or hat rested on the coat stand.

While she waited, she made lists. Lists of letters she needed to write—to her mother, first; postcards she needed to buy; errands to run (the post office, the bank, the market, she needed one of those brightly colored straw bags she saw all the women carrying in the *puestos*); and then there were the lists of the sites she'd like to visit—Palacio Nacional, the museum, Chapultepec, Coyoacán. There were her obligations to her hosts, the Zaragozas, too, incorporated as she'd become into their family activities, though more and more feeling as if her presence merely meant an excuse for them to have a party. Add to this whatever she might need to do for her father—find him first, speak to lawyers, if she could, embassy officials, or maybe the Mexican authorities to see if his years in Mexico would amount to any rights as a Mexican citizen, gather the letters she'd taken from home, the one her mother wrote, too, and see what she might be able to do. She looked at her list—or several lists. Each scrawled across a different part of the page. They each represented some fraction of her very self and she was overwhelmed to see such stark contrasts spelled out before her.

The irony of her new employment was not lost on her. A little absurd really. She surveyed the various forms on the little desktop set of shelves to her right. Forms for duties and taxes, country of origin and country of destination, embarkment and landing. She felt the tragic comedy in the fact that she would spend most of her days here ensuring the safe passage of fruits, clocks, guitars back and forth across the border, but not her father. If she thought too much about it she knew tension would grow, turning to tears, and, well, she'd be no use to anyone in that state—no use to Mr. Davies, the Zaragozas, her father, and least of all her mother. No. Best not read too much into it for she'd have to keep herself together as if she were made up of a fine network of strings, calibrated and tuned with just the right tautness and tension. Too much strain and she'd snap.

SUDDENLY, THE DOOR BURST open and in sauntered a tall lanky man who stood as if on a tennis court. A bounce to his stance. His straw-colored hair swirling to the left and combed down on the right. He bounded into the room, leaning on her desk, hands splayed.

"It's a straightforward and simple process," he began without intro-duction, noting she had been surveying the forms. "For each import, you use the light blue one here," he said, pointing to the pile of light blue forms to his left. His thin, long fingers seemed to match his long limbs. "For export, you use the pink ones here. Fill out all the information re-quired, place the completed forms on my desk. I sign. You mail off and we're done."

"Yes. I understand," Vera said.

"What else? I'll need you to answer the phones, of course. Take dic-tation. All that sort of thing, which I assume you know how to do?"

"Yes, of course."

"Good then," he said, and disappeared into his office with the same abruptness with which he'd entered.

The morning went by with Mr. Davies making a few outings, asking her to fill out some forms before he left and then a series of phone calls for which she took messages. She cleaned out some of the desk drawers and reorganized the papers and notebook on top of her desk. On her lunch break, when she could be sure the office was quiet, she took the time and privacy to write to her father. If he did receive her first letter, sent Gen-eral Delivery to the post office, then he must know that she was now in the city. She would write to him again. She would schedule a meeting and then what? She'd no idea. She'd only ever known him as a young girl, and through his letters, and those much more directed to her mother. As the years continued, they grew more distant, formal and as if written by a stranger. How odd to think of him as that—a near stranger. She was learning the possibility of, the power of, contradiction; one could have a fundamental connection—father, daughter—but still be two mere strangers.

She sat at the typewriter. Its rounded metal keys more cumbersome than the machine she'd learned on back home. She pulled out a piece of stationery paper from the top drawer of her desk and began. *Dear Father, I've arrived in Mexico City.*

After a few mistyped words, going back with the delete key and typing over the misspelled letter, she was able to continue with few mistakes, detailing her trip, the state of her mother, how her brother would be arriving in a few weeks' time, on account of the fact that he'd finished his service work and was able to study in Mexico City on the G.I. Bill. *Your son a member of the U.S. Navy!*, she'd typed with an exclamation point. She'd gotten halfway through typing the letter when she'd realized it was ridiculous to be writing in such detail when she'd be able to tell him all of it in person. Was that not the very reason for her visit anyway? She laughed at herself, tugging the paper from the roll. She began again. She would not go all astray. She'd stick to the point of her letter—to secure a date, time, and place to meet. She would not clutter it up with details, and when she'd finished and reread it, she was concerned about the tone, thought it sounded much too brusque, formal, and, due to its brevity and directness, cold. But it would have to do. Lunch break was over. This is what she wrote:

> *Dear Father,*
>
> *I've arrived in Mexico City. I'd like to meet at Sanborns in the historic center. 6:00 pm on Thursday, after my work hours. Please do come and meet me there.*
>
> *Love,*
>
> *Vera*

. . .

SHE WALKED THROUGH THE shadows cast by the street's wrought iron railings, fitting her feet within the coiled squares of their Greek eternity symbol design. Her day began again, though only Vera knew this, slipping away from work and delaying her return to the Zaragoza family so that she could meet her father and begin what she knew was sure to be a laborious process of getting him home.

She counted out her steps as she walked—fast and chin tucked. Her new straw bag hung heavy off her shoulder, her market purchases from the morning pressed into her hip bone.

SANBORNS. 6:00 P.M. Casa de los Azulejos, the House of Tiles. The street noise and pedestrian traffic faded as she walked into the now louder din of the restaurant. The inside coolness. A break from the dry and dusty streets. She looked at her shoes and was surprised to see how much dust had gathered on her otherwise black, polished, T-strap heels. She looked around, but in searching realized she might not recognize him. Of course, he'd sent some photographs home, but the last one she'd seen was five years ago. Would she recognize him? Would she be able to pick out her own father in this city of what seemed to her millions, narrow it down to here, at this moment, amid the overcrowded clatter of Sanborns? All the tables of tourists, mostly Americans, she could hear that from the language, though Mexicans were here too she saw as she let her gaze draw arcs back and forth over the main dining area.

She knew it was him in an instant. The full mop of charcoal, nearly white hair. The rather thin figure, hunched over his cup of coffee. His gaze rising every few seconds in a way one knew that he was waiting for someone. He sat back in his chair for a moment and then leaned forward again, shoulders drawn into his small frame. She took a breath, pulled herself up and walked straight to his table, her hands falling onto the tabletop, dropping her bag, and saying with more emotion than she'd realized,

"Father, it's me, Vera. It's Vera." Her cheeks hurt she was smiling so hard, barely realizing his own reaction—a little stunned, a little confused. He opened and closed his eyes in a way that seemed to blink back tears. He rose and smiled, grasped her hands, and then they embraced. She could feel how slim he was, not the robust, thick-necked man she'd always thought of as her father. But he was still tall, taller than she, and that somehow gave her comfort. The years may have diminished his strength and width, but not his height. He sat back down and extended his hand in a gesture for her to sit. She did so, sitting across from him and smiling what she knew was her brightest smile. Then began an odd period she would only later be able to define as her father's shock. She watched his face, his eyes still with that blinking, glazed-over sheen. He placed his hands on the table and she saw that they were dirty. Dirt under the fingernails, grease maybe, she thought. Calloused and dry too. He had a deep gouge across the fleshy part of the back of his right hand. She imagined a razor or barbed wire had done that. But her eyes were drawn to his thumb, smashed in, crushed beneath the nail bed, and the nail itself a deep purple. He noticed that she'd seen and Vera looked away from his hands, but it was too late. She flushed and felt a triple shame—that he'd caught her staring, from her own sense of remorse, and finally the sudden fear that she'd offended him. Oh, dear, poor father, she thought, but then tried to change her expression lest he think she pitied him. If she knew one thing from her mother, he did have a kind of pride. "Stubborn, just like Vera," her mother always said. But he could not speak. He kept looking down at the silverware. Back up to her. She was now conscious of the people next to them staring at the odd exchange. His eyes were so blue. As blue as Leo's. The gestures too, just like her brother's—the furrowed brow, the slight squint to the eyes, even the way he brought his hand up to his hair, rubbed his nose. This was her father. *Solemn*. It was the first word that came to her mind. In the blue eyes, sometimes frantic, searching. A handsome, if worn face, she thought. She wanted him to speak, but she felt she had to contain herself, not throw too much at him at once. He seemed able to process little bits at a time and this frightened her as much as he seemed frightened, overwhelmed himself. Finally, he began.

"Vera? How can this be?"

"It's me."

"Vera, Vera." He shook his head, looked down at his hands and then said, "Truth or faith."

"What is it you're saying?" She did not understand. His thick accent, harsh on the English, jagged. It had surprised her. She had not remembered the sound of his voice. Her father's voice.

"Vera. In my language—it means truth or faith. So you choose."

"I never knew."

"You don't know Russian? Your mother didn't tell you?"

"No. We went to Russian school, but we learned very little of the language," she said. He frowned and shook his head. Disappointed, as if she'd caused him a mortal wound.

"Truth or faith?" He then smiled. "Choose."

"Well," she laughed, remembering that he did always have a kind of trick or game to play with her, "with truth I'd always know. So, I'll take faith."

"Smart girl," he bellowed, beaming. He hit the table with an outstretched hand. "You've grown so. A young lady."

"I should hope I had grown. It's been fourteen years."

"It has been fourteen years," he repeated, nodding his head and looking down.

Silence.

She crossed her legs. The restaurant was crowded, filled with businessmen, workers, the American tourists with their binoculars, sunglasses, and heavy black cameras dotting tables cluttered with Coca-Cola bottles. There was a couple next to them. The woman was looking at a map. The man was far back in his seat, nodding to the woman's suggestions that they go to see Teotihuacán not today, but on Sunday. The restaurant's high ceilings enveloped the drone of conversations. The chandeliers hanging by chains as thick as wrists. It was noisy. Chairs scraping. Waiters called to each other and from the street came a steady stream—cars, pedestrians on after-work errands, halts, beeping. In the fading daylight the darkened storefront windows, as still and serene as a lake in the morning, doubled the dusk's movement.

"You look so like your mother."

"People do say that. Of course, I never see it."

"You do. You have her hands too," he said, picking up one of her hands, turning it over in his own and patting it gently. "And your mother. How is she?"

"Happy to know I'm here. She'll be even more happy to know I've met with you. Of course worried too."

"Yes. She always did worry herself," and he began to fiddle with the silverware before him. "Tell me, Vera. You traveled all by yourself, all that long way?"

"Took a plane, flew Pan Am."

"All by yourself? You should be careful, traveling alone, such a young woman."

"People travel all the time now, Daddy."

"Still, you must watch yourself."

"I do."

"When did you arrive?"

"A few days ago."

"And you are staying in the city?"

"Yes. With a Mexican family. I work too."

"Work?"

"I told you in my letter."

"You must work?"

"It's the only way I could come here." He frowned again. This time an expression of deep perplexity. He could not hold her gaze for too long, as if the very sight of her confused him. Instead, he would study her face with intensity, leaning on the table, and then he'd shift his gaze—now to the silverware, or to his hands, or to the left and right of him for a while, now retreating in gesture and in mind. She watched him and waited for him to come back to wherever he went in his thoughts, deep into memory she assumed, but what it was he was thinking about she couldn't fathom. Her mother had told her so little, and when she ever did begin to recount their story she'd begin to cry and this upset both of them so much that Vera never pressed her further. Now she saw that she might have difficulty with her father too. She'd try to help him though. If he could be home, with her mother, with all of them, surrounded by the family, given work, something to occupy his fine mind, as her mother always called it, then nostalgia (the Russian disease, her mother said) would fade and he could focus, she hoped, on the present, the here and now.

"Here is a little something from Mother," she said, pulling a small pink envelope from her purse. It was a check for ten dollars. He opened the envelope, looked at the check, and shook his head, a deep frown showing the long creases along the sides of his mouth. She knew he had worked, in the copper mines of Cananea, until the Depression hit and he'd lost his job, but now she had no idea how he took care of himself, if he did at all.

"Daddy. Tell me what you do, where you work, how do you take care of yourself?"

"If you send my designs to the patent agencies, like I've told you to do, she wouldn't have to work."

"Where do you live?"

"She could have a house, you see, and then a garden. Like we had in the Ukraine. Oh, you could spit on that soil and something would grow." He laughed and she couldn't help but laugh too.

"Why don't you do as I say?" A sudden anger in his voice, which had a deep baritone to it and a tendency to resonate. It caused her to jump, others looking at their table.

"Daddy, please." She lowered her voice, hoping that he'd follow her lead. "Where do you live?"

"In the center here. A boardinghouse."

"And for work? You are not at the electric company any longer?"

"Repairs."

"I see."

"I do okay. I need very little, you see."

"Yes," she said, but could see right away that he'd need several things—a new pair of shoes for certain, a new suit, a haircut.

"Daddy, I have some pictures. Of the family, the boys, Mother and me. That is, if you think you'd like to see them."

"Your mother?" he asked, an expectant, pleading look.

"Yes. I have photographs, of back home," she said, reaching into her purse. "I have a whole bunch of them right here." She pulled out a large white envelope, placing it on the table and pushing it toward him. He didn't motion for it so she picked it up once more and removed the packet of photos bound by a thin grosgrain blue ribbon. Her mother had done that, she thought, and then felt her eyes well up thinking of what she'd make of her husband now. She undid the ribbon and began to place each photo before him. One at a time.

"Wait," he said, hand raised, "I would like to order some more coffee."

"Yes, yes, yes of course. In all the excitement I'd forgotten where we were," Vera said, looking up from their table, sitting tall in her chair, trying to beckon one of the waiters. The orders were placed, Vera doing the ordering, her father sinking back in his chair, staring at the silverware, never once looking at the waiter, even when addressed directly. She observed him when their coffees arrived. He used half the slim carafe of cream, and, from the blue and black ceramic sugar bowl, four heaping spoonfuls of sugar, stirring and not bothering to remove his spoon from the cup. He slurped when he drank, hunched over his cup, he seemed unable to sit upright and drink from the mug as she did now. Coffee spilled here and there from the rim.

She moved their coffee cups to the side of the table and brushed away the sugar crystals that had accumulated in a fine granular surface. She laid two photos down at a time.

"This here?" He pointed to one photograph. Vera winced, closed her eyes and then told him.

"Yes. That's Mother."

"Julia?"

"Yes. Daddy, we sent you photographs. Over the years, did you receive them?"

"How changed."

"Did you?"

"Oh, yes. I got them all."

"Good," she said, doubting this as she watched him look at her mother's photograph, searching out the face he'd known.

"This is me with Leo, you see," Vera continued. "We are at the park. This was about, oh, five years ago."

"Yes, yes. Beardsley Park, is it?"

"No."

"No?"

"I think this is—"

"Beardsley Park, yes. I courted your mother there. We walked and walked till dusk, every Sunday. Without fail. Has she told you that?"

"Yes," Vera lied, finding it difficult to explain that her mother rarely spoke of him, and when she did out would come a torrent of tears and her lips would draw into a fine thin line. Braced is how Vera always thought of that expression.

"This is Leo's photo from the Navy."

"The Navy? Let me see here," he said, sitting forward, smiling now. "So changed, so changed." A group of men stand up to leave, a loud crush of chairs scraping. One of them is calling for the waiter, a booming *"mesero"* echoing.

"Daddy, you'd like to come home, right?"

"If they'll let me."

"I'm here to make sure that happens."

"Oh now, how? What can you do?"

"Well, I will start with the Embassy."

He considered this, nodding his head, which went from an affirma-tive, to a kind of defeated shake of the head. Then he leaned close to her, his voice lowered to a near whisper.

"If you do get me home," he said, his eyes wide, "will your mother accept me?"

"Oh, Daddy. What a silly thing to say. Of course she'll have you. She's written letters her whole life to get you home."

VERA AND AUSTIN left Sanborns, the crowded clatter of the place at their backs as they stepped into dim streets.

He was walking too fast for her.

"Father, please slow down"—she laughed a bit—"your one step is equal to my three." He stopped, satchel beneath his arm, his body pro-pelled forward. His face as Vera drew close was expectant. Eyes elevated with some inner blaze of thought she could not fathom.

"The windows close soon," he explained, and then she fell into step with him and then lost pace again, his stride though smaller still overtak-ing her own. He dashed through the post office entrance forgetting him-self, and doubled back to wait for Vera, clearly unused to having a companion, she thought. They walked through the lobby and he led her to one of the side tables, elbow high. A few others milled about them, but for the most part, the post office, near closing hour, was quiet. She watched as he opened his satchel, rummaging through to find his letters, the envelopes. His fingers marked faint smudges along his, for the most part, clean, unblemished drafts.

"Daddy. Your fingers are a mess. Let me help you," she said to him.

"I didn't notice," he said, dropping the papers and turning over his hands.

"No. Of course not, but you certainly can't send them with such a mess of prints on them. Look how your fingerprints are all over this one." She took a draft from him and inspected it a bit more closely. She sighed. "Here, give them all to me," she said, spreading out the papers, envelopes, and letters, each addressed to the Ambassador, one to the Patent Commissioner, Washington, D.C., the General Consul, D.F. He stood empty-handed next to her, watching. She knew these letters and the repeated pleas and explanations, how he'd applied for citizenship, how he was married to a citizen of the United States of America. They were the same letters he'd send home to them all, the same ones that made her mother down for days. To see them here now, while she was standing right beside him, made her want to shake him and make him see that no amount of his inventions would allow him back in. But she didn't want to bring all that up just yet and spoil their reunion. She felt her eyes smart with tears. She gritted her teeth. There were the specifications for each invention—the electric welder with its cylinder and flame. He was mailing off the propeller designs too. To Vera, they were all a geometrical conundrum. A series of circles and arcs. Arrows and numbers. She could sense him, see him out of the corner of her eye, watching. He was making sure she was careful, that she was placing the correct drafts with the correct letters. She knew, and it broke her heart to admit it, that all these efforts of his were futile. She wanted to take his hands and plead with him, tell him the truth, "These inventions will not get you into the U.S." Oh, but it would destroy him she knew.

"Daddy," she began instead, "you know, you're sending so much of yourself to these patent agents, and now the ambassador too?"

"They will soon see," he said, cutting her off, not meeting her gaze. He nodded his head with a little grunt of confirmation, his eyes focused on the designs she was placing in the last of the envelopes. She set all the slim bundles one atop the other and then slid them down the table where he stood shifting his weight. She watched him in periphery. He took the envelopes in hand, head cocked, eyes narrowing, double-checking the addresses. He looked to her now and smiled, taking two steps back. He turned to cross the large, empty lobby to the bank of postal windows. A wide stride, the anxiety in the bend of lanky, thin joints. She drew her hand away from the table, feeling a heaviness descend as she took her time walking to the main entrance, all the while wondering and worried about who exactly her father had become.

. . .

THE PROPELLER WAS FOR his Sonnie. They were good ideas. Useful inventions—for engineering, for ships and building. He was ashamed of their presentation now. He'd tried to get the best paper, always in shorter and shorter supply, his own funds hardly covered one ream. He'd had no proper presentation materials to work with either. He had explained as much in the patent letters. Once, years ago, he did have a typewriter—a broken, discarded one that he'd found behind a printing house. He'd taken it back to his shop, fixed the keys, though the *E* never worked, so he'd had to painstakingly insert a series of hand-printed *e*'s. He'd not re-alized how many *e*'s one used up in the course of official correspondence and soon empathized with the typewriter's former owner, deciding to also discard the old, ineffectual machine. He hadn't used a typewriter since. Relied instead on his fine print—neat, capital letters. The letters were legible, if a bit amateurish. But any good patent agent would soon see the value in his ideas and not take it as an affront to the profession, or at least that is what he hoped.

And now these fingerprints. He hadn't even considered those. Perhaps all these years no one ever looked at his designs because they were such a mess of smudges and blotches. Or had some shrewd patent clerk, seeing the unimpressive presentation of Austin's ideas, seen a way to take advantage, to polish up these very drafts, passing them off as his own? These damn men in power, with positions, he thought, raising up his foot and stamping it down, muttering under his breath. My God, what if Vera was right about the fingerprints? He felt a fool, a deep shame. How had he not been more careful?

He was still standing in front of the post office, clasping his satchel in one arm, his other hand stuffed into his pocket. He'd said good-bye to Vera and she had promised she would return the next day. Vera. His own daughter. Dropped into his life in an instant. He watched her leave. She kept turning around. A reassurance. There was a knot in his stomach, wondering how he could be sure of her promise. He walked across the street, deciding on the long way back to the boardinghouse, feeling somehow more vacant now that she had gone. He'd begun to feel joy while with her at Sanborns and to now be back in the city—alone—returned him to his usual state. It seemed all the more unbearable now knowing he'd had a rightful connection to someone here. He now meant something to someone—his own child. Her sudden presence made the years rush at him. He thought of all the time he'd been in the city, and wondered if it would simply amount to one of many stories of this country—one enfolded into its highways, *colonias*, ruins, parks, waters, the cantinas and *pulquerías*, the markets and storefronts—or was it his story? He found that he really was unable to separate the two. True, he had tried to preserve himself, to attune his body, which had its own memory, to seasons left behind, but he soon learned the futility of such a practice. The city had worked over and through him—its vastness as indifferent as the ocean. We are defined by our surroundings as much as by our pasts, the way a river stone is worn smooth by currents. Mexico City had left its mark, indelible.

He continued walking. His antidote to solitude. He walked as the old walk. Miles a day. He walked to occupy the hours, to evade loneliness, to practice patience. And he was still walking on this day to deflect the sharper sting of loneliness that pervaded his every footstep, walking to reach the next day when she would come back to him again and take him for a proper meal as she'd said. He walked through three *colonias*—Centro, Zona Rosa, to La Condesa. He was now passing stores selling tawdry rubbish and bric-a-brac. Windows piled high with bags, beads, feathers, dried eucalyptus, branches, packs of cards, baskets, clay pots. He stopped in front of one storefront. His face in the glass. The gauntness of it. High cheekbones even more defined. A sadness in the corner of a blue eye. His thoughts thrust up against the store window, his mind holding a history that suddenly seemed to merge with the storefront wares on gaudy display—the bright green garden hoses, yellow wire bird feeders, spools of copper, pinwheels, baby dolls, coffee cans.

What if she was able to help him? Bring him back? He gave in to the idea, lingered for a moment on that possibility. A kind of ideal he sees suddenly as a shining triangle, a certain, clear shape of something that had been vague and shadowed, but then another stream of thought came to him like a cloudburst; it shook him, caused a shudder. What if he would die in Mexico City? He sat with this, the discomfort of it palpable in the tightening between the shoulder blades, at his neck. A gentle wind swept some marigolds off a rooftop. From a shrine, he thought. The golden, oblong petals falling looked like they were disintegrating and happy with their descent. He smiled, the release visceral. Don't let your mind get into brooding, he scolded himself, thinking of the world he'd built up around him here. He knew that it was not quite a bad life, even if he'd never forget the life that now lay back in a distant past, nearly imaginary, though he could see the street still, the house and those windows, and now Vera was here. His own Vera. His baby girl now a young lady. Something lodged deep within loosened. He kept walking, unmoored, lightened, the petals continuing to fall from the rooftop in an orange cascade behind him—a falling he could no longer see.

HE STOOD NOW AT the corner of his street, could see that someone sat in the alcove of the window, legs crossed as he has often sat. He took a few steps, waiting to focus his gaze. Were they Jack's polished shoes? No. He recognized the leather sandals, the curve of those calves.

"Austin." Anarose walked toward him now. "There you are. Why are you closed?"

"Please, come inside," he said, opening the grate. She shook her head no, remaining out on the sidewalk. Then she leaned back against the wall, arms crossed. She was pouting.

"I need to speak with you."

"I saw you," she began. "On my way here. Standing at the post office with some *gringa* woman."

"I can explain."

"I feel I have a right to—"

"No. You must listen to what I need to tell you." She did not look him in the eye. He walked into the shop, she followed and he turned to her.

"She's my daughter."

"Your daughter?" Her arms fell to her sides, palms open, released. Her eyebrows arched.

"Yes."

"I thought your family died."

"*Die?* Who told you they died?"

"They were killed, *no?*"

"By who I'd like to know!"

"I hear from the women in the neighborhood. They all say you lost a family, well, I just assumed."

"No. They're alive. They are in the U.S."

"And you. Here," she said. "So you will make your fortune, yes, and you will go to your family too. It's as I said, right? Leave Mexico."

"It's not as simple as that. I'm not allowed into the country."

"Tell me, why don't you cross the border?"

"I must go legally."

"It's quite simple if one knows the areas."

"You don't understand."

"You know something—you are a man with loss of your own making," she says, backing out the door. He watches her leave, her footsteps slow and certain, her back rigid and arched as she walks away in what he interprets as impatience.

HE JUST TOOK NOTICE, hardly realized, but there before him was Chapultepec, some of the locals already filtering out to venture home while the Americans were still in the park, playing ball. He'd no idea how many of them were down here—actors, screenwriters. He strolled closer, could hear their banter, the jokes of others gathered nearer to the attempt at a field.

A solid crack of the bat against ball like a firecracker. He shielded his eyes, trying to follow the flight of the ball. It had been struck far back to one of the men in the field. He could smell the clean scent of grass as he continued walking.

He thought more about Anarose. He had not wanted to hurt her, hardly knew himself what his intentions were except that she was a soothing balm to a long struggle. He didn't expect her to understand, but her words lingered with him—a loss of his own making. He was looking at his life in reverse, wondering if she was right.

An hour passed. He'd found he had traversed nearly the entire park, wandering back the way he'd come in, by the ballplayers, watching the last of their game.

"They do this every evening," Austin heard a voice behind him. "In Cuernavaca too. Poor guy. That would've been a home run."

The men were running in from the field, all drawn together like beads on a string, and the others ran out to take their places, forming the outer and inner half circle. Austin turned to see Jack approaching, stepping up behind him.

"But it's good for them, I guess. A little diversion, a little leisure." Jack shrugged his shoulders and then kept talking. "Fear of blacklisting just about destroyed some of these men." He shakes his head in reflection. "I admit, I do feel a bit sorry for them. Can't even do the work they love in their rightful country. Just hanging out, 'waiting out the political climate, waiting out the climate,'" he said. "They've been here not even a year yet, some of them. But you, Austin. How have you done it?

"Work," Jack said, answering his own question. "I mean you work all the time. Can't tear you away from it, those damn drafting papers and always on the lookout for more. Your inventions and letters. It's like building a fortress only to realize you aren't protecting yourself from anything, you've simply locked yourself inside." Shouting and laughter came from the field and they both looked up. Cheers erupted among the players.

"Someone just ran into home," Jack said. He grew silent and continued watching the game, then sighed. "Not sure what's got into me, thinking about all of this. Suppose watching them all this time, and you too, not knowing if you're coming or going, or staying, and meanwhile the years truck on by, and before you know it—" He broke off.

"Oh, God, I've made you upset and I didn't mean to."

Silence. They watched the game. The light continued to fade and the men were now mere dusky outlines on the field. Austin could make out the white ball, could hear the sound of the bat as it hit the ball—sometimes a solid, full sound like splitting wood, other times more of a light snap.

When the game was over Austin, without a word, turned away from Jack and began walking toward the park's exit.

"By the way, we know your daughter is here," Jack called after him.

"What? What did you say?" Austin said, circling back.

"Your daughter. We know she's here. Vera."

"And?"

"She's involved in your goings-on, I have to watch her."

"She's not involved in anything. You leave her alone."

"Orders. I don't have a choice. We know she's going to try to help you, work on your behalf to get you reinstated, but it won't do any good."

"You don't know that. She's an American. She's my daughter."

"Doesn't matter. We both know it will be a waste of time," Jack said, hands in his pockets as he turned on his heel and began walking away from Austin, past the players who were gathered in small groups, talking, laughing, the sun now down, the evening rising so that as Austin stood there he saw Jack, a faint trace of blackness in the growing dark.

. . .

SHE COULD HEAR THEM all filtering in through the front foyer, voices echoing against the red flagstones. The click of all those heels. Everyone, she could tell, was talking at once. Greetings. Kisses. Slaps on the back. Clapping hands. Laughter. Trilling voices. Shrill. Combined, it was a distant din that traveled to the back of the house, gliding down the dark, shadowed hallways and swirling around her like a threatening gale.

The Zaragoza family and their guests continued to gather. Some, she could tell, had filtered through the dining room to the back garden— their voices coming to her through the window. The mariachi band started to play. Its chords and refrains adding a layer to the laughter and talk, the cries of recognition and embraces. She started for the door then stopped, her hand falling away from the doorknob. She stepped backward and sank to the floor, lying down, first on her side, head nestled to her arm, and then on her back. She needed just a moment.

Her body relaxed into the wood floors. She could feel the night air through the windows, the smell of something burning. Voices continued under the drums and horns. Out the window the garden's ivy clung to the walls, the leaves large and sinister, like winged creatures. *If you'd sent my designs to the patent agents, she'd have a house, a garden.* His words angered her. She felt guilt too. He'd lost the ability to know what it meant to have a house and garden.

She knew where to find him now. He'd given her the address of his boardinghouse, his shop, and she had planned to meet him again, though she had to admit she was spent by only their first meeting. Why had she come here again? She had to remind herself—out of obligation to her mother, to her father too. But she'd try to help him in some way. All her life she'd felt pulled backward, toward Mexico—a thread tied her to it while another self pressed forward, trying, striving to build up her own life. She could see the sky purpled like a molding above the adjacent homes' rear façades, doors and windows, walls and landings, these shadowed, silent witnesses to her determination, which she'd keep secret from all of them. She would get her father back into the United States.

Vera stood up and clicked on the lamp near the window. She bent to tug at the hem of her dress, smoothing out the wrinkles. Vera had changed into her faux silk dress and watched now as it changed from burgundy to an iridescent pale green, to copper in the full glow of the lamplight. With a firm hand, she worked on the back of her skirt. She liked the sound of the pleated silk, like billowing, starched sheets—*thrash, thrash, thrash.*

Vera wondered what her father would be doing now, if he would be okay without her. She'd promised she would come the next day and he nodded his head and frowned again and then pinched her on the nose and she said oh, but he just laughed and reminded her he used to do that when she was a little girl. Yes, she remembered, she'd told him, though she didn't. She didn't have the heart to tell him that she'd forgotten. He clung to such shards of memory so fiercely. Why not allow him to have at least that?

"I'll see you tomorrow. We'll have a proper meal," she'd said, and she turned away and began walking, looking back after him as he stood on the post office steps watching her walk away. *In his own world*, she thought. But she shook off the tears she felt brimming, fixed herself a bit in the mirror, refastened her hair, and was ready to join the other guests.

While the house was large and of many rooms, the rooms themselves were small. There was a cozy warmness to such small rooms—the wood beams, the adobe walls thick as torsos made it cool in the summer and warmer in the winters. The food was set out on silver and copper platters. The candles were lit, reflecting off wineglasses, ruby red tequila glasses, and the several oval and round ceramic plates that covered the walls. The room smelled of tobacco, bitter coffee, vanilla musk perfume, grilled corn. Someone was calling for a toast. "*Ssh,*" people said. Glasses clinked. Quiet settled as if someone had cast a mesh blanket over the room. Last-minute footsteps could be heard in the hallway and foyer. She could hear early clinks of glasses. Sighs. Humming. Little quiet moans. A welcoming toast. How she loved this family. She looked at the father in his navy blue sweater, a white and blue striped scarf tied around his neck for warmth. His hair was thick and white and his silver cuff links and wedding band shone in the candlelight. He was a kind, dignified man, like all the Zaragoza men. Why couldn't her father be this way?

Some of her older friends back home—employers and teachers— told her that it wasn't her responsibility, that there was no need, and that the loss, the feeling of absence, would dissipate, that, in time, it would leave her almost when she least expected, and that she really need only worry about her own life now that she was an adult. In an act of defiance, she made sure not to forget, but rather to take it upon herself to come to Mexico City, find out what happened to him, and how she might get him home. She couldn't bear to think he had not a soul to help him here.

She was there, at the party, but distant. Back and forth between two states, two positions—guest and spectator—until she found the right balance, hovering on the edge, balanced, so that she could be both at once. When she felt this liminal state she had an urge to rush away, go to a room by herself and close the door. But she willed herself to stay still. She would not run away.

. . .

"I AM HERE ON behalf of my father——," she began.

She had been at the embassy for two hours. Ushered from one waiting room to the next. Told to take a seat until her number was called. Repeating her predicament to a blank-faced, pale clerk—three times in total. She now sat in a larger room filled with the gentle, muted rattle of typewriters and phones ringing, the line of clerks behind a glass that stretched the length of the room. She sat in the first row of wooden benches and prepared to wait, running over exactly what she'd say, letters and papers all fastened together securely in her bag. The woman seated next to her made pleasantries, explained how she herself had lost her passport and was worried that the embassy might not be able to replace it in time for her to leave on her next trip. Vera had smiled and reassured her that it would be fine.

"Let me stop you right there," the man said to her now, placing his hand up. "Is your father with you? We need to see the person in question." The clerk had a weary look, one of exasperation. Vera had not finished her planned speech and her pulse throbbed at her temples. She faltered a moment, tucked her hair behind her ears, once and then another time. The clerk grew impatient.

"Miss. If you're here on behalf of your father we need to see him."

"No. I'm afraid he's not here. It's just me. Of course I can return with him, but I wondered if I may speak to an authority on immigration matters."

"You can speak to me."

"I have several letters here explaining our case." She began to pull out the bundle of papers. "You see, my father was deported from the U.S. on incorrect charges."

"Incorrect?"

"Yes. He is not, that is, he never was, an anarchist."

"Anarchy?"

"Yes. It's quite a difficult, complex situation, but, well, you see, my father has lived alone here in Mexico City now for fourteen years. We have tried to get him reinstated to the U.S., and he's tried himself, but nothing has come of it. I'm now here and would like to try to work on this in person. On behalf of my father."

"You're on a tourist visa."

"No. Work visa."

"I see. I'm afraid I can't look into this any further without the subject."

"The subject."

"Your father, miss."

"Right. Yes, of course. Well, I can bring him with me."

"I suggest you do that. You'll need to gather what documents you have there. You'll need forms. This packet here," he said, handing her a folder. "You say he was deported, on anarchist charges?"

"Yes."

"That's quite a serious offense," he said, all this while looking down at his paperwork. "If you're saying that it's incorrect you'll have to request an appeal on the deportation, a waiver."

"How do I begin an appeal?"

"We'll look into the file on our end, and then you'll need an appointment. We will review the file with the subject. Of course, he'll need to submit to some questioning. All normal procedures."

SHE LEFT THE EMBASSY, walking down the steps and standing on the sidewalk, her eyes fighting to adjust to the bright light. She stood still for a moment, thinking of what to do now. Return to the Zaragozas'? No. She couldn't do that. She needed some time to herself. To her left she saw the woman who had sat next to her greeting a friend she saw approaching. She then waved to Vera.

"They've replaced my passport for now. What a relief," she said. Vera congratulated her, smiling. She watched the two women laughing and speaking in loud American voices, clomping away in heavy heels, sunglasses cut in slim, cat-eyed ovals. She turned away, her smile dropped. To her right, a bus careened past, overcrowded with men clinging to the outer windows and back bumper. It left a strong stench of gasoline in its wake. She looked back at the embassy, its sleek modern structure, all that silver chrome, and she felt a sudden contempt for her country. The brutes, she thought. They'd kicked him out. An appeal? She'd not known of this, but it seemed promising. She'd have to get his documents of course, and if she brought him to the consulate would he manage? She felt the vast city around her, all these buildings and people and her father tossed among them like a pebble among the waves. And he was not bearing up, was he, she had to admit. Not bearing up at all. She crossed the street and sat on a park bench in the shade, now wondering about what distances of mind and heart he could have traveled to be here, in such deep, desolate solitude among the inhabitants of this city that it made her feel parched and spent and herself nearly on the brink of despair. She took a deep breath, tucked her hair behind her ears, and stood up.

The walk from the embassy to her father's boardinghouse took a good half hour, but she'd resigned herself to proceeding on foot, knowing a good walk, a change in temperature, scenery could prompt a change in mood. She passed some fine stores along the *avenida*, and she could see her image in the two-paned glass storefront where she paused to look at a dress in the window. Her silhouette reflected in double against a sky traced with cloud formations, which today were large, white, and godlike—a cavalcade of clouds. She soon crossed Avenida de los Insurgentes, having to pay attention as she walked, stepping now into the avenue, the noise and brightness of the sidewalks filled with street vendors, traffic moving at the pace of sludge, sirens. She was eager to step into the calm streets of the Condesa, passing the one lone man standing on the median who was selling wildflowers as cars passed. Vera could feel the heat of the day beginning as the hours tipped toward two.

"*BUENAS TARDES,*" she called.

Austin sat forward in the alcove of the front window.

"Out here," he said, walking to the door, eyes on his shoes.

"There you are," Vera said. "Didn't you see me?"

"Yes."

"And you didn't bother to call to me."

"No."

"Why ever not?"

"I wanted to be sure it was you." He smiled.

"Well, I'm terribly sorry I'm late. I got held up at work," she lied. "I raced back to change my shoes, my feet hurt so, and then came here straightaway."

"A busy young lady," he said.

"Now, I promised we'd get you some new shoes. You can't manage in those shoes."

"I do just fine."

"Just fine is not good enough."

"Whatever you say."

"Well, I don't know about that, but I know you need new shoes."

"You came all this way by yourself?"

"Yes, Daddy. I've told you lots of people travel nowadays. It's not like it used to be. And women too. Oh, you can go all over by yourself and it really is no problem. I'm in one piece, aren't I?"

"Still, you must be careful. I don't like that you are out at this time unescorted."

"Not you too! Please, I'm just fine, you know. The Zaragozas never let me go anywhere by myself, except to work and back of course. I don't need you telling me the same thing."

"I always was the protective type. I can't help it. When you were small, you would wander off on your own, all the time. Where is Vera, where did Vera go? We'd find you eventually, but the fright of it. In Mazatlán you liked the ocean, always running along the shore, not scared of the waves a bit. 'Not so close to the water,' we'd yell to you and to your brother too. We were so frightened. Do you remember?"

"It's such a long time ago now. No. I can't remember that far back. It's hard for me."

"I see it so clear. You came up to my knees then. The water will swallow you up, I used to say. And now look at you."

"I think we should get you some lace-up shoes," Vera said. "Not loafers like you have now because it seems you slip out of them. Lace-ups would do. Some nice new oxfords, if they have them. The Zaragozas gave me two names of stores."

HE FOLLOWED VERA TO the shoe store off the main avenue. There were racks of shoes outside arranged by colors, browns on one side, blacks on the other, and butterscotch along the rack closest to the window. He stood looking at these when Vera called for him to come into the store. It smelled of leather and coffee. Vera stood talking with the shop-keepers, he could hear—a mix of Spanish and English. They were smil-ing and listening to her with patience. They took to her, he could tell, with her wide smile and forthright American-ness, curls bouncing on her shoulders as she talked. He slunk in behind her, admiring the shoes of leather, smooth and thick. They ordered him to take a seat and Vera told him to take off his shoes, his feet all misshapen with large bunions that he knew would hurt in the new shoes. He could hear them whispering in the corner, conspiring over something. Vera came toward him, bent down and swiped up his old shoes before he knew what was happening. He watched as Vera threw them into the trash basket.

"Vera!" he yelled.

"Yes, what is it? Is everything okay?"

"You've thrown my shoes away."

"We're here to buy you new ones."

"It doesn't mean I can't still wear those."

"You won't be walking around in that pair. The soles are flapping off!"

"They worked fine," he said and sulked, he knew, feeling the corners of his mouth droop.

There was the matter of his clothes too, she told him. He should have a new suit, she'd said as they left the shoe store, his feet clad in a new pair of tight oxfords, slippery on the sidewalks. He sat on the windowsill of a storefront and removed his pocketknife, cutting grooves into the pristine, unblemished surface of his new, treacherous shoe soles. Three diagonals across and three on the opposite diagonal like hatch marks.

"What are you doing?" Vera asked, doubling back to stand before him now.

"They are making me slide. They'll be the death of me."

They walked two stores down to the men's clothing shop, where the shopkeepers descended upon them with questions and their measuring tapes. The suit he was wearing hung off him and the tailor began pinching back the material, clucking his tongue in disapproval, insisting that Austin should take a size smaller than the suit he wore now. Austin protested. He liked layers and a jacket too small might prevent him from being able to wear an undershirt, a button-up shirt, sweater, and vest. His argument was ignored as the man produced a suit two sizes smaller than the one he was now wearing.

"Try it on," Vera said, coaxing him into the dressing room, which was really just a sheet hung over a rope that stretched across the corner of the room. Austin changed in the triangular space, elbows and knees at odd angles, emerging with the suit, still too small he could feel. The store clerk shrugged his shoulders, closing his eyes as if he'd grown bored with them now that it was clear they wouldn't possibly purchase anything.

"We'll take it," Vera said.

. . .

THESE FIRST DAYS OF visits led them into and through the monuments of Mexico City. He did not want Vera to meet him at his boardinghouse. He didn't want her crossing the city on a bus all by herself. Instead, he sometimes met her outside the Zaragoza home or they met in the Zócalo, the Alameda, or in the plaza of Bellas Artes. Other days she insisted on taking a walk through Chapultepec, along the paths of ahuehuetes, he acquiescing to these longer walks. Other meetings were scattered amid café tables, sometimes a cantina or within the sinking marble of Bellas Artes.

ON A TUESDAY, Vera took a day off work and brought him on a picnic, out of the city. She saw that he could not stop smiling. "I can't get over that you are here," he kept saying. He'd brought his sketchpad and removed it from his satchel. She watched as he sharpened the pencil to a fine tip, printing out equations, numbers and symbols. She had prepared pepper-and-egg sandwiches, hard-boiled eggs.

"You know, Father, Mother has tried to help you in every way she can," she said, offering him a sandwich.

"Yes."

"I can't remember a week that she didn't send you a letter or go to the lawyers or the congressmen. She was always at it. And they'd given her such hope too. It was always only to be a month, a year away, and then you'd be able to come home."

He sat still, looking not to her but straight ahead.

"We'd get a lead, a senator would give Mother some hope and look into the case for her," Vera continued. "And, of course, that takes time, you well know. A few months would go by and we'd hear that it was possible, that some other office was taking care of it. Then a few more months would go by and we'd learn it was impossible due to your subversive activities, as they refer to it."

"I've had no activities!"

"We know this, but the government doesn't. They see your file in Washington and you're automatically denied entrance. No exceptions. But listen here. I've made an appointment with the embassy. We'll set this all straight. I have enough letters of support and Mother's letters and proof that you'll be an upstanding citizen."

"I'm an applicant for American citizenship."

"That doesn't qualify as being a citizen."

"Well, it must count for something. I've filled out all the documents, all the required papers." Silence. And then he turned to her. "Your mother. She's never come to visit me."

"She's had to work, Daddy. She's had to raise us, you know."

"If you'd all sent in my inventions to the patent agencies, I'm telling you, you'd all be taken care of. She wouldn't have to work."

"The patent application fees are an expense."

Silence.

"Does she have a house and garden?"

"No."

"Where does she live then?"

"We live in a small two-bedroom apartment, with other families. In the same house."

"In the same house?"

"Yes."

"And no garden?"

"No."

"Don't be too upset, Father. It's not so easy to have a house and garden in America."

"And why not?"

"Mother does not have enough for those things."

"I see." She watched him absorb all of this, a strain in his eyes, his jawline tense. "If I were there, she'd have a proper house." He stood up, paused a moment, and then, without a word, walked ten or so paces away from where she sat.

. . .

LEO. THE YOUNGER OF the two siblings. He has far fewer memories of his father. He is more uncertain of what to expect, his only contact since a young boy being letters he received, the same letters that made his mother begin to peck and poke at the typewriter and made him and Vera share a complicit look that said, "Father." The memories he did have were vague, dreamlike—hanging off his father's solid neck, laughing. Sometimes too a certain cast of light as it fell through the doorway or a smell of oil grease, copper. Sounds could conjure a moment of the familiar that even he did not realize meant—father.

FIRST, THE ZÓCALO. Broad shot, from a height, to give the impression of how large it is. This city square, which takes—watch him—one full minute to cross on foot. Next, settle on a figure in the crowd. The shoes first. The shadow he makes. Other footsteps surround him. Music. The sun bright. It causes confusion. Shapes are indistinct. He is still walking across the Zócalo, crossing the street and about to enter the courtyard of the Palacio Nacional. The Palacio Nacional, which sits on the western side of the Zócalo like one side of an ornate bronze frame. His first day in the city, in some shade-of-gray suit, his Baedeker guide in his front pocket.

He walks now through a wrought iron gate, the sun throwing thin lines of shadow along his suit. He had not expected the sun to be so harsh, and he skirts the palace courtyard by taking the long way, walking the perimeter of the sun-drenched square, staying beneath the arcade. On the opposite side, he can see the interlinking arches, the empty spaces like blackened mirrors—pleasant in their symmetry; eerie in their darkness.

Inside, he is flanked by other tourists. Exclamations, loud and soft. His head aching from the change in altitude, so high up, the pressure mounting. He follows other viewers up the staircase (wide), the grayness of the stone at his feet in contrast to the Rivera murals, the chaos of all that color, and the faces, bodies commingled in clashed arms, struggling embraces. One had to love these faces, wise, solemn faces, with a whimsy and mysticism he longed to understand. He lingers over the eyes, the hats, the animals, even the fire and the blood.

"There you are," Vera says as she walks up to him, her heels clomping against the stone floor. "Almost took you for a distinguished gentleman," she teases.

"How are ya, kid?" he says, arms open. A hug, a kiss on the cheek.

"And Mother?" she asks.

"Your letters—she reads them over and over," he says, looking over her shoulder then up to the top of the ceiling, settling back down. "How's Father?"

"I've told him you're coming. He seems to understand." She raises a hand to her forehead, pressing her temple before tucking her hair behind her ears.

Silence.

Almost without his realizing it they are walking, he following her for two paces before they are side by side. The whole history of Mexico at his shoulder. The dryness in the air causes him to cough, his head aches still, a tight pressure that the guidebooks say could last ten days or more. He will need to drink water, lots of water. He may be tired, listless even. He cannot tell if this sudden tightness is a claustrophobia, altitude sickness, or the disorientation of seeing his sister in an unrecognizable setting.

They have walked back out of the palace, falling onto the square, and he can feel the Palacio Nacional at his back, panoramic in its breadth. Vera has been talking as they walk, and he finds himself nodding in agreement, but he's not sure what she has been saying. He is trying to focus now, can see her peering at him, surveying how he's taking it all in, what his reaction will be. He winces, looks to her and offers a semblance of a smile. Now, back out amid the city, he finds that he is caught between two sensations, a surge of adrenaline, taking in the new—the light, the dust, the sounds, the dirt, trying to connect or feel some sense of his father—and a sinking feeling, a low drumbeat of his heart, slow. He continues walking next to his sister. They will meet their father in less than ten minutes. He has not seen him in fourteen years. First, though, he will need a drink.

THEY ENTER SANBORNS, the lunchtime crowd surrounds them as they sit across from each other.

"Do you want a drink?" Leo looks first over one shoulder, then another. There is no waiter in sight.

"No."

"Are you sure? One *cerveza* with me. It's after two o'clock already."

"No. I'll just have a coffee." Vera, he knows, is already worried about the time. They should stay only fifteen, twenty minutes, she should already be hastening their departure.

"Come on. Just one with me." Leo sees a waiter. He raises his arm, waves. The waiter's expression—noble, but annoyed.

"Oh, I really don't think I could."

"It's late in the day already. Just one *cerveza*."

"All right, all right."

"Two *cervezas*, *por favor*," Leo says. The waiter is mute. He nods and turns away.

"Well, *café*, *cerveza*, what's the difference, right? If you want me to, I can change the order."

"No. It's okay," Vera says. "We can't stay very long."

"I know," Leo says. He is looking around the place, elbows on the table, his eyes now meet Vera's. A pause. "How is he?"

"Okay, I guess." And then. "Well, not okay. Lives in his own little world really. His damn inventions and paper. And it's difficult to explain to him how the immigration system works. He thinks being an applicant for American citizenship somehow gives him some rights. It's difficult to make him see any different."

"I see."

"He's much changed."

"I don't remember him before the change so—"

"I've told him you're coming. I've told him we'll be there this afternoon."

"Good."

"You look like him."

"Really?" The waiter brings the beers, a bowl of small limes cut into tiny equilateral triangles.

"Yes. Same eyes. Startling, really."

"Shouldn't be much of a surprise."

"Yes, well. You'll see. It's a bit of a shock."

It is here over these limes, and within the crowded, teeming Sanborns that Leo reflects over the word—*shock*. He'd had a shock acclimating himself to this city—dust and sunlight. The dirt, the grime and noise. He'd not been prepared for it. He'd spent the last years on a naval ship, two years in the war. He'd served his country. When he was discharged after V-J Day, he like the other boys thanked Harry for saving his life. Then the G.I. Bill and the promise of college courses wherever he'd like to go. Vera had urged him to come to Mexico. But damn it. He shook his head, looked at his sister, out across Sanborns, back to his drink, picking up one of the limes and crushing it between his thumb and forefinger. He'd served his country and they wouldn't let his father in. The bastards.

"We should just drive him up to the border." He takes a long sip of his beer, looks away and then back to her. "Just get in the car and go," he continues.

Silence.

"I've already been to the embassy. I've scheduled an appointment. It's not easy to get one, you know," Vera says.

"Come on. We've been through this so many times. You know they won't let him in."

"We can try again."

"I think you're fooling yourself."

"Well, why shouldn't they? We're here. We can vouch for him. We have to count for something. We're his children." Vera has peeled the entire label off her bottle of beer, a pile of gold and brown paper crumpled before her. She sits back in her chair, sipping her beer. She is seated in profile to him now. After the embassy visit, she says. If it doesn't work, if the appeal doesn't work. We'll go then. He listens to her talking, the words, *embassy, appeal*. He looks to her now, his sister. She seemed to run on several cylinders—vigorously alive, Leo always thought, forever in gear and so precise in her attempts, with every *i* dotted and *t* crossed. Just like her mother, really. Relentless. In pursuit of something that he could see was like trying to move a mountain when he'd just as well break the law instead. What help had the law given any of them? That's what he kept trying to show, the damn injustice of it all. The bastards.

THEY TAKE A CAMION to the Condesa, the bus driving through shadow and light, all these trees amid so much dust. It doesn't make sense. Dust on his shoes, a fine dust seemed to have formed on his upper lip. There is wrought iron and green, medians full of plush ground cover, the curving circular streets, the dust. Everywhere there is dust. He had ideas about his father, imagining just what Mexico might be like, but he'd never expected so much green. Or dirt. Crippled street beggars too. *He's worn down his mind, worn down his mind.* He can't get the words out of his thoughts. His mother was the first to have said it. He'd overheard her in what she must've thought was a private moment. She'd read one of his father's letters, instructing her to send his designs to patent agents, to the U.S. patent commissioner. Leo can see the letters now—thick blue ink, drawings for machines with pipes and pulleys. She would say it softly at first, after reading the letter, holding it down by her side, her other hand wrapped around her waist, her gaze off and away and then the shake of her head, her lips pursed and frowning, *worn down his mind*. It's what neither of them now had the courage to say. It's what they didn't want to believe. It's the truth.

The bus drops them on a quiet, tree-lined street. Storefronts open. Rusted tin signs set against sidewalks or hanging from chains. Hand-painted signs on wooden placards of red or yellow. He follows his sister into a small vestibule, open to the street, the floor filled with sawdust and dirt. Lights off. He can see a frail man sitting behind the counter, who now turns as Vera approaches. At once Leo sees the eyes that seem to apologize for themselves in each blink and, my God, how diminished and fragile he seemed. And before he knows what is happening, there are words of greeting. "So tall," he hears his father keep repeating. "You were my little rolling ball." He laughs, and there are tears forming in his eyes, the blinking, his hand raised to his forehead. And then the clumsy, uncomfortable hug. The startled recognition. The nervous smiles. An accent unexpected. He is asking him to take off his hat, stay awhile. He does as he is told. His father next to him, nearly the same height now. He keeps opening and closing his eyes, shaking his head. A gesture of disbelief.

Vera was right. They look alike. No surprise there, to his mind, but the experience of it is an altogether different thing. Shyness. He'd not expected that either. A kind of sneaking for a glimpse, a real gaze at the face and then, as if overwhelmed, having to turn away. Neither can hold the other's gaze. His eyes, his gestures had been Leo's alone for his twenty-one years, and to see them sketched on another makes him angry. "The imposter" is what he wants to call his father. Already on the defensive, an element of distrust in someone who looks so like himself.

This first meeting. It is not how he had imagined it. Years and he had just stood before a doorway. It happened so fast. He wants to go back and review. That doorway was now the doorway. One, two, three steps and he was in the same room, inhabiting the same space, the breathing air, the space of his father's days.

"Vera has you all fixed up," Leo says.

"She does." He nods, a half smile.

"New shoes. New suit," Leo continues. And then. "We will do what we can, you know."

"It is appreciated," Austin says. His eyes draw them both in, but his tone of voice pushes them away—keeping them a little at a distance, suspicious, as if, at any moment, they may vanish.

"I'll get us a sandwich," Vera says.

"I'll go with you." Leo begins to follow her.

"No. Stay. It's just across the street. I'll be only a few minutes. Stay."

"Yes. Of course."

Vera leaves. They both watch her exit. Leo has no idea what to do, where to stand. He puts his hands in his pockets and then takes them out again. He sees the shop, the two rooms filled with clocks and radios. His father sits in a chair alongside the counter, he still standing. Leo walks, more paces, before the window, the ceiling low, the light weak, and the chimes above the door seem, in this decrepit place, a small luxury. He has not prepared himself for, what is this burning sensation, a singe at his throat and torso, radiating out toward his shoulders—shame. To see the space of his existence, to witness how close to the bone his father lives, he can almost hear these things rattling within silence and solitude.

Their talk turns to Julia. Does she ask for me? Yes. Does she work? Yes. Too hard. Leo can feel his father tracking him with his eyes as he walks back and forth. Is she waiting for me? Yes.

"Father, enough of all that now," he begins. "Listen to me, I've been thinking. I know Vera has an appointment with the embassy. We're all scheduled, but if we can't make any progress, if it comes to it, I think we should try crossing the border." His father meets his gaze now, a silence stretching out along the band of light that falls into the shop. Leo can see the dust motes spinning wildly, holding on to the air in desperation. He looks away from his father.

"I'll drive," Leo says.

"Was there ever any question about that?"

"I'll drive. We'll go up to Sonora," Leo continues. "You know those towns. We can make it a nice trip—a good long one. Get out of the city. And we'll drive and drive. Maybe even make a segue to the coast. We'll take that coast road along the Sea of Cortez. All the way up to Nogales. It's just route 15. We'll head west, first through Toluca and Tonalá, then to Guadalajara, Tepic. I've mapped it out here in the guidebook."

"I don't know." His father is shaking his head, jaw set, his face, body with a confirmed resistance, Leo meanwhile still pleading. He draws closer to his father now, leans forward and then pivots on his heel to pace.

"We'll take it nice and easy. We can go to the ocean maybe, you know? Then it's just to route 15 all the way up—Culiacán, Hermosillo, Cananea, Nogales. And we'll just cross right there, pretend like we're simply crossing home to Arizona or California to get our *visas de turistas* fixed."

"And if they stop us?"

"They won't."

"But if they do?"

"You really think they are going to bother with you? We'll give the border guards a little something, what do they call it—a *mordida*, right? Grease the palms, you know? I'm telling you it's easy, easy."

"Yes, yes. I've heard this—'it's easy, so easy,' but no," his father says, leaning on the counter now. It is cooler out, the early night coming on, and a breeze finds its way inside. The beads sway and click.

"Father," he says, "why do you have to be so damn good? It might help more if you were a bit of a jerk, you know—not so upstanding," he continues, and then laughs to lessen the harsh tone he hears in his voice. Vera passes in front of the window, and then, in a moment, she enters. How out of place they both seem. Distinctly Americans, Leo thinks. In contrast to their father—his accent, his manner. Suddenly he is acutely aware of how their consonants are hitting hard against their teeth.

"Look," says Leo. He is taller than his father, just a bit, fills out his suit more though he has a lankiness of youth. "Now, we came here to help you. You can't go on living like this. We'll simply get in the car and drive. They'll have no idea and you'll be with us. God, Vera and me? You can't get more unassuming than the two of us."

"You? You've practically got 'blacklisted' stamped on your foreheads," his father says, shaking his head. "I'm not going back like that. I want to be legal."

He watches his father, hears him repeating, "I want to be legal."

"More than you want to be home with us?"

"They are two different things," his father insists.

"Father, please stop being so stubborn and idealistic." Leo feels the words through his gritted teeth.

"Stubborn? Idealistic?" His voice is loud, booming. "If I go illegally, maybe the first day, the second, or in a year, they will get me, they will find me out—" He breaks off, shaking his head. "And then what? Back to Russia? For what? Live out a life in a camp? No. I will work on my inventions. I will go legally."

"Don't you see they'll never let you in legally. I can even see that. It's been over ten years! You have tried their way, with their rules. It has not worked!" Leo can feel the excitement in his voice, his heart racing. "Has it?"

"You do not know what I know," Austin says, matter-of-fact.

"What is it that you know, that you are so certain of, that you know more than we do?" Leo asks.

"I know what they are capable of," Austin says. The same flat, steady tone.

"Who?" he snaps, and then as if thinking out loud, the thought just coming to him, voice lowered, near to a whisper, he muses, "All these years and you've fled other countries, crossed other borders, and now this last one, this one you won't cross."

"You don't know—these men. They know things. There are some people I know. They have power, you see? You understand? You don't know what they can do. They came for me when I did nothing wrong, nothing! What will they do to me when I actually break their laws?" His voice rising.

"Haven't they already done enough? Besides, don't you see, there is no 'they,' they won't do anything to you, they won't bother with you. You can go, you can—"

"You don't understand, you don't realize. These men!"

"All right now," Vera says, placing the sandwich she purchased on the counter. "Enough! Let's settle in and talk before we get into any plans." She turns to Leo, her voice lower. "Don't upset him. He gets agitated enough, be gentle. It's not so easy for him."

"It hasn't been easy for us, for Mother," Leo grumbles.

"Don't you think he knows that, feels that every day of his life?"

"He's just drowning in his own sorrow is how I see it."

"Can you blame him?"

Leo is standing in the doorway now, back to the inside of the shop, hands stuffed in his pockets, he can't stop fuming, but feels tears come into his eyes.

"It's his own fault."

"No, it is not and you know that's not true. He's trying in his own way."

"What way is that? His inventions? Useless scribblings by an old stateless Russian. That's what they are!"

. . .

"YOUR NAME, SIR."

"Austin Voronkov."

"Austin Voronkov. Is that your full name? In Russian?"

"It's Ustin Alexandrovich Voronkov."

"What country are you from?"

"I'm an applicant for U.S. citizenship."

"But we'll need to know your country."

"Russia," Vera says.

"The Soviet Union?"

"No. He is Russian," Leo said.

"I see. Well, Russian."

"Yes."

"And you come here today with your son and daughter."

"Yes."

"And please, your full names."

"Vera Voronkov. Leo, Leon Voronkov," Vera said.

"I see here you are requesting an appeal, a waiver?"

"Yes."

"For deportation, a ruling from 1920."

"Yes. That's correct."

"Anarchy. Mr. Voronkov, you've been found guilty of the charge of anarchy. Do you agree to this?"

"Yes. That is correct."

"And why the appeal at this late date? Your date of deportation is 1920. It's 1948."

"I would like to join my family."

"Your family is here."

"I'd like to join my wife and children in the U.S."

"You do know that we can accept a waiver and appeal form, but it's Washington that deals with deportation cases?"

"Yes. We understand this," Vera said.

"Anarchy. A serious offense."

"His political leanings have changed," Vera said.

"Look here, I'm not an anarchist."

"It's a mistake, you see," Vera began.

"I'm an applicant for U.S. citizenship," Austin began to speak, but Vera placed her hand out to stop him.

"An applicant, perhaps, but if you were deported"—the immigration officer tilted his head to the side and then tipped his glasses down his nose, staring at Austin—"well, you see, it's not just a simple application for U.S. citizenship."

The room was tight, confining, low-ceilinged, and the one window faced a brick wall. The hallway was dim and every once in a while he could hear footsteps clatter past. His head felt tight. His pulse in his neck throbbed. He was taking deep breaths. They were asking him questions. He answered. He could hear his voice, though a strange echo brought his words back to him and he kept his eyes on his hands, could feel Vera on one side of him, Leo on the other. They too were talking, when they had something to say—sometimes leaning forward to emphasize a point, other times sitting back in slumped exasperation. The clerk was of some higher office than the petty clerks who sat within the outer room behind the glass partition. No. It seemed they had moved farther into the building. Closer to the seat of power, yes. Austin imagined that somewhere within this entire structure was a central office with one man seated in the middle, aware of what went on within all these rooms with windowless doors. And he heard the words come to his lips, almost without realizing it he was talking, in response to a question. He heard his words echoing still, but he seemed to be speaking and taking deep breaths, gasping as he continued talking, telling the clerk, "Look here, look here," and going on at once about his wrongful arrest, hoping that the unseen surveillance would also hear, about the weeks spent incommunicado, the interrogation and the deportation. "Thrown out back to a country intent on murder and starvation!" And he explained his long travels as a Russian émigré, following with the others to Odessa, across the Black Sea to Constantinople and then onward to France—Le Havre first, before Paris. Then the Nansen passport. He produced it from his satchel. A many-folded, wrinkled booklet of gray disintegrating papers. And the long waiting process through quotas. He heard himself asking the clerk if he knew about quotas. The young man blushed and looked away from Austin, who looked to Vera and Leo before continuing on, explaining that the quotas meant only a certain percentage of ethnicities were allowed into the country in any given year. "Two percent," he said. Two percent of the U.S. Russian population for any given year would be allowed in. They never made the 2 percent, they never made quota. And he spoke of the journey from Russia to Veracruz and Mazatlán. Desperate for work, he took the lighthouse work, then the copper mines, waiting to be reinstated. Two months. He told the clerk about the two months, how it was only to be two months, which stretched into one year, then two before he moved to Mexico City, and now, the lousy brutes started stealing his designs and drafts. "You men and your power," he kept repeating like a refrain. He told the clerk about how he knew that the U.S. government had been watching him, sending this Jack to ensure his inventions wouldn't get to the patent agents or to the commissioner, making sure that he wouldn't try something tricky like crossing the border. They'd cornered him in. They'd blocked him out. He was breathing more heavily now, quite out of breath. The man was behind the desk, staring. Vera and Leo too were at him, saying, settle down, whispering. *It's all right, Father. Settle down.* Someone brought him a glass of water and he drank half of it in one full gulp, spilling some down his chin and onto his shirtfront. Vera rose and was talking, nearly whispering to the clerk, who'd risen himself, both near the now open door.

"Can't you see? He's quite in need of being with his family," he heard her say, and then the clerk: "If we allowed for every person in need of being with his or her family, the country would be overrun." Words whispered. Hushed. Hissing and then a louder voice.

"Is there no way to make an exception, considering the circumstances?" Leo stepped in. "We'd like to have him home."

"We can't risk his becoming a ward of the state."

"We won't let that happen," Leo said. "Besides, he can work. He's an engineer. We can provide for him if it comes to that."

"That's not a guarantee."

He watched Leo and Vera talking with the clerk, bodies tilted forward on an angle, pointing, looking at each other, to him. Leo sprang back in anger, prowling, muttering in disgust. Vera kept pleading.

Anything to be done? Anything? he heard her say. They were only two, three feet away from him, but their words were garbled and distant. Suddenly, there was more conferring, whispering. The senior clerk was speaking in a low, nearly muffled voice. A tone of graveness. Then their eyes, all of them, turned to him. He recoiled, averting his own gaze out the window to the bricked wall, each edge of brick fitting neatly into the others.

"There is one thing," the clerk began, and then looked to Austin and gestured for Vera and Leo to step out of the room and into the hallway. More low voices. Austin still sat drinking the glass of water. He was not sure if he should follow them outside, or stay where he was. He stared out the window, again the bricks sat in their tidy formation. Footsteps began far down an unseen hallway and he could hear them approaching. Under the door a line of light, shadows of movement, whispers, low voices. All voices talking about him, no doubt—planning, colluding. To what end? For what purpose? His own children now siding with these clerks? He no longer knew what to think.

The clerk walked back into the office with a purpose. No more of his vague, vacillating stance, his unwillingness to assist, to listen. He was making phone calls. Vera leaned over him, bent toward him in a gentle way, talking to him. "Another glass of water, Father? The man is preparing for you to answer some simple questions, yes?" Was that all right with him? Well, it had to be, Austin thought, nodding his head. "We will be right outside, just right here," Vera said, as she and Leo left the room. Yes. He understood. Fine, fine, he nodded. He took a sip of water and set the glass down.

Soon, a different man was ushered in to sit behind the desk. He wore a tweed jacket and a maroon shirt whose buttons were like opaled seashells. His mustache was black, but his hair was graying and he had large black eyes set far back into his head.

"Mr. Voronkov. Are you ready to begin?"

"Yes."

"I will present you with a series of images here on these cards and you then tell me what you see. The very first thing that comes to mind."

"Yes. All right." He sat up straight. The young man before him presented a flash card. An enormous black butterfly lingered on the page, and the butterfly morphed into a face. Two eyes, there in the empty section and the features forming—nose, mouth, the cheekbones—and then it melded back to its insect form, wings, antennae. The next card similar, though as he stared, seeking out some image, any image, it seemed to crack, a split down the middle, turning black and dark, some terrible, horrifying darkness of nature, beguiling and yet dangerous. He could hear the pencil faintly scratching along the page as the doctor wrote his responses. Next, a mouth. Wide, open, its smile malicious and, at one instant, benign. The next one, eyes hovered above, red and pulsing, demonic in their stare. Clouds came next—threatening, treacherous clouds, violent as if they would touch down out of the sky causing havoc like gods wrapped in pastel colors. He spoke in a fast spurt of words, the doctor goading him on. *Say the first thing, the very first thing that comes to your mind*, he scribbling furiously, taking down what he said, no doubt, to use it against him, Austin suddenly thought. The cards flashed before him, first one and then another. Some black and gray. Others colored—a light pink or red, gentle watercolors with a strange, eerie wickedness about them.

"Who are you and what do you want from me?" Austin asked, rising now. The door opened, Vera and Leo stood in the hallway. Austin looked to them and they were walking toward him. He cowered back and then shouted, "Who are you and what do you want?" They were coming closer, and behind them others had gathered in the doorway, had stopped in the hallway to peer into the office, all staring at him as if they might take something, some fiber of his being, something crucial, and he felt the floor giving out from under him—a sudden rush. He had to sit down for a moment, just a moment and he fell into the chair, grasping its sides, knuckles white. The men gathered in the doorway were clerks, all with manila files, suits, and hair combed back. The light from the hallway white and monotonous now and their feet like his own, caked with the insistent dust of Mexico City.

Out of the corner of his eye, he saw a man walking far down the hallway, past the men who had stopped to look at him seated in such a vulnerable, unforgiving state. His walk was familiar, a kind of calm, nonchalant stroll amid the commotion of those crammed in the doorway and hallway, all peering deep into him. That pace, that gait! Austin knew it. Jack! His suspicions had been right after all. He grew silent, his breathing calmed. He looked blankly at Vera and then to Leo, each stood on either side of him now. Leo was talking to the clerk still, papers spread out on the desk. Austin saw his satchel leaning up against the side of the chair and in one swift move he lunged for it, tucked it tight under his arm. He stormed out of the room, excusing himself among the people lurking around the door and down the hallway. He could hear Vera now clattering behind him, other voices close and then distant. The bastard was still walking down the hallway, oblivious and nonchalant. When Austin stepped out of the room, he could feel hands on his arms, but he threw them all off. My God, his designs had never even reached the ambassador! He pushed past the men who tried to block his way, pressing,

pushing, and passing until they finally gave way and he tore down the
hallways, slipping for a moment, dipping down before he caught his balance, grasping for the wall, steadying himself, all the while hearing
the commotion at his back, voices—*Mr. Voronkov, Father, Father, Mr.
Voronkov*—but they faded as he now made his way back out to the vast
lobby with its lines and shuffling papers, clicking of the typewriters and
murmurings, the din of simultaneous speech. He kept running until
he found himself outside on the embassy steps, the cars flashing by. The
park sat calmly before him, people strolling amid its delicate lanes, the
dark green glossy in the sun. No Jack. Austin raced down the steps and
crossed the road, the traffic screeching to a halt. He walked into the park,
looking left and right, his satchel beneath his arm. The damn thief, taking his designs, ensuring they'd never get to the ambassador. It was unconscionable and he'd confront him and say, "Look here, you cannot do
this to a man! You cannot torment him so, disrupt the natural course of
his life and ruin all his chances," for that's what had happened, Jack ap-
pearing in his life as a reminder, a deterrent. The bastard. He'd tell him
though, and they'd all soon see. He was Austin Voronkov, inventor. He
was not an anarchist.

. . .

LEO SAT WITH HEAD BOWED, the weight of it all, picking over what
had happened. The *pulquería* was dark. The broad shadows of the maguey and palms fell across the narrow sidewalk and through the open
windows whose shades were pulled only halfway down. Overhead, fans
whirred through the intermittent clink and clatter of glasses passed, pul-
que poured.

Drinking, he could feel layers unearthed. One atop the other. Whole countries turned over and he felt gratitude. He stood on the man's shoulders. The old man had unknowingly sacrificed his life for their lives and oh he'd make something of himself. He'd get out of this terrible, wrenching situation with a mother who cried anytime his father's name was mentioned, and a father who'd *worn down his mind* in Mexico City.

Damn them. He had been in the service—the Navy—and this is how he'd been thanked? Unable to bring his father to the United States. Part of him wanted to hit the man, hit it out of him, make him see clearly, make him realize that they could go, that no one would bother with him, no one would come for him, and then the opposite urge to offer sympathy and some semblance of comfort, but how, how? This old, thin man raving about his inventions. Damn it. They were useless. *Scribblings by an old stateless Russian*, he'd said, regretting it now, but, well, it was true. He'd spell it out, draw it out right there and say they were no use. And he would then put the man in the car himself, put him in and drive up to the border. Put him in against his will if he had to. Drive up through the states of Mexico—Sinaloa, Sonora. And they would cross, like any Americans going back after a good time below the border, or to renew their tourist visas. Or they'd get him a fake passport. Yes! That was an option too. And then he saw the scene in his mind, it bloomed before him, the place he'd go—a small room downstairs, a basement one entered from the street or back alleyway. A postage stamp of a room. A small half door and a man seated over a desk with one of those magnifying glasses affixed to his eye, hunched over papers, fake seals. The intricate, painstaking work of forgery. And then damn the U.S. Embassy! It had all been too much for his father. Why had they put him up to it, to face it? How had they not realized he wouldn't be able to handle it? An appeal seemed all well and fine if it worked, but why had they believed coming in person would work, when all this time their mother's letters were simply futile attempts, amounting to nothing?

His mother's letters. Where were they? Who had they gone to? Missives sent into some abyss was how he saw it, but there she had sat over the years—the old cumbersome machine, teaching herself to type, more point and peck. But she'd done it, and she'd written so many letters pleading their case, their family's case. And his father's damn inventions, drafts sent to patent agents. Pay the price and they'd handle the administrative hassles—a waste! Oh, but one had to break the rules in this life, one had to at least have more moxie, more willingness to not always toe the line. One had to break out, take some kind of active stance. Once he was with them all, once his father was back home, Mother would take care of him. He'd come around then, he'd find rest. *Worn down his mind.* It was true, but they would put him to some kind of work—a mechanic maybe, or working as an engineer, maybe at the Sikorsky plant. Surely, they'd take him. He could do numbers and figures, understood all the mechanics of engineering. He had excellent drafting skills, that Leo could see from the designs, the precise measurements, all these fractions scribbled in the margins. They'd take him. It would work. *Worn down his mind.* And then, well, he'd be an upstanding citizen of America as he'd always wanted to be. He'd decided. He'd put the man in the car himself, if it came to that. And he'd drive, he'd be the one to drive.

. . .

IT IS LATE. It is early. It is 2 A.M. Austin can hear the thunder in the distance as he nears his boardinghouse. He has walked from the cantina, a dull numbness in his feet as if his steps are upon not concrete, but soft felt. He walks to the stairs, holds the banister, and struggles up the steps. He falls. It is the fall of a child, tottering, but not bracing, more collapsing, limbs pliant. He is muttering, his tongue thick in his mouth.

> *"Mr. Voronkov, can you tell me where you are from?"*
> *"Where were you born?"*
> *"In what country do you have citizenship?"*
> *"Where do you work?"*
> *"On what street do you live?"*
> *"What is your permanent address?"*

The thunder grows louder as it moves over the mountains, encroaching upon the city.

"These men and their power and position," he mutters to himself, "with their stamps and papers." It is in rolling succession, the words come, phrases streaming through his mind.

> *"Are you an anarchist?"*
> *"Do you have anything against the government?"*
> *"What is your country of citizenship?"*

He stares around him, startled, dazed. He has reached the top of the stairs, his chest tight from exertion and now releasing as he stumbles for the door to his rooms. Darkness. The thunder louder now, closer, and then a sudden downpour like the far-off cheering of a swelling, enormous crowd. As his eyes adjust, he can make out the gray-white rain forming a veil over the window. He walks to it. The taxi still parked at the end of his street in all its sinister stillness. He is drawn back to his room, can now see the table, and in the next room, his bed, dresser, and a flash of light in the oval mirror. He is suddenly unsure how he got here, standing in the middle of his room. The wind outside is strong, strong enough to shake the windows. He is sweating. He races to his table. His drafting papers lie scattered. He begins to take the designs—under the floorboard, the bed, next, behind the dresser. He gathers them, laying them out on his table. Such definite marks—points connected, measurements taken. Something would be made out of them, something tangible, of worth. He grabs his satchel on the floor and places it on the table. He gathers the designs into a tight bundle and stuffs them in his satchel, fastening the buckle, struggling with it, bent over it, pulling and tugging. His head swirling as he stands upright, placing the satchel snug under his arm and taking a deep breath, waiting for the room to steady, bracing himself on a chair, then on the doorframe. In a moment, he is out of his rooms, racing down the hallway, taking the stairs two at a time.

Outside, there is nothing but the rain and wind, which, when it barrels down the street, creates havoc—trees bent, leaves damp and strewn, the wheezing, whistling is incessant until the wind calms for a moment, silence resuming except for the now steady pelting rain. The rain is cold and already his hair is drenched, his shirt too. His shoes begin to rub his bare heels, the water seeping through the soles, he conscious of a sting, knowing the skin has chafed and torn. No matter, he thinks, walking, his satchel beneath his arm still. He holds it tight, close to his body as if the wind might snatch it away from him, its contents strewn over the Condesa, blown away on a terrible gust and lost. No cars. No lights. The streetlamps black. He stops at the corner of the Parque México in its glossy green oval of trees, wet in the rain, benign and lush amid the blackness and damp around him.

Beneath the trees' cover, he gets a respite from the rain, wipes the water out of his eyes. He stands still, listening, the rain here dulled, its softer patter on the canopy the trees make all hushed for a moment. Where exactly is he going with his designs? He had it in his mind that he'd bring them somewhere, but to where or to whom he's suddenly lost. The post office? Perhaps. But it is closed. To the U.S. Embassy? He can't go back there. He stands clutching them still, the satchel wet.

"Why did you ever go through with it?" He hears Jack's voice, the same abrasive baritone. In the darkness, Austin can't make him out. The trees and night more dark than ever with all the rain.

"They insisted. I had no choice," Austin says, his voice in a strained whisper and then growing louder. "They believed they could help me."

"Of course it wouldn't work. I told you it wouldn't make a difference."

"If they'd just make an exception," Austin says.

"Impossible. You heard what the clerk said, if they made allowances all the time, the country would be overrun. And now you are left with one option."

"What is that?"

"You know." Austin can't see, thinks for a moment he may be going blind, all is so dark. He places his hands in front of his face, fingers spread, palms wide. He brushes the rainwater out of his eyes. He can see his hands before him, the rain, wet on his jacket, his satchel.

"Crossing," Austin half whispers. "It's what they want me to do."

"Do you want to?"

"I have no other choice."

"There are consequences if you cross."

"If I'm caught."

"What makes you think you won't be caught? With me following you?" But Austin keeps searching, trying to find Jack, back and forth across the clearing in the park. But after each time he hears Jack's voice, only the rain in its hissing race to the ground makes any noise at all.

"I trust my children," Austin says into the emptiness.

The rain bursts and then settles to a now steady hush as his thoughts continue to do a frantic series of about-faces—crossing, not crossing—while he grips tightly to his designs. They now seem useless in his arms. All these days and years, held together by the thinnest of strands, strands that had multiplied to form a web over actuality, over his own reality. And now here, he tears through the fine gauze and for a moment the years in Mexico are as clear as glass. An existence made out of nothing but his own pride, fear and folly, a stubborn certainty, a blind, sheer will that his inventions would bring him to the United States, to be an American inventor, to be a father, to be a husband. Meanwhile, they had moved on without him, and his soul feels hollow, scraped out. What use was he? What use his inventions? The yearly attempts? He is weary, now conscious of a deep exhaustion in body, mind, and soul, and he stands still with his satchel in hand wondering at where he is going and why.

All the years come at once, bold and forthright, fall right into his palms—the weight of them and likewise their lightness—and he is now forced to see them, how they've changed, the faces within his mind, and he looks to find perhaps that they no longer exist in the way he needs them to. To see them now, here, is to see himself now—the clear truth: the wasted years, hollow, dry years, and they had accumulated, one after another without his even noticing, one turning over to the next effortless change of a waiting life, one built around the loss of them, but also the loss of all his possible lives, his hopes, what he'd wished for in America, then again in Russia. And perhaps on the third try, in Mexico, he did not have the strength to imagine another way of being in the world without them and so instead set himself headlong into getting back to them, all of it in a state of perpetual striving for if not a life of that then what? Nothingness. He is staring into it now, a crevice in time, which seems to him of navy and blue. Darkness—a place that has its own rules and reasonings, its own strange logic.

. . .

THUNDER WHEN SHE HEARD it had always been in her general surroundings, not so far off that she had to wonder about the noise as she did now, lying awake. The low rumbling seemed to come from outside the city itself. One or two A.M. it must have been. The distance, the nonthreatening clash of hot and cold, no lightning yet, made her wonder what exactly she was hearing and, because she was wide awake, she was listening, hearing it travel, incremental and growing louder as the storm drifted closer, still no flash of light, just the rumble. Hollow. Like distant drumbeats. And she thought of all that air and cold and heat and when exactly the rain would come.

She drifted in and out of sleep, holding on to a thought only to lose it as she dozed off, waking to find her mind settled on something else—a vague idea about her father, about Leo, she fighting to nail it down before it passed. And then feeling the fatigue of the day, how much it had offered to think about, and she seemed to be staring into the very truth of her father's life.

"A nervous condition, severe mental strain. It's to be expected," the

doctor had explained when her father ran out of the embassy. The clerk
had suggested the psychological evaluation as a way to lend some support to the appeal. If it was a positive evaluation, the appeal would be
viewed favorably, would give him more of a chance with the appropriate
authorities. "Common among refugees, émigrés," he'd said in an effort
to comfort them and then later, "But with the anarchist charge and this
condition, I'm afraid he will be categorized as 'unfit for entrance.'" Oh,
but it was all their doing! If anyone had blood on their hands it was
them—these men in power, these governments and embassy clerks! It
was their fault, and she'd said as much. She was ashamed now suddenly
at her own rage, remembering how she'd sprung forward, lunged at that
young doctor, pointing. "And it's no wonder! It's your fault!" It was gut-
tural, instinctual, a kind of cry, plea. And now they are left with Leo's
idea. The best chance they had really. Crossing.

She had dozed off again and then was woken by the wind or what she
thought was the wind, but when she heard a faint calling, she knew it was
him in an instant.

"DADDY, WHAT ARE YOU doing here?" she asks, looking over her
shoulder and back again as she stands in the doorway.

"Are you drunk?" she says, drawing close to him, trying to get at his
scent, his neck and mouth. He looks at her, his stare vacant, confused.

"Father," she says, taking him by both arms. "How did you get
here?" She pulls him into the courtyard.

"I don't know." He looks past her.

"Speak softer, please. Come," she says, taking his wrist and leading
him to the dry corridor between courtyard and house, not wanting to
disturb her host family.

"We made a decision. I let you all go," he says, trailing behind her. "I wanted you to go. It seemed the wisest thing to do then. It was the consulate who told us."

"Okay. Yes," Vera says, standing in front of him now, smelling the sharp, bitter scent of tequila as he struggles to keep his eyes steady on her.

"They told us," he continues, resting his head now back against the wall, closing his eyes. "I should've known not to listen to it, to trust it. But then, they'd told us two months at most. It was too good to turn away from. Never in the world did we think they'd not let me in. Every year it seemed more of a possibility, especially in the first years. A year— so little—one stops counting. And now?" He looks to her and looks away, lips pressed tight. "What do I have to show for myself? I've amounted to what? I'd like your mother to think I had made something of myself." He does not look at her.

"You are her husband. Once you are home, you will work, your inventions—"

"Mere scribblings by a stateless old Russian." He groans.

"It serves you right to think of them that way," Vera steps back from him, drawing her robe closed before folding her arms across her chest.

"What good have they done me? Leo is right. Besides, I'm still here aren't I?"

"We will drive you. Leo has said he'll drive. I'll go with you. We'll all go. And you'll see how easy—"

"How can you know? You don't. I cross the border and I'm illegal. A pawn. Wait for them to get me. How can I be a father and a husband when they think I'm an anarchist?"

"What does it matter anymore? It was years ago. No one will bother with you—"

"Julia, Julia, my jewel. She's worked her whole life. And what kind of husband and father have I been to you? Not able to make a scrap to send."

"You'll simply be with us."

"I kept hoping. I did work. Drafts and drafts. You've seen them. There. Look," he says, his satchel left out in the courtyard, its leather darkened by the rain. "They are all for you. The designs, my inventions. It has all been for you, but I've been able to offer you nothing, provide you with nothing. Is that a father, a husband?"

Vera watches him, his shoulders curved inward, his head bowed so that he glances up to look across to the wall beyond her. "Do you know I applied for my first papers? I did. I took English classes. I registered for the draft. I took out my first papers, an applicant, you know, an applicant for American citizenship."

The rain has stopped, but the sound of heavy, residual drops falls from the trees, their soft echoes resound off the flagstones, the stone walls.

"You've allowed *us* to be Americans," Vera says. He seems to take this in, offers a little laugh—in spite, in gratitude, she's not sure which, and then he stares directly into her eyes.

"Oh, Vera, but don't you see, I've forgotten even why." He scowls.

Silence. She speaks softly, her words forming over the last of the rain.

"Perhaps it is time now to come home and find out why, to remember why."

. . .

THEY STAND WAITING LIKE CRIMINALS. The Cadillacs slide, curve through the morning city streets, which are damp still from the night's rain. Car windows streaked white, then black like enamel. Austin has a cigarette at his lips and in his hands a book of matches, a compact square that he flicks loosely as he passes it through his fingers.

"He said eight, right?" he says out loud.

Vera nods, offering a murmured yes of confirmation. She is wringing her hands—she would be. He is pacing, the pebbles beneath the sole of his shoe making a pleasant scratching sound on the sidewalk. The city is slowly filling as the cars amble by through thin morning air that is fumed by the sweet, thick scent of gasoline.

He watches the street. Far down a man on a bike approaches, his head peering out from behind a tower of packages—cotton sheets of periwinkle and pink, boxes, flowered oilcloths yellow and red and blue. His shoulders tense, rise. He turns his head and sees Vera in profile, her back to him.

"Why are we standing in this sun? Come, let's cross," she says over her shoulder. She begins without him, he falling back behind her, pausing to allow the bicyclist to pass. He has moved from the sun to the shadows of the trees, and the leaves cast a pattern along his face. He enters into the full shade, the cooler relief of Parque México. The knotted, arthritic tree roots have cracked through the cobblestones so that the ground is uneven. She sits on a bench and he sits beside her.

A Cadillac passes, the buttercream chrome and silver of the hood ornament unmistakable, like a mermaid or angel, hair billowing through water or wind, a sense of resistance, of pressing onward.

The cars keep passing. He begins counting. Cadillacs in new models—the slim, dashing lines, the silver grille plate, the spearmint white tires blur. He's stuck now with the distraction of it—Packard '38, cobalt blue; Cadillac Sixty Series, blood red; a black one, slick as the top of a piano. Out on the Avenida Amsterdam someone is leaning on a horn. Too early. Others follow, someone pressing in fast bleats. It startles Vera and her shoulders jump from the suddenness of it. And he too. His blood seems to freeze and then course fast through chest, neck, temple, settling into a bloom of heat across his sternum. He thinks momentarily of simply walking across the street, getting up, sliding away farther into the park, away from their plan. He turns to see Leo. He's hanging out the driver's side window of a light pistachio green sedan. His hands wide and stretched along the bulge of the car, tapping it—one, two, three, four—full, hollow sounding. In one hand he holds a navy blue booklet.

Vera stands, her torso blocking him from the sun. Then, the click of her heels, slow and dragging as she makes her way to the car, placing her palm down on the hood as she steps down from the sidewalk.

"I'm sorry I kept you waiting," he hears Leo say.

"We didn't hear you drive up," Vera says.

"I cut the motor and let it coast in." Leo is out of the car now. He's opening a pack of Wrigley's Spearmint gum. Austin joins them, following up behind Vera. Leo offers him a piece of gum.

"No. No, thank you." Austin's eyes are on the passport. It looks real enough.

He has packed nothing, or nearly nothing. He has only one bag of minor effects. That and his satchel.

Leo hands him the passport. The rectangular book lay in his hand— navy. The way he'd envied them at one point. Paper is stronger than one imagines, he thought to himself, flipping through the book now, slapping it against his palm a bit. Deep navy and crisp as the Atlantic and he remembered walks along the Long Island Sound, then a remembrance of possibility when he'd felt young, strong, enterprising, and in love. That was what the passport in its dashing, brash navy blue seemed to say, all neat and clean and almost as serene as a sea.

LEO IS WALKING TO the car. The doors are heavy, clicking open, a solidity to the metal handles, the button no larger than a thumbprint. He'd borrowed the car from a buddy. One of the kids lent it to him. It would be doing him a favor too. He'd drive it up across the border and meet a friend coming for a visit. The friend would bring it back down—a perfect exchange.

Leo watching as his father aims for the door.

He nods reassuringly, swiftly, and he opens the front dropping into the passenger's seat with difficulty, his legs too long. Leo instructs him to readjust the seat, and then he settles in himself. The car smells of leather, Wrigley's Spearmint, and a faint hint of perfume, which has left a gauze of flowery spice.

"How long are we looking at?" Vera asks.

"A day." Leo turns to make sure Vera is in the back now. He sees her staring out the window, a heaviness at her lip, mouth, at his too, but they lock eyes and in the weary smile is a reassurance. He knows her worry, her anxieties, and he is trying to paint over all of this with his own calm, feigning it yes, but someone must be composed.

THE DRIVE, THEY'VE TOLD HIM, will take more than twenty-four hours. He didn't have a say in it all, was following their lead. First, they will drive all day from Mexico City to Guadalajara, onward to the west.

They will need to stop a few times, for gas, food, and rest, staying one night in Mazatlán. Leo wants to see where he was born. Then it's MEX15-D up the coast, until they reach the Sea of Cortez, onward to Hermosillo and then through Santa Cruz to Nogales.

Leaving a city as day begins is a humbling experience. There is—in the early light, in the first sounds of passersby, their footsteps and conversations—a promise. It is hard not to think about what one will miss as the activity of the day, the day in the city you are leaving, continues, as its inhabitants go on with so much busyness, flurry, and to do and to be, no one aware that you are leaving, no one to know you have left. But, leaving a city uncertain of return? It would go on. A body removed, deposited elsewhere—the city's indifference to your absence, the days rising and falling, piling up without you.

Anarose. Only she, he imagines, would wonder at his absence. He sees her now on the line, the first time he'd seen her. The fatigue and almost boredom of her stance as if she'd long been waiting for something, for anything, to happen. She had a face of her country—a pouting mouth that burst into smiles and laughter. She may come to the shop a few times more, enter and stand in the emptiness and perhaps pass her hand across the counter, leaf through papers, and maybe something about the way the things sat on their shelves, more still than usual, the sense of settled dust, would tell her that he'd done it, that he'd finally gone. He hopes she can in some way forgive him for balking. He'd half opened a door, peering inside, and then, on second thought, he'd turned away.

As they drive the sky spreads out before them. Blue, with the sun's glare threatening to whitewash. All the space, uncluttered by buildings, sets his thoughts open almost like the way he'd felt when standing before Julia those many years ago.

"I will know you when . . . ," he'd said to himself, and who is that brash boy now, he wonders?

VERA DOES NOT KNOW why she'd agreed to all this. Perhaps they should simply go on without her, she'd said to Leo. But he was so determined, had insisted. True, it was a last-ditch attempt, and she'd heard about others crossing with no problem, why shouldn't it be just as easy for them?

They have passed the city limits, are speeding outward. The sun lines the rearview mirror. She catches her image, a view of her profile. Her forehead creased, the eyebrow broken from the furrowing, the hollow of her eyes squinting against the haze. Leo is fumbling with the radio, leaning forward, one hand on the wheel. She can see the jaw muscles flex, moving up and down working over his Wrigley's—the small tight rectangles he'd brought from the States.

Her father is still and silent. If it were not for the occasional turn of head, one would assume he was asleep. Vera brought her knitting needles and draws them out now, her hands beginning to move in successive darting stabs, the click of the needles pleasant and soothing over the hum of the motor, the crackle of the radio. Leo has settled on a bolero station. He is singing along.

It is a clear day, if blustery. The inside hood of the car, the leather ceiling and arc of it cut into her view of the sky, which is blue and searing, tranquil for a Mexican sky, though clouds are forming over the four peaks of Iztaccihuatl, the white woman. The city gradually slips away from them, as if undressing, shedding asphalt, cement, steel, and brick. The embassy, shop, Mexico City—it all lies far in the car's wake now, discarded as they merge onto the four- and five-lane highways—the great valves. The other cars have fallen away too and soon they are driving, one lone car on a road far from Mexico City. The country now dotted with small, flat-roofed adobe houses of white and yellow, the flat landscape—maguey, dark, gangly against the sky.

Nervous condition. Unfit for entrance. She cringes, remembering the scene. The unsuspecting, nearly oblivious doctor. The phrase keeps running over in her own thoughts. *Well, and no wonder!* she'd said, rising, and Leo telling her to calm down even though he too was seething, she could tell. She'd broken into a sob, left Leo there to continue talking with the doctor, stunned and speechless. She'd stormed outside, pacing back and forth, her hands wringing, teeth clenched. Her eyes flecked with the first of that night's tears. She didn't know what was coming over her, years of frustration on behalf of her father. Well, they'd go, they'd just leave, all three of them, just drive up to the border and cross, as Leo had said. She'd stood still for a moment, never believing something like this would come to fruition. How fully she'd imagined that she'd be able to simply do the paperwork, make her pleas, and they'd follow the processes and procedures and surely allow him in legally. But this now, this she'd not prepared for—now forced on this drive. She'd never really thought of the actuality of it. This drive. What it would mean. How it would be. It was always just a possibility, like when one watches another's final breaths, anticipating what is to come, but the actual final severance, when it happens, is still a shock. No. One needed to adjust to the change now, to the reality of it, which is what she's trying to do, knitting still, stitching it all up into some semblance of understanding, resigning herself to the decision; she'd be with them on this, the final, decisive push across the border.

. . .

AUSTIN HAD IMAGINED IT many times. Just how it would be—the day, the weather. But here they were, driving. One can only prepare so much—the day marked, the time chosen, the clothes, the people positioned, even the route that Leo had prepared. But all this thinking and preparation was an attempt to precipitate what would happen—the tricky complexities of the events of one day. What he had not expected was this quiet, his relative state of what he can only call calm, as if he were, for the time being, suspended in a hammock strung across a canyon whose depths he only half consciously knew of, like a memory, and only when bothering to do that hard, arduous work of recall would he remember and dare to sit upright, peer over the edge, to look down into the vast chasm that, all the while, had lain beneath him.

The steady driving. The sun through the open window. The hum of the motor. Combined, all had a lulling effect, so much so that for full moments he could drop into a tranquility and strange stillness, the crossing in a future moment. A swell of numbness in his chest, stomach. They were worried—Vera and her panicked needles, Leo's hand on the steering wheel, fidgety. And he, Austin, has his hand out the window. He'd never even considered that they would be traveling together, embarking on this together. He'd always seen himself there at the border, faced with it—alone.

Rooms come to him—the shape and color of the dining room where he would see Julia. The violet light of a winter afternoon, the gauze of white curtains. The two large picture windows looking out into white, the gray branches of what were to him now foreign trees. And then in an instant the lighthouse. The peace of those mornings. Awake and working, hearing her voice below. The barracks house with all its wood and emptiness. His boardinghouse, alone in Mexico City. Then, he'd never have contemplated the need for such a trip that they were all embarking on now. Then, when he'd clung so fiercely to the belief that the embassy would soon grant him a visa, that his inventions would get him to his family. That terrible, old room, the shape of it, the bareness with white light from the windows. The dresser with bits of crumbs, an orange peel. The bed strewn with papers. He gathering them, placing them in his satchel, trying to take as much as he could. Vera had sat him down.

"You don't need these, Father," she kept saying. "You're coming home now." He hears her voice still . . . *home, mother, rest.*

THE CITY FADES AWAY from them, its pull has loosened and they are driving faster now through the midmorning sun. Vera cannot imagine what her father is thinking—a kind of still preoccupation grips his whole body, his being. There is agitation in his silence. Reserve. It is as if, she thinks, he is storing up energy for the crossing. She can hardly imagine what it will be like, nor what it would be like for him. A simple crossing of some line demarcated by mere governments. She feels a dropping within, a hollow in the stomach as they leave the land plateau on which the city sits. The descent like staggered, labored breathing.

She looks at her father, quiet in the swath of sun that blazes in a tight, neat square along the passenger's side. His legs drawn up, his knees knobby, his hand out the window, and his gaze set forward. How, Vera wonders, could we think this would be a good idea, this faux joyride with the inevitable success or failure—crossing, not crossing—only two, three days away? She suddenly feels as if she were riding alongside a train pulling out of a station, struggling to keep up as the train picked up speed, the engines in full gear, falling back.

The country out the window is dry and rugged. One American-like highway cuts through the cactus farms. The landscape shifts to vast fields of brush and brown. Soon, they drive through green, through mountains where roads are tight and winding, filled with steep climbs and descents, switchbacks and hairpin turns. The drops down are fast and she feels the falling in her stomach. The windows are open. Her hair, which she has tied back in a loose knot at the base of her neck, flies in tendrils that whip her cheeks, lash her eyes so that she is forever brushing the hair from her sight lines, removing a tendril from her mouth. They pass through cool swells and then through sunlight.

She has only ever seen one picture of her mother in Mexico. She is standing, unsmiling, on a dirt road. Her hand is raised to her brow shielding her eyes from the sun. A maguey sits behind her and off to the side. Vera realizes that she is nearly the same age as her mother in that picture, with the Cananea landscape at her feet. Her eyes, though shaded, seem to struggle in the bright light of the desert. There was a softness and mildness to her features in that picture, incongruent with the stark extremes of the Cananea climate—arid, dry, desolate, and the sky massive and brooding above her, clouds like giants, and the land too, flat and vast and stretching far out behind her so that it reached the horizon, which seemed to vanish into the sky—Julia swallowed by it.

Vera remembers too, and one could miss it if one did not look closely enough, but there in the foreground of the photograph, imprinted on the ground at a slight diagonal, is the photographer's shadow. Her father, no doubt.

Her mother had a similar picture of her father. They must've

switched places, he taking the photo of her and then the awkward exchange of some cumbersome camera—the repositioning, the laughter.
She maybe struggling with the weight of it. The heat. And the same
shadow lies across the foreground of this photograph too, she remembers. But the shadow, of course, is different in this picture. It's not his. It's
Julia's shadow. The prescience of photographs.

She looked at her father again. He, unlike her mother, did not seem so
unfit for that severe Sonoran landscape. He'd become weathered, burnished by the Mexican sun so that his face was rugged and tan now, his
hair silver, wavy.

THEY SPEED THROUGH GREEN. On one side of the road, it is a straight
drop down. On the other, the mountain rises gradually. The trees here
all adorned with garlands of orchid vines. He can pick out the orange
trumpets, the spider lilies, the tiger orchid of red and orange.

They are driving forward toward a past, the past that he'd come to
meet that would take him from Mexico. There is a finality in this traveling even as they try to make it bearable—retracing his past journeys,
the towns he used to know nearing: Guadalajara, Tepic, Mazatlán,
Hermosillo.

His other travels return. The pier at Trieste. The wide-bottomed ship
like the sheen of a whale, or what he'd imagined was a whale. Then, he'd
had his first sight of open ocean, the roar and rush of the waves, shouts of
men loading crates and trunks from the dock, large hoisting lines and
foreign voices. The awful Atlantic crossing, and then the steamship back
to Russia, the trains to Kherson and away again, a boat across the Black Sea
to Constantinople, a boat to France, a train to Paris, and the steamship to

Veracruz. He skips through the years so the images gather, one bound to the next as if looking at a child's flip book. Another man may find in it adventure. From a different perspective, vantage point, perhaps it was, but he'd wanted a home and what was that but to wander day in, day out among the same knowable streets, frequent shops of a neighborhood, to be seen and known.

THROUGH DENSE GREEN Leo spots the ocean. It is a curved inlet, a bay of blue. Like a puddle of ink among mountains.

"The Pacific," Leo says. He is sitting forward now, slows down the car, pulling it to the side of the road.

"Careful," Vera says as branches tickle the hood of the car, threatening to poke through the back windows. Before he's even put the car in park, Leo has opened his door, jumping out. Pebbles crunch beneath his shoes. He cut the motor, but the radio is still playing, and he can hear it softly behind him, guitars strumming, the high-pitched voice of a female singer—something about remorse or resignation.

He is grateful to see the ocean, a half circle of turquoise, the horizon beyond a swath of white and a fine, deeper blue like an outline. The late-day sun causes the water to flicker white, scalloped as if by white wings. He looks out upon the place where the very circle of his life began, or straight path, or whatever geometry it would come to be, and he casts himself back to here—to Mazatlán—hoping to have some sense of recognition. One should know, he'd always felt, become intimately acquainted with, the place of one's birth. He tries to recall a memory, any memories of this place.

He picks a leaf from the bushes and drops it into his pocket. Later, he'll place it in his notebook and he'll write out beneath it, "First sighting of the Pacific in Mazatlán, Mexico. 1948."

THEY DECIDE TO STOP for food and a chance to stretch limbs. They will spend one night here, waking early to continue toward the border. Like all sea towns, the town itself, at midday, is deserted. It is lonely driving through the silent streets. Vera feels an eagerness to abandon all the metal and glass of the car for the salt air. As if he'd precipitated her thoughts, Leo veers off the back street, sidling up along the crumbling sidewalk.

Vera adapts. She can already see how this town works—its rhythm and colors. While on first impression the old city seems empty, devoid of motion, the activity of the town takes place in the shade, making it difficult to discern. Is a store open or closed? Is a restaurant serving food or does it sit abandoned? Has it been inoperative for one year or ten? But slowly, nearly imperceptibly, movement begins. In fact, it had always been there, and now, readjusting her focus she can see, in the shaded areas—beneath awnings that line the square forming strips of gray, blue—a dog's tail wagging, a white-aproned waiter removing glasses from a just-vacated table, the flutter of a green parakeet's anxious wings. A long line of old men sit against the ochre-colored façade of a tobacco shop. They are like a daisy chain of paper dolls, every third one with a cane. The old men stare at the three newcomers. It is perhaps the most excitement they have witnessed in some time, Vera imagines. She smiles at them. One responds with a nod of his head. The others sit motionless, save for a yawn, a hand swept thoughtlessly across a brow, canes tapping in a waltz rhythm—just because.

They are walking across the plaza. Leo falls behind.

"Are we idiots?" he yells out.

"What?"

"Only Englishmen and mad dogs—"

"It's better than being in that car."

Nearing the ocean, Vera hears the crashing waves. She walks slower here. Gone are the furious, furtive steps of her Mexico City self.

The real life of the town takes place on a meandering strip of board-walk, the *malecón*, which, like the sand, rocks, and waves, traces the curves of the coastline. By noon the fishermen's day is long over. Their boats strewn like the used crayons of reckless children—spent and worn wood of primary colors. Red, blue. The fish is now in the stalls—bull fish, shrimp. Gruff fishermen sit hunched over the work of mending—reweaving the frayed and broken ropes of their fishing nets. Vera likes the names of the fishing boats. Some are women's names—*Ibari*. There are other names: *El Faro del Sur, Vamanos, Sal Marina, Sand, Pearl.*

AUSTIN, VERA, AND LEO eat sandwiches they purchased from a stall on the sidewalk. They eat in silence. Austin knew the lighthouse was down the *malecón* and up the hill. Within walking distance. They'd pass right by it. But he didn't want to bring attention to this fact, didn't want to tell them. The scent of the salt and sea air is like a burning. A trace of sulfur too makes him think of grief, thick and briny. He feels like a ghost here on this coast, looking upon a fragment of his life that should no lon-ger be disturbed. Like a sleeping lion. Julia's presence like sunlight. One couldn't get away from it. He had dragged her across half the world, for what? The few years of peace in that lighthouse? Perhaps that was all they were meant to have? He shouldn't be here. He'll never return, he knows.

To hear the waves hit the shore in their constant, unrelenting pulse reminds him of the drive ahead. He wonders how he will sleep, knowing what awaits him the next day. Could it really be that he need only step across? Step across and simply return and all the inventions, struggles, patent letters, trips to the embassy, post office, walks in parks—all of it, the years of separation spent in effort to return, all the empty years, one strung to the next in a chain of worn-out hours, a solitude abated by a simple triangle of boardinghouse, post office, embassy, drafting papers and designs, lines drawn and erased, tequila downed and bottles discarded—all of it could end? He wonders at that: end. He feels as if he's peering deep, looking at some image hidden within one of the cards that doctor had shown him, and suddenly, here stood, here emerged, the thing, the truth, and he fights to hold it clear in front of him, examining it, turning it over, before it goes back down and hides within the rest of the ink blot—there, there. Without *it*, without that fight to rail against something, what would fill his days, who would he be, what purpose would his life have served?

He wonders if his clothes might still hang in the closet. He'd imagined them one hundred times or more. Was the image to Julia like a dead man's clothes? On narrow hangers. Had she kept them? One shirt, maybe? In his imaginings, when he does dare to think of standing before her once again, he can only see himself seated at a table with a single glass of water placed before him, Julia standing in the doorway watching. The wood is dark, walnut wood. A strip of lace cuts the table in two. And there are, he imagines, candles. Beeswax yellow. They are lit and dripping wax onto the lace, on what might be, he thinks, a quiet, cold Sunday at 4 P.M. The soft sound of cars beyond the window, the sun reflecting off a windshield might cause a ripple of light across the table or ceiling corner. They watch it come and then fade as if someone else had walked into the room and turned the corner down the hallway. A glass of water. That's what he envisions. She would set the glass of water before him and stand in the doorway, watching him perform a simple enough act, drinking a glass of water. No ice. And he sees himself sitting before it, watching the way the glass and water distort the tablecloth and table and, when he holds it, his fingertips. And perhaps the glass is of fake, cut crystal so that the water reflects colors like a prism and he would drink the water and set the glass down, and she would fill the empty glass and return it and they would repeat this until one of them said a word, except the problem was that he could not think of what either would say to the other.

Tears had rolled down his cheeks, a steady stream. He had not even known he was crying.

IN THE EARLY MORNING as they drive from the state of Sinaloa to Sonora, they pass a sign that reads, "Why leave? You'll come back." They pass it in silence.

If it works, he'd complete the circle. In this final arc—one that would cut through Sonora, Arizona, New Mexico, the upper part of Texas, onward, to meet what was now the tip of the crescent, or sickle. Life's geometries. These patterns that can shape one's experience, that are perhaps set into place long before we have a chance to redraw our own boundaries, life lines, engineer, assemble, invent our own geometries.

The car moves beneath him, and he likes the steady hum of the motor, the breeze mild, gentle warmth along his eyelids, with his forearm out the window in the sun. The anticipation of what is to come still far distant, even if only one mile, two as they near the state of Sonora.

NOGALES.

"Has the place changed?" Leo asks. "It's been what, over ten years since you've been back here?"

"Nothing was here," Austin says. "Nothing."

Cantina Nogales.

The main street is bustling, but it is a leisurely, relaxed pace. His father is anything but, though one wouldn't know it. Leo realizes that he is the kind who gets still, silent when nervous, holds it inside, his heartbeat racing, his body seemingly calmed, though gripped, he can tell. If Leo were to touch him—an accidental brush of arm against arm, a mistaken nudge of shoulder—he'd jump as if licked by fire.

The car is moving more slowly. The images flicker past. Buildings of white, blue, yellow. There are new storefronts. Windows, porches filled with copperware—pots, bowls—punched tin stars, serapes, hats, paper flowers in red, pink, orange, and yellow. Men stand slumped under shaded awnings. Some are seated on the short two steps leading to a store entrance. Others lean against a banister, a support beam. Most wear cowboy hats, white or brown. Other faces are shaded by wide-lipped sombreros. He can spot the Americans, the Mexicans. The Indios though—they are in the sun, their market wares spread out on hand-woven tapestries and cloths. Heads turn as they drive slowly past the buildings.

"There she is. U.S.-Mexican border," Leo says, pointing. He watches as his father follows his hand. It is the first sign noting the border. A small bronze plaque, the words and images in bas-relief. A line divides the sign in half, two arrows point toward each other symbolizing the two countries, the boundaries or *límite*.

Silence. Leo can hear the radio turned low, a man's deep voice, the rhythm imperceptible. He hears thwacking too and sees a woman beating a rug—red, yellow stripes draped over the banister; clouds of dust billow and sparkle in the sun.

"I don't know about anyone else here, but I sure as hell need a drink," he says.

CANTINA NOGALES. 2:00 P.M.

"There was a carnival they used to have in Cananea," Austin says to Leo after they've been seated, drinking. Vera, after one drink, decides to go to the market, and, in her absence, Austin begins to talk, share his thoughts—an idea, impression, something he's trying to articulate.

"Really?" Leo says.

"Do you remember?"

"No."

"I don't expect you to," Austin says. "We used to take you every night when it was in town. You'd never seen so many lights." He shakes his head. He looks up to Leo who takes a sip of his beer, looks down and away. "We thought you might be scared, all the lights and music, but no."

Austin understands now that Julia was right. How would they all have survived? But still they could've gone then, just kept walking out into that darkness until they'd seen some lights, a town in Arizona.

"Should've crossed then," Austin says out loud.

"What are you saying?"

"Just remembering."

"You can cross now," Leo says. "That's what we're here for. Listen, Father. They'll think we're just American tourists coming back over the border after some rolls of the dice, you know? A night out on the other side—that's all. We can look like that. Hell, we can smell like that. Or we can just claim we're renewing our tourist visas. It's half true. *Mesero*," Leo calls over his shoulder, "*cerveza*."

Austin looks at his son, a young man now. A veteran who'd seen the war. His youngest sitting before him, now twenty-one years old. He shakes his head. The waiter sets down two beers. They sit in silence. Somberness descends, or, and this is more true, it dominates—all this talk suddenly seemed a way to feign normalcy. Beer bottles move to lips and fall to the table with a solid click. He wonders what he could offer them all now, almost sixty. What would become of him when he went back? They were no longer children, had managed well enough on their own, at an age when they wanted to, should be able to, strike out, away from their family. He knew it well. He'd crossed an ocean to do it.

And he'd realized it on the drive here. Some of those views just break one's heart—such a lovely drive, even the desert, how he'd hated it so in Cananea, but he sees its beauty now. It holds so many of his memories. (One has to love that geography, or at least it should have a significance— not indifference; never that.) And he thinks of the feeling that can come over one when traveling, when one is really speeding onward—eyes closed, half dreaming—and you know, you are certain, that you are moving forward, but somehow the monotony of moving, the velocity, speed, all of it, the slight pressure in the chest, can make you feel like you're going in the other direction, as if some force were pushing you lightly, gently backward. And you wake up suddenly, disoriented to see that no, you are moving forward, the road rushing alongside of the car at a shockingly fast pace. And it occurred to him somewhere between Hermosillo and Nogales: when he thought of them or of Julia, he saw them as children, two, six, and eight and Julia as twenty-five. He'd never thought of the actuality, of what it would mean to go back. It was not a reclaiming of those years, was it? The ones they'd lived here, that was it. They are not children. And he is no longer thirty years old.

"Go live the rest of your life. Go live the life that was taken from you," Leo says.

It was taken from him. He had a right to reclaim it, he sees that, now, here, but what would he say to Julia? What would it be to behold her? He wishes instead that he could arrive unannounced. He'd like that, prefer it maybe. To spy upon her, maybe slip in unnoticed, acclimate himself to the sounds and scents. Would she recognize him? Maybe not. He could arrive, step into her sphere, open a door for her, pass her among the aisles of the corner store perhaps, or follow her down the sidewalks of Main Street to the nickel movie house, or track her through Beardsley Park. He'd want to see her before he felt the eyes of recognition, or—and this harder to acknowledge—eyes empty and unfeeling, uncertain who he was, a cold unfamiliarity, indifference, and then, perhaps even a shame.

THE BAR IS PROTECTED from the sun by wicker shades and Leo can see the shadow of them along the stucco wall—like lead pencil tracings, hatch marks. The light enters, diffused as if through oilcloth. He has a chill, for inside is cool and it feels good to sit next to the window, warmed by the light. Outside, a truck passes. The tinny music from its radio enters for a moment, lingers, and then leaves. He can hear too the sound of horse hooves, though the horses are not in his sight lines and so he hears only the breathing and the steady, strong, clomping steps along some part of the dirt road. He is tapping his fingers on the table. He is bouncing his leg. Every once in a while he slaps his hand down hard on the table's surface, which is of striped wood the color of patinaed copper. When he does this it startles all the inhabitants of this small square of being— the bartender, his father seated across from him, the white dog fast asleep in the doorway, the old man seated in the corner who is nearly inanimate, so still, save for his jaw and its incessant chomping.

The bartender is busy. Leo watches as he takes strips of copper wire from a small pile assembled on the bar like pickup sticks. His thick fingers have a surprising dexterity, bending and twisting the wires into coiled circles and squares, the finished work littered across a piece of cloth. The bartender looks out the front door and Leo turns to the window to see what has caught his attention.

"*Trabajadores migrantes,*" the bartender explains.

"They do this every day?" Leo calls out. The bartender nods. It is a solemn sight, bodies tired. It's in their faces, eyes drawn, lines at the cheeks, a haggard step even if some are smiling, laughing in their exchanges, others anxious to simply get home, walking with a tired deliberateness and direction. They are dust-covered. It is in their hair. A fine film coating their skin, and their words, Leo imagines, might form over granules of sand.

"The mass exodus," Leo says, pointing out the window, his father turns to look as well. The workers are returning from fields and farms in the United States, walking back home. Some on a truck, workers in their chinos cinched at the ankles with rope.

"See, they do it every day," Leo says, looking to his father, who is following the workers with his eyes, back and forth, back and forth as the stream continues.

"Do what?" Austin says.

"Cross the border."

The bartender has turned on the radio. It crackles and then the music comes on loud. Leo and his father look up, the horns of a *corrido* blaring, and Leo can make out, in the tone, the voice breaking nearly, a pathos. Revenge for a death perhaps, a stolen first love.

"Perdón," the bartender calls. He readjusts the volume to a more palatable level.

VERA CARIES A BUBBLE of a pot, a terra-cotta *olla*. She bought a straw bag of stripes—vine green, aquamarine, orange, and bougainvillea pink. She is crossing into the shade of the bar's storefront, nearing the steps, her face no longer burnished by sunlight, feeling the gray and blue, the light at her back now. Her entrance is a flurry. The dog, who has been asleep for what seems like days, sits up and stretches, back legs bent, front legs drawn out before him, standing now to walk, a little reluctantly, though with curiosity, toward Vera who is setting out her purchases on the table before Leo and her father.

"It's suddenly like Christmas," Leo says, offering a nervous laugh. Vera sets down the bowl, a series of string animals. "A chicken, an armadillo, a turtle, a donkey, a horse," she says, turning each one from side to side before placing it on the table. She is smiling, her father is beaming and picks up each animal and then the smile vanishes.

"Now we'll really look like tourists," she says. "Everything okay here?" she asks, looking first to her father and then to Leo.

"Fine, fine."

"It's going to be perfectly all right," Vera says, though she herself is not sure of that and wonders if she sounded even half convincing. She watches her father's eyes, how they seem to fight now between sorrow and fear and then focus, draw to a still point on his beer bottle, the drink nearly finished. She sits down across from him, grabs Leo's beer and takes a long sip. Leo motions for another round. The dog has seated himself in front of their table, chin rested on the ground, eyes cast toward Vera. She reaches down to pet him a few quick times on the top of his head, along his neck. He moans and then lets out a sigh.

"Shall we have a tequila?" Leo says.

"Now?"

"Yes. Take the edge off. We're all about to jump out of our skins."

Vera turns to the window in her habit of looking elsewhere when searching for an answer, as if her words lay not within her mind, but beyond her—across the street, whispered amid the couple that just strolled by the open door, or within the store, lying patiently between sacks of coffee beans, or sealed inside the cars creeping by, these traveling vessels of glass and metal—and, upon finding them, returns proudly to present her found, much-sought-after words.

"Why not?" Vera says. "And then we will go."

The bartender brings the tequila and he places the glasses down with a kind of reverence, pausing with a hesitation in his presentation as if he knew their gathering was not one of merriment. He must see lots of people at the outset or returning from back and forth across the border, Vera thinks. She finds herself wondering now about how many others before them have stopped before crossing—other families, illegal immigrants unsure of return or reunion.

.   .   .

THE MUSIC STAYS WITH HIM, has impressed itself upon his memory so that as they leave the bar, the last song, almost without his realizing it, lingers. The tequila has worked itself through him so that instead of a singed dryness within his heart and throat, he now feels a rounded, soothing sense like a kind of balm. He was sweating, felt the wetness seeping through his shirt. He took off his jacket, following Vera and Leo out on the porch, in the shade, scorched by one lengthwise rectangle of sun.

The car sat in wait. Its pistachio green somehow brighter so far from the colored cacophony of the city, out here, where all is the color of almond. Something about it breaks his heart, sitting waiting for them— the curve of its fenders gleaming silver and streaked white from the sunlight. He hears Leo saying something about the time, and he repeats the hour, 3 P.M., and he feels his words fall like stones. Except for that exchange there is no more talk, only a bubble of anxiety seems to work across his body and he is fighting to catch his breath, seems unable to get enough air, his thoughts, voice blanched.

Hope for this moment had carried him through twenty years of the country's two seasons—dry and rainy. It had passed along from one day to the next, a circled gleaming glass like a water droplet, brimming, about to burst. It had moved from the dry season's days of whiteness and heat—orchids blooming, withering—to the rainy, when even the drying leaves were replenished by the torrents of rain that would gather and then slide in sheets across the city or the Sonoran countryside. It pervaded his rooms so that it was there among his drafting papers, within the curve of a pencil stroke drawn in the coolness and shadows of his boarding room while the sun blazed whiteness over the city. It was in his path as he walked out hours among the parks of Mexico—Parque Alameda, Chapultepec, Parque México, Xochimilco. It was even in the clouds that gathered heavy and violet and full, baring the rain that pummeled the willows and ash trees, and caused the branches to hang low and burdened, sodden and dank with, first, the June rains and then all the downpours of July and August.

And now it was here.

WHAT WAS IT THAT he had said to her, that phrase that etched itself within? Here it was now, blooming. She was hearing it again. Something about separation. Her father had been talking about when they'd first returned to the States. Without him. Ah, yes, here it is, the sentence complete: "Separation comes quite suddenly." He had said it once when they were walking in the Alameda. Yes. That was it. And here it was— separation, only this time they were leaving together. It felt like a slow dropping of a string. First, one inch, then another. Here, we walk to the car. Here, we open the doors. Here, we sit, turning on the car. Ten. Nine. Eight. Vera seated in the back. Her father in the passenger seat. Leo walking at a painfully slow pace to the driver's side. She got angry at that, how he was demonstrating that he was calm and collected. He even taps the hood of the car as if part of some ritual. He smiles, but it's a wan smile as if he too will soon brace himself like Vera, like her father, who are holding themselves together. But one has to do that. One has to summon up all the atoms, make them line up, these little things we are made up of, line them up and drop oneself into the moment. See it through. After all, they'd come this far. They were not going to turn back. He was going with them. They were nearly already gone, across the border, and she felt it like the switch of some internal knob. It was the same certainty of instinct that she'd come down to Mexico City with—something silver, knife sharp, shining. These little slivers of—one glimpsed them if one listened carefully enough maybe only a handful of times in life—clarity. It was so simple suddenly. After all this time, a simple yes, no; a going toward, a moving away from; life, death; crossing the border, not crossing; the United States, Mexico; the past, present. So much of the rest was a constant state of hesitation, preoccupation, decision making, analysis of thought and feelings, action. Only—and this she felt was one of those moments—when she sat as if hovering above herself, above them all in this car, watching, listening, pulling back to take it all in, this moment, did she get in and around the emotions that flashed, vibrated, and trembled within her. They were leaving Mexico. They were taking their father home.

The car keys clink in Leo's hands. The car starts. A grumble of gears, ignition, sparks before easing to a low and steady motor purr. How many years she'd wished, how tightly she'd clung and clutched to the hope of bringing him back. She thought of all the years they'd had to endure without him and it seemed a shame to her that there ever needed to be any such thing as leaving, as parting. The car was pulling away. A simple, basic image. One car now driving away, she still imaging it from above, taking it all in—the taillights red through a haze of billowing dust. It was so simple. One sees such images all the time.

"THIS IS HOW IT'S going to be," Leo begins after a silence. The car is creeping forward, he's pressed his foot on the gas pedal and he can see Vera seated, settling into the backseat.

"It's a white booth, no larger than a cottage really," Leo explains.

"The line of cars might be long. We'll see. Maybe, maybe not. But we drive up and stop. The two border guards will step out of the booth. They'll ask for our passports. It is absolutely imperative that you do not speak. If you speak, they'll hear the accent and then it'll be all over. So, not a word. They might inspect the car, look in the trunk, but mostly they just let the cars go through. And like I said, they'll smell the tequila and beer. They'll figure we're just some gringos crossing back over the border after a good time—simply on our way back home. Okay? And if it doesn't work, there's always the *mordida*, a little bit of money never hurts these fellows."

"Yes."

Leo is driving slowly as he talks, making sure his father is grasping each word, the full scenario, outlining it all for him so that there'll be as few surprises as possible. He can feel the heat of the steering wheel beneath his hand, with his other hand he is gesticulating, pointing.

"You ready for this?" he asks, though his own heart is pounding in his chest, the sweat beginning in a line across his forehead.

"Yes. Nervous."

"Don't be nervous," Leo says, feigning composure.

"All right."

"We turn down here and there's no going back."

"I know."

"All right. Let's go."

They creep forward. The sun is in his eyes, and he pulls his visor down. In two seconds, his father does the same, and out of the corner of his eye he can see the pack of Wrigley's tumble into his father's lap, the slim compact rectangles the color of nopal leaves. His father has jumped in his seat and Leo reaches down to help, all the while steering.

"Sorry about that," Leo says, laughing, bending forward to pick up some packs that have fallen on the running board.

"Well, take a piece," Leo says. "And leave a pack out in the open? Leave it right here," he says, patting the dashboard. "Make you look like a true American." Vera laughs, Austin too. He watches his father fumbling with the packs of gum, gathering them and placing one after another back under the visor, arranging them in a neat row beneath the red rubber band Leo had used to secure them into place. He readjusts the visor. Leo reaches over and removes a pack of gum. He hands it to his father.

"Go ahead and open it," he says, holding it before him, watching as his father takes it in his hands, opens it, the red string breaking through the thicker green wrapper. The pleasure of the silver sheen and scent of spearmint. He unwraps the foil and folds the gum into his mouth, chewing. He places the pack on the dashboard, on a straight line. Leo moves it a bit, sets it on an angle, on the diagonal to look more casual, he doesn't know why, just makes him nervous otherwise. He puts his arm out the window, banging the outer door with his palm.

"All right now, all right," he says as he turns the car around the corner and toward the border crossing. "You ready for this?"

"I think so," his father says, offering a half smile.

AUSTIN'S WINDOW IS OPEN. He can hear the tires on the road, the gentle idle of the engine at rest, then the sputter of gas and the idle again, back and forth—time enough for thought, an action of reversal. The border patrol shack is white. A freshly painted white. Black trim. A hand-painted wooden placard announces the current exchange rate: twelve pesos to the dollar. The border guards stand outside the customs house, disaffected and bored. Their badges and buckles glint gold and white under the 3:30 P.M. sun and the wide sky hovering like a dome, the same sky he's stood under all these years. He can hear Leo telling him to be calm. He adjusts his neck collar and feels the tightness at his mouth, the way his jaw moves up and down over the gum, tasteless and growing stiff, brittle. That, and his heart, full and constricted as if struggling with all the fear and doubt and hope and guilt wrangled inside of him. All the while he can hear Leo saying, "easy enough," "easy enough to cross."

They drive past signs. *Principia Región Fronteriza/*You are entering border region. *Mercancías Generales/*General Merchandise. The searchlights are dead during the day and he can see the other cars go before them, stopping at the window, an exchange of words, a quick once-over of papers before passing through. It was easy for them—one, two, three had been allowed admittance. He can expect the same. What were the chances of being stopped? He quickly works out an equation of probability, but knows now that he will have to leave it all to chance or to have some faith and that faith will have to carry him across the border, yes, but also the many miles through, and once again on the train trip, and even more so when walking down Main Street, searching out the old street, a right and then left, two blocks down, stepping through the gate and up to the front door. Would it last? He already feels faith waning. He is tiring. He does not know if he has the strength to see it through. It is a lot to ask of one man.

He sees some Mexicans at the pedestrian crossing—women with their mesh bags of yellow and green, handwoven, their low-heeled black shoes are covered in a film of chalky dust. He watches their faces burst into smiles, an ease coming over them as they entered their side, their country, free to giggle at some complicity, remarks about the border guards no doubt, he thinks, their white shirtdresses and bobby socks, hair cropped short, clipped to the ear or held back with barrettes. They come together and disperse, walking in single file now, their silhouettes thrown into relief against the flat barren fields that stretch to the dry brown foothills in the distance—a terrain that seems to shame the meager customs house, which sits tiny as a toy beneath all the austerity, blatant, serene.

"Identification."

"Yes, sir."

The guard's sunglasses, cracked and fixed with tape, hang from a rope around his neck.

"Where you people headed to?" he asks, his voice a low growl. He turns one passport over in his hands, examines the paper, looks at the picture, back to Leo and back to the picture again. He does the same with the other two. Flips through the pages, runs his fingers along the front embossed seal.

"California," Leo lies. The border guard places his hands on the hood of the car and hangs down so that his face is framed by his forearms. His sunglasses hit the top of the open window.

"Which way you headed?" he asks, talking to Leo, Austin's eyes on the dashboard as he feels the guard's gaze make a once-over of the car.

"Eight-nine," Leo says. " Then the Pacific Coast highway."

"You may have some trouble then," the guard says. Austin cannot move, his hands are suddenly shaking, his mouth parched, but he keeps chewing the gum, finds it a welcome distraction, chewing in a series of threes—one, two, three, one, two, three. He can see the guard standing to take a step back from the car, pointing across the border.

"Accident," the guard says. "You can take your chances, but you might be backed up there for miles."

"Thanks. We'll see what happens," Leo says.

"All right. Go on ahead," he says, waving them through. Austin's heart is beating, and they sit in silence, a bit stunned, as Leo maneuvers the car through the crossing point, driving a few yards before speeding up onto the highway. Austin is unable to speak. The sun in his eyes. He shakes his head, rubs his forehead, brings his warm hand to his neck, cracking it a bit as he turns it left and then right.

Leo is laughing, Vera sits forward, her hands resting on the seat back. She is talking to him, asking him if he is okay, joining in Leo's laughter.

Austin knows he should be thankful, that he should be flooded with relief, that soothing balm, and not with what he feels now. A tenseness along the shoulders, in the chest as if he'd stored up all this energy to cross and had not yet felt its release. From the interstate Austin can see the scalloped outline of a general storefront, the rounded cupolas of restored missionary churches, whitewashed and pristine, colored by the amber light of the setting sun.

"Stop the car for a minute," Austin says.

"What? Here?" Vera looks around.

"Stop the car. A minute, please."

"Sure thing."

"I just need to step out for a moment."

Leo presses on the brakes, the car slows as he pulls it gradually to the side of the road, but not slow enough so that the car skids a bit on the gathered gravel. A cloud of dust encases the car, some coming through the windows. Austin closes his eyes, feeling the car roll to a stop. He places his hand on the warm silver door handle, clicking it open and stepping out to stand at the side of the road for a moment before making his way down the embankment—four strides and he's in the field. From behind, he can hear Leo and Vera talking, getting out of the car now, doors slamming shut and the certain sound of someone sitting on the hood, the tin dented with a little popping.

The cacti are scattered before him like pieces on a chessboard. Some of the crown cacti rose to his height, their late-day shadows long and slanting, like his own.

"Hey," Leo shouts. "How does it feel to be in the U.S.?"

"Good," Austin calls over his shoulder, waving a hand up in the air. He walks about twenty paces, stands still for a moment, dragging his sole along the ground, disturbing flies from their dusty slumber. They flitter up and loop, coming to rest on some safer surface.

He is in the United States. No voices, no sudden arrest, no men to take him, no guns or bayonets, blackjacks or clubs, no tumult of questions. What had he expected, now safely across? An onslaught of something—joy maybe. But he doesn't feel that. Some change in the weather at least as if all the minutes, years might gather and fall back to him like the distinct drops of a sudden rain, heavy and laden in descent, spattering the dry fields and mountain ranges, the parched cacti, soon soaking his clothes, his skin.

That did not happen.

Instead, the sun sits above the horizon like a bored and discontented child who will not go away. He puts his hand to the back of his neck, squeezing the tightened tendons, staring at the random scatter of cacti along the hillocks in the distance and those closer to him.

He could have crossed years ago, kept on walking that night when he'd found his Sonnie in that field, so much like this one here, sweeping him up so that the boy could hang off his neck. He'd moved then amid that open field as if wading into the dark, unknowable ocean. That was when they would have needed him—then—when he could lift him, throw the boy over his shoulder, when they were all just little tikes. And now? To go back he wonders if they can forgive him his absence. It had all been for them. *I love . . . I miss . . . I pray for health . . . years . . . time. . . .* What did it all mean, all those years? He'd once been the young man who'd written so ardently, "There is nothing in the world stronger than love of heart and soul for only in it there is life and happiness." He thinks of Leo's and Vera's efforts, but he knows he is right, this will not be a reclaiming of those lost years. He is in the United States; he's never felt more foreign. He had tried. He had succeeded and yet he had failed. He turns to Vera and Leo, thinks of Julia and feels loss and gratitude and then remorse and guilt and the bitterest of sorrows, regret—he could not be the man they wanted him to be.

He picks up a stone, can feel its coarse warm skin. He tosses it up and down in his palm and then throws it like a discus toward a crown cactus. He misses. He picks up one stone after another, watching each hit the earth so that a little cloud of dust billows up from the impact, butterflies now scattering in their anxious flights. He throws the last stone, and it is like throwing down a gauntlet. He looks back to the car. Leo and Vera sit waiting, silhouetted by the curve of the horizon. How they'd grown. Two adults. They'd come for him, to bring him here, to bring him home. He pauses. Looks around. It is as still as any winter he has known.

ACKNOWLEDGMENTS

I am grateful to several people who, combined, created a network of support, encouragement, generosity, advice, and friendship that helped me to write this book.

Thank you to the Hunter College MFA program and to Susan Hertog, whose generosity allowed me to study at Hunter on a Hertog Fellowship. Special thanks to Peter Carey, Donna Masini, Colum McCann, and Tom Sleigh, whose courses served as inspiration and whose care and community buoyed me through a period of difficult loss. I am also grateful to all of my Hunter MFA colleagues. My deepest gratitude is reserved for Colum, my adviser at Hunter, who saw the potential for this novel early on.

Thank you to Salman Rushdie, whose advice, example, and feedback on this novel challenged me and helped me to grow as a writer.

Thank you to Francisco Goldman for daring me to always write closest to the emotional truth.

I am also grateful to John Freeman for publishing an excerpt of this novel. Thank you to everyone else who helped in that publication (my first), including Patrick Ryan, Ellah Allfrey, and Michael Salu.

Thank you to my wonderful agents, Caroline Michel and Rachel Mills of Peters, Fraser and Dunlop, and to everyone else at PFD; their enthusiasm for this novel is greatly appreciated.

Thanks to my amazing editor Andrea Walker for her intelligent and insightful editorial suggestions, which helped me make this a stronger book. Special thanks also to my current editors, Virginia Smith and Ann Godoff, for their input and guidance and for providing me with continued support at The Penguin Press.

I'd like to thank Elaina Ganim for her reading of an early draft of this novel. And thanks also to Corinna Barsan, who read some of the very first pages. Their friendship and encouragement were crucial during the intial stages of this project.

For her friendship and perceptive observations and critiques, I'm deeply grateful to Maria Venegas.

I reserve special thanks for Nicole Parisier, who read my early fiction, encouraged me to continue writing, and offered me a seat at her dinner table for several much-needed meals during the writing of this book.

Thank you also to my former professors at NYU's Gallatin School of Individualized Study, Julie Malnig, who taught me the craft and joy of research, and Bella Mirabella, who has continued to take interest in, and support, my creative endeavors. I'm also grateful to Gallatin's Lauren Kaminsky for her help in researching Russian history.

In researching the Palmer Raids of 1919 and 1920, I'm indebted to the following history texts: Robert W. Dunn's *The Palmer Raids*, Constantine M. Panunzio's *The Deportation Cases of 1919–1920*, Kenneth D. Ackerman's *Young J. Edgar: Hoover, the Red Scare and the Assault on Civil Liberties*, and Christopher M. Finan's *From the Palmer Raids to the Patriot Act: A History of the Fight for Free Speech in America*.

Thanks to Abby Gardner, who believed that this novel would see the light of day even when I wasn't so sure, and to the entire Gardner family for offering me a home away from home when needed.

To Alison Clarke, who once long ago made it possible for me to have a room of my own, thank you.

For their friendship, time, shared laughter, and encouragement, thanks also to Wen-Yuan Betts, Sarah Eggers, Antonia Fattizzi, Dara Feivelson, Allison Lehr, Soledad Marambio, Meagen Marcy McCusker, and Brenna Sheehan.

Thanks to D.B. for helping me to piece together my own narrative.

Thanks also to my cousins on the Manko side of my family, Thomas Selleck, Laura Selleck, and Susan Selleck, and, of course, to my Aunt Ollie (Olga Selleck). I'd also like to acknowledge the Manko boys, Gregory, Danny, and David. We all stand on the shoulders of the man on whom the main character of this novel is based, and their encouragement and support was essential while writing this book. Special thanks to Laura, whose research helped locate important primary source materials.

My deepest gratitude is reserved for my immediate family. Thank you to Paul and Kate Manko, and especially to Paul, my brother, who read several drafts of this novel and whose wonderful, keen instinct for story helped shape this book. To my grandmother, Louise Ciccone, your love and warmth fill my heart and these pages; thank you. To my aunt Diane Ciccone, thank you for your support and encouragement and for always being there when I need you. Love and thanks to my mother, Carol Manko, for her unwavering belief in this novel and in me and in all of my dreams, whether they required a pair of pointe shoes or a pen. I could not have done any of it without you. I'm also indebted to my father, Harold Manko, who passed away while I was writing this book, but who instilled in me a love of story and an appreciation for the arts, which led me first to dance and then to writing.

Lastly, my greatest debt is owed to the man whose life story inspired this book, the late Austin Manko, who, I hope, will not be forgotten, and also to the late Julia Manko, who, with grace and strength, fought to keep her family together . . . across several borders.